I0675019

Also From Cohesion Press

Military Horror:

SNAFU: An Anthology of Military Horror
– eds Geoff Brown & Amanda J Spedding

SNAFU: Heroes
– eds Geoff Brown & Amanda J Spedding

SNAFU: Wolves at the Door
– eds Geoff Brown & Amanda J Spedding

SNAFU: Survival of the Fittest
– eds Geoff Brown & Amanda J Spedding

SNAFU: Hunters
– eds Amanda J Spedding & Geoff Brown

SNAFU: Future Warfare
– eds Amanda J Spedding & Geoff Brown

SNAFU: Unnatural Selection
– eds Amanda J Spedding & Geoff Brown

SNAFU: Black Ops
– eds Amanda J Spedding & Matthew Summers

SNAFU: Resurrection
– eds Amanda J Spedding & Matthew Summers

SNAFU: Last Stand (late 2019)
– eds Amanda J Spedding & Matthew Summers

SNAFU
WOLVES AT THE DOOR

An Anthology of Military Horror

Edited by
Geoff Brown
and
Amanda J Spedding

Cohesion Press
Mayday Hills Lunatic Asylum
Beechworth, Australia
2019

SNAFU: Wolves at the Door
Cohesion Press 2019

An Anthology of Military Horror
Geoff Brown and Amanda J Spedding (eds)

Editorial Team:
Adem Besim
Jen Bourke
Shannon Carter
Cathy Curtain
Bryce Gordon
Jaime McDougall
Luke Poulter
Phoebe Ward

Set in Palatino Linotype

Cohesion Press
Mayday Hills Lunatic Asylum
Beechworth, Australia
2019
www.cohesionpress.com

Contents

Taking Down the Top Cat - R.P.L. Johnson 1

Skadi's Wolves - Kirsten Cross 19

Semper Gumby - Steve Coate 37

Ancient Ruins - John W. Dennehy 47

The Fenrir Project - David W. Amendola 64

Project Lupine - Brian W. Taylor 82

Werwolf - W.D. Gagliani & David Benton 100

Jester - Jennifer R. Povey 151

The Wild Hunt - James A. Moore 159

Taking down the Top Cat

R.P.L. Johnson

Night fell in the jungle: greens sinking into blacks, shadows growing up from the valley floor like a dark liquid pooling in the deep places of the world.

Sergeant Jared Naylor scanned the compound through his binoculars as he waited for the rest of the team to make their way up the narrow game trail. From above it looked like a holiday resort. The main house nestled into the wooded hillside, its sprawling size artfully hidden by sculpted gardens that led down to the river. A helipad and boathouse on the river completed the picture. It looked more like an eco-retreat for detoxing celebrities than a drug lord's stronghold.

"Man, I am in the *wrong* business," said Garcia. He gave out a low whistle as he stared down at the luxurious compound.

"Well today's your lucky day, Private," Naylor said. "I hear there are going to be a few vacancies opening up in his operation pretty soon."

Germaine McDowell lumbered past, toting the heavy MG4 as if it was a kid's BB gun. "Of course that would mean you'd have the mighty fightin' Delta Force bearing down on your ass right now," he said.

Garcia shrugged. "I heard they ain't so tough."

Mac gave him a friendly shoulder check as he walked past. "Some of them ain't," he said.

"Zip it," Naylor said. "Save the bull session for the ride home. I want it tight and quiet from here on in."

He checked his watch; they were right on time. Not bad after a ten-mile hike through dense jungle. This hadn't been a usual infiltration. Their target was Hernando Ramirez, head of the infamous Cascajal drug cartel. Ramirez was notoriously paranoid, and his compound was miles away from any road and well off any commercial flight path. They couldn't afford to give him any warning, so they had been dropped two valleys away with the rest of the journey being made on foot. Other squads were hiking in from the south, and under Emcon Alpha, full radio silence, timing was everything.

"There's the boathouse," Jim Lowe said, the last man in their four-man fire team.

"I see it," Naylor replied.

The boathouse was their way out. Getting away from the compound had to be as fast as their approach was stealthy. This operation was strictly off the books. The chain of command went from Naylor to his Captain straight to the commander of Delta and then to a D.C. suit. Naylor had been working operations like this for years but still got nervous when he thought about who was ultimately in charge. A Mexican drug lord might kill you, might even torture you first. But those Beltway cats would sign your death warrant with no more thought than swatting a fly if they thought it was in their interests. They couldn't afford to get caught in Mexico. If they did, the unofficial war on drugs could become an international incident.

Fortunately Ramirez's lavish lifestyle extended to a collection of motorboats in his private boathouse. That was Naylor's objective: hold and secure their way out while the other squads took out Ramirez and his key lieutenants.

They made their way down the hill. If anything the undergrowth was even thicker on the south-facing slope and they were forced to hack their way through the bush.

Naylor swung his machete against a particularly tangled knot of vines when the blade struck something hard. He pulled the vines and they came away like a living tapestry, an interwoven blanket of tough, woody tendrils. Behind was a huge boulder of yellowish green rock just like the outcroppings they had seen during their hike. But this wasn't just some slab of bedrock protruding through the topsoil, it was a huge stone head.

"Well, would you look at that," Garcia said. "Olmec, I reckon."

"Listen to him," Mac said. "Just 'cus his gran'pappy swam the Rio Grande forty years ago, he thinks he's some kind of expert on Mexican history."

Naylor examined the huge artefact. The features had been smoothed by time but Naylor could still make out the broad, fang-filled mouth of the Olmec jaguar God.

"Well in this case, I think he's right," he said. "This is Olmec country, and they liked their carvings sure enough. I even saw one like this in a museum in Guadalajara one time."

"You know, I heard Ramirez was into all this shit," Lowe said. "Collects artefacts, even makes out like he's some kind of champion for the native Olmec Indians."

"Yeah, I heard something similar," Naylor said. "Seems like being a drug lord with more money than God isn't enough for him. Ramirez likes to pretend he's some kind of mystical badass, Lucifer and *Sante Muerta* combined. I guess it helps to keep the locals in line: stops the coca farmers from selling the crop to the other cartels. It's all bullshit designed to keep the locals away from his pleasure palace."

"Pleasure palace," Garcia repeated. "I like the sound of that. Like I said, I'm in the wrong business." He patted the giant stone head as they walked past. "I'm going to tell Ramirez about this, he might want to add it to his collection."

* * *

They hit the boathouse at the stroke of 2:00am. There were two guards on patrol, both were chatting and smoking on a small jetty that jutted out where the river widened in front of the house. Both caught three rounds each from the suppressed MP5s carried by Lowe and Garcia. They collapsed in unison, hearts shredded, blood pressure crashing and pitching them into a deadly faint while the rest of their body caught up to the fact that they were dead.

Naylor ghosted forward to secure the bodies, afraid one of them would pitch over into the lake, raising an attention-getting splash. But they both crumpled into their own footprints, empty eyes staring up at the sky.

Naylor crouched over the bodies, scanning the boathouse through night vision goggles. There was no sign of movement, and no sign either of the simultaneous attack Naylor knew would be happening right at that instant on the main house.

That was good. Silence meant things were going to plan.

"Mac, get that SAW up here. Garcia, start prepping the boat."

The two men moved with smooth, practised efficiency. Mac heaved a crate onto the jetty and set the big machine gun up on its bipod while Garcia started to check over the motor launch Naylor had picked.

"Lowe, give me an overview," Naylor said.

"On it."

Lowe took out a small drone, a quad-rotor hardly bigger than his outstretched palm, and pitched it into the air like a softball. At about twenty feet its four tiny propellers spun to life with no more noise than a family of mosquitos and Lowe flew it towards the house, controlling the tiny drone with what looked like a wireless game controller with a built-in screen.

Naylor know what to expect, but he asked anyway.

"How's it looking?"

He could see Lowe's smile as his teeth flashed green in the night vision.

"Sergeant, when this is over we can sell the video to the Stockade to train new Operators."

"That good?"

"Textbook."

"Hey Garcia," Mac hissed, "you still want to join the cartel?"

"I've changed my mind," Garcia replied. "I hear the retirement plan's kinda rough."

Gunfire, coming from the main house. Naylor recognised the distinctive agricultural clatter of AK47s and in reply, the faster buzz of a Delta machine gun. Sounded like the cartel had finally woken up. Well, that was to be expected eventually.

"Stay tight," Naylor said. "Garcia, how are we going with that boat?"

"Two minutes, Sergeant."

"Damn," Mac said. "I could throw a rock in downtown Jersey and hit three guys who could jack a boat faster than you."

"Can it," Naylor ordered.

He crept over to where Lowe was still piloting the drone. Its night vision camera clearly showed the main house. There was no sign of the other Delta squads, but staccato flashes of light strobed in the windows in time to the clatter of gunfire on the night air.

More gunfire now, mixed with screams. Animal sounds ripped from human throats. The night was alive now with movement and noise. The old dance – predators and prey.

Something wasn't right.

A voice came on the secure Delta short-range network, breaking radio silence with a garbled scream.

"Holy shit! Get back, get back, get b—"

The fast, pneumatic flutter of suppressed gunfire swamped the panicked voice: not a controlled burst, but a full-auto spray that emptied the clip in seconds. Then the screams cut short with a wet, ripping sound that reminded Naylor of his mother de-boning a chicken.

A growl. Naylor tried to imagine what could be done to a human throat to make such a noise, but failed.

The screaming carried on the still jungle night. Naylor stared at the drone's screen, willing it to show him what was going on. But whatever it was, it was happening inside the main house.

He listened closely. He had heard his share of gunfire and screaming, but this was different. The screams had a panicked edge, not cries of pain, but animal yells of terror. The gunfire was wild and sporadic. He expected that from the cartel guards, but he could hear the familiar crack of Delta-issued Berettas. The two squads that had stormed the house had ditched their rifles and were using their sidearms. That was bad.

The comms was alive with voices now: radio silence forgotten. Naylor heard desperate pleas for help and snatched fragments from open microphones.

"What the fuck was that?"

5

"Oh, God... Oh, God..."

"Where d'it go? Where d'it go?"

"What the fu—"

"Fall back! Fall back!"

The roar that echoed across the compound was as loud as thunder.

"Boat's ready, Sarge," Garcia said.

"Okay." Naylor broke radio silence to send the coded signal that their way out was ready. He didn't know what was going on at the main house, but now they could complete the mission and exfiltrate down the river as planned.

His call was answered by another chorus of shouts and curses over the radio, punctuated by gunfire.

"Get ready, people," Naylor said. "Whatever's happening in there, they'll be coming in hot."

"Copy that," they said in unison. They had all heard the pandemonium over the radio. They knew that whatever clusterfuck the mission had turned into over at the main house was about to descend on them.

They waited: trying not to listen to the cries on the radio; trying not to picture the fire fight, the dark, confined corridors of the house lit by the deadly strobe of muzzle flashes, the bullets, ricocheted fragments and splinters ripping into flesh. And definitely trying not to picture whatever it was that was making that fucking roar!

The noise grew even more chaotic, if that was possible. The gunfire had almost completely stopped and the shouts had turned to sobbing screams. But throughout it all, unchanged, was the deep-throated roar and that other noise: the chicken-bone sound of tearing flesh.

Finally, even the screams died away until there was only one voice, breathless and pleading.

"Please... please..."

Silence.

"Sarge?" Mac asked. He was still scanning the path back to the house through the holographic sight of the MG4.

"I know, I know," Naylor replied. If anyone was coming back to the boat, they'd be there by now. Instead there was only silence. Even the radio was quiet.

"Boat's ready, Sarge," Garcia reminded him.

Naylor knew what he should do. He should pack up and leave, get his men out of there. Those were his orders. But just as he knew what he should do, he also knew that he couldn't do it.

"Mac, you stay here with the SAW. Guard that boat. The rest of you, on me."

Naylor led the way up the path to the house. If anything, the silence was worse than the screaming they had heard just moments before. Lowe had placed his drone into a hover. It would keep station there without any human control, giving them an overview of the battlefield. But it wasn't telling them anything. The house still looked quiet. There was no sign of movement, not even from the cartel's guards.

"I got a body," Garcia said. "Not one of ours."

Naylor looked at the corpse as they passed. It was indeed one of Ramirez's men; he was still clutching his rifle, but didn't look like he'd got a shot off before his throat had been cut. Naylor appraised the work with a professional eye. He was starting to put together a picture of what had happened. The approach had been good, the guards taken out swiftly and silently. Whatever had gone wrong had happened inside the house.

They reached the main door. The black cavity stood like an entrance to another world.

"Hey, Lowe," Naylor said. "How good are you with that drone?"

"You want to go inside?"

"You got it?"

Lowe broke out his controller again and the three men took cover behind the stone carvings that flanked the main entrance as Lowe flew the little craft inside.

He was good; the drone flew steadily along at about head height, giving them a real picture of what it would be like to walk down the corridor. At first there were no signs of trouble, the house looked just like Naylor expected from their briefing: an opulent villa with broad corridors lined with paintings and statuary that reflected its owners love of the local, Olmec culture. Small versions of the stone heads they had seen in the jungle sat on mahogany tables; tapestries and jade masks hung from the walls. Everything was painted in a palette of jungle greens and deep black from the drone's night vision camera.

"Back up," Naylor said. "There, just there."

"We got a casualty," Lowe said. A broad staircase led down to a basement level. At the top of the staircase a soldier lay slumped in a puddle of his own blood.

"Gunshot to the throat," Lowe said. "He never stood a chance."

So far, so bad, Naylor thought. But casualties were to be expected. What else had happened? What else could make two fire teams of hardened soldiers descend into panic?

"More bodies," Lowe said. "Bad guys mostly. Looks like quite the fire fight."

Naylor nodded. Delta had come in, taken out at the guards at the cost of one of their own and pushed on into the house. But that was about as good as it had gotten. Lowe stopped calling out casualties after the first half-dozen. They lay where they had fallen, cartel guards and the Delta operators. The walls were daubed with blood, and doors and doorframes shattered by automatic gunfire. Instead of an expensive villa, the lower level looked like a war zone. The expensive tapestries and artwork was smashed, fragments on the floor amid the brass of discarded shell casings. Here and there grenade damage had started fires amongst the wreckage. The flames glittered green in the night vision giving the place an otherworldly, eldritch air.

"What the hell happened here?" Lowe asked.

Naylor looked at the bodies. They had been torn apart.

"Grenade do that?" Lowe asked.

"Don't think so," Naylor replied. "I'm not seeing any blast damage. Looks like they were cut."

"What the fuck?" Lowe said. "Who the hell were Ramirez's bodyguards? Ninjas?"

"I heard one time, this guy in Columbia, he kept a whole zoo. He had lions and all kinds of shit," said Garcia.

"You think animals did this?" Naylor said. "Think maybe Ramirez let them out?"

"Well I've never seen a bullet open a guy up like that."

The drone pushed on down the corridor.

"Signal's getting weaker, Sarge. I don't know how much farther I can go without losing the drone."

"Copy that," Naylor said. "Keep going."

The little quad-rotor flew down another short flight of stairs; the only sound in the house was the whine of its tiny electric motors. The stairs opened into a large room – the biggest they had seen – but instead of Garcia's zoo this place looked more like a museum. Glass cases lined the walls, most of them shattered and cracked, their contents indistinguishable from the shards of broken glass and debris that littered the cabinets.

There was movement at the edge of the screen. A black shape that Naylor had thought was a shadow suddenly slipped away out of the frame.

A figure moved behind it, a soldier, lying against the wall, one leg stretched out in front of him, the other folded beneath him, broken or dislocated or both.

Naylor watched the man's eyes as he tracked the departing shadow with a look of barely contained horror. He was alive.

"Shit! It's Miller," Lowe said.

Miller saw the drone. With a quick, desperate look back at the departing shadow he mouthed, *Help me!*

Miller's eyes darted to the left. A split second later a black shape moved in front of the camera and the drone was swatted from the air. It tumbled into the wall and the screen went dead.

"What now, Sarge?" Garcia asked.

Naylor didn't answer. He had seen something. "Lowe, give me a playback of the last few frames."

Corporal Lowe rewound the last few seconds of the tumbling drone until the image stabilised.

"There!" Naylor jabbed at the screen. An instant before the drone was hit it had caught an image, a pattern of blotchy black rings."

"What is that?" Garcia asked.

"Jaguar," Naylor replied. "It's a jaguar."

"So what do we do now?"

"What do you think?" Naylor asked. "We go in."

* * *

They followed the route the drone had taken, the scene looking eerily familiar through the green night goggles clipped to Naylor's helmet. They descended the stairs, checking the vital signs of the bodies they passed, but there were no more survivors. Perhaps there were more inside. Perhaps it was just Miller. Either way, Naylor was going to find out.

"Holy crap! Just look at this place," Garcia said as they descended the second flight of stairs.

It was the room they had seen with the drone. Ramirez had created his own museum inside his house. Naylor had seen this kind of thing before. Some of these guys had collections that rivalled anything in the Smithsonian.

Ramirez's taste ran to Olmec artefacts and guns. Stone heads of various sizes lined one wall of the room along with fragments of frescoes and larger carvings. Each was lit with tasteful up-lights and labelled with a small plaque. The other side of the room looked like a cross between a jeweller's front window and an armoury. Naylor had never seen so much gold. There were gold plated rifles and matched pairs of jewelled pistols. There were older weapons, lovingly restored and, just like the Olmec masonry, each item was labelled with obsessive care.

Garcia whistled. He picked up a gold-plated 1911 semi-automatic with mother of pearl grips.

"Stay focussed, Garcia," Naylor said. "We don't have time for rubbernecking."

"I know, I know. But man... just one of these things could set a guy up for life. And two... Well I'd—"

It hit Garcia high, springing from the shadows four-footed like a cat, although Naylor had never seen any cat that big. It was bigger than a jaguar. It was more like a bear, although slimmer and sleeker and faster.

It sprung on Garcia, knocking him sprawling with its speed and sheer weight and riding him to the ground, crushing the breath out of him. Garcia didn't even get a chance to scream before it bit down with its huge jaws. There was that noise again: the wet, crunch of snapping bone. Naylor squeezed the trigger on his MP5, more out of instinct than conscious thought and the muzzle flash lit up the green-black flank of something squatting on Garcia. It ignored Naylor's shots. He saw the muscles bunch under its sleek pelt as it worked its massive jaws, twisting and pulling and then it was gone, leaping away through a doorway leading to another wing of the museum.

"Holy shit! Garcia!"

Naylor was at his side in a second while Lowe covered the doorway with his MP5. But Garcia was already dead. His head lolled at an unnatural angle, his neck half torn away by a terrible wound that had opened him up from chin to collar bone.

"What the fuck was that?" Lowe shouted.

Naylor didn't know. Some kind of animal, Garcia had been right about that much. A tiger maybe? He could think of nothing else with that combination and size and speed and predatory savagery.

"Just watch that fucking doorway," Naylor said. "You see any movement, you light that fucker up, you hear me?"

"Copy that," Lowe said through clenched teeth.

Naylor quickly padded the last few metres to where Miller still lay slumped against the wall. He was unconscious. As well as his broken leg he was bleeding from four parallel slashes across his chest. Naylor slapped him, hard. It barely roused him. He stared past Naylor with unfocussed eyes.

"Wake up, Miller, dammit," Naylor said and slapped him again.

That seemed to work.

"Out! We've got to get out," Miller said.

"No shit," Naylor replied. "How many of those things are there?"

Miller grimaced as Naylor helped him onto his good leg. "Just one."

"One!" Naylor thought of the bodies littering the upper levels. "You're wrong. Ramirez must have had a goddamn zoo full of those things. No way one animal could do all this."

Naylor hefted Miller onto his shoulders in a fireman's carry, ignoring the man's cries of pain.

"You don't get it," Miller said. "That's no animal. We took out Ramirez's guards, followed him down here when he ran. I... I saw him change. That thing is Ramirez."

Delirious, Naylor thought. Stress and blood loss. They would have to get him back to the boat and stabilise him. Get some saline into him to get his pressure back up before they could get any real answers out of him.

"Jesus Christ, I saw him change!"

Naylor started back towards the stairwell feeling naked without the comforting weight of his MP5 in his hands.

"Contact!" Lowe shouted and fired a short burst down the corridor.

"Just keep it off our backs. We're outta here," Naylor replied, grunting with the effort of carrying Miller.

Suddenly Lowe was firing. The room lit up green from the light of the muzzle flash on full auto. Naylor saw movement: he caught a glimpse of something tall filling the doorway, walking on two legs like a man but the head and thick, powerful neck were anything but human. A second later something hit him from behind. It felt like he'd been hit by a truck. He fell into one of the shattered cabinets, felt an immense weight crushing the wind from him and grinding his face into the glass shards. He could feel its claws ripping, snagging in the tough webbing and pulling him left and right with immense, animal strength. Then suddenly the weight was gone and Miller's screams were echoing down the hallway.

Naylor rose shakily to his feet. Miller was gone.

"It just took him," Lowe said. "I emptied a full clip at it and it didn't even slow."

"Which way did it go?"

He didn't need an answer. The creature's deep, rattling roar rang out from somewhere behind them, chilling Naylor to the marrow.

He raised his weapon and stood back to back with Lowe. *Let's see you sneak up on us this time.*

"We're leaving," Naylor said. "Stay together, keep it tight, all the way back to the boat and we're gone."

"Copy that."

The roar sounded again, closer now.

"It's picking us off, one by one," Lowe said.

"So stay together. Don't give it that chance."

They stumbled through the debris-strewn room towards the stairwell. Naylor nearly tripped a couple of times but didn't dare take his eyes from the holographic sight of his rifle and the arc he was scanning back down the hall.

He saw movement, a subtle shifting of the shadows. Whatever this thing was, it had a jaguar's stealth. The shadows embraced it, pooling around it like a liquid cloak. He saw the gleam of yellow eyes and loosed a few rounds at it, drawing out another roar, a deep animal noise that plucked a bass note in his guts. Suddenly he became very aware of his place on the food chain and knew that it was not the top.

The old dance, predator and prey, but this time they were on the wrong side.

"We need to go faster," Naylor said.

The creature rose onto its hind legs. This was no jaguar; this was like no animal Naylor had ever seen before. It had the head of a big cat complete with yellow eyes and snarling lips pulled back to reveal long, interlocking fangs. But the head and powerful, sinuous neck rested atop human shoulders and long, muscular arms. Naylor could see the muscles on the thing's chest. It was built like a power lifter, but under the sleek, black fur the musculature was human. Only below the hips did the cat-like form reassert itself with long, seemingly double-jointed legs ending in huge paws.

It roared, jaws opening impossibly wide, fangs glistening.

Naylor fired; he flicked his MP5 onto full auto and mashed the trigger. The creature hardly seemed to notice. Lowe turned around and opened up; Naylor could see the creatures flesh rippling where the rounds struck it, but they were as ineffective as a handful of thrown pebbles.

It kept coming.

Naylor's gun ran dry; he quickly popped the magazine and slammed a new one home, knowing as he did so that it would do no good. Eleven men had tried to kill this thing and eleven men had failed.

The creature swiped at them with one clawed arm. Naylor heard Lowe scream, felt blood splash hot against his skin and then the creature's follow through picked him up and hurled him into a broken display cabinet. Splinters of wood and glass stabbed into him and his desperate, outstretched fingers stubbed painfully into something heavy lying in the shards.

The creature stepped over the moaning form of Lowe as he writhed on the floor and reared up before Naylor. He could smell it now: a warm, animal smell, like the steam off the jungle floor after rain. He could see the rosettes of its mottled fur, black against the deep purple of its pelt. He saw its yellow eyes on him and its paw raised, claws extended for the killing blow.

"Get down!"

It was McDowell. He was standing at the base of the stairs, cradling the big MG4. The muzzle flash stabbed out into the darkness and tracer rounds hammered into the creature. It screeched in rage and covered its face with one huge arm. Naylor could smell burning hair where the hot tracer rounds hit it, but just like the nine-millimetre slugs from the MP5, McDowell's barrage didn't seem to be penetrating at all.

Naylor had to get out from under the thing. He clutched the weight under his hand, not caring what it was, and swung upwards. Gold glittered and the thing in his hand carved a bright arc upwards through the green-tinged darkness and bit into the creature.

It screamed with rage and clutched at the bloody stump where its right arm had been. It looked at Naylor with an expression of pure hatred and then it was gone.

"What the fuck was that thing?" McDowell asked.

"That was Ramirez," Naylor replied. Crazy as that sounded, he was certain it was true. Naylor had seen some weird shit in his time. He knew the world wasn't quite the way most people thought it was, but the differences could only be seen around the edges, in extreme situations in off-the-grid locales. The kind of places he found himself in more often than he liked.

Miller had not been delirious; Ramirez had changed. Somehow after his guards had been defeated the cartel boss had become that creature. He had killed the rest of the squad and now he was after them.

McDowell helped Lowe to his feet. His uniform was shredded from hip to shoulder, the ragged torn edges were soaked in blood. The creature's claws had bit deep into the muscle of his chest and stomach, but he was still alive.

"Good job," Lowe said nodding towards the thing Naylor still clutched, white-knuckled in his hand. It was a knife, a golden knife. Blood flecked the ornate curved blade, as rich and as red and the rubies that studded its hilt.

"Looks like you hurt it," McDowell said. He was right; the creature's severed arm lay where it had fallen among the splintered remains of the display cabinet. Only it wasn't really the creature's arm. Naylor looked at it closely: the fur was patchy and dry, flaky leather showed though the many bald patches. It was smaller, too; a dry, desiccated thing, quite unlike the powerful, vital creature that had nearly killed him.

Naylor picked it up. The skin came away in a roll and a human arm fell out onto the floor, leaving him holding the paw and tanned hide of a jaguar's forelimb. The skin tingled in his hand. Naylor could feel the power in it just waiting to be set free again.

"What the fuck!"

Naylor quickly searched the shattered display cabinet. So far the golden knife had been the only weapon able to injure the creature. Maybe there were more. He found nothing but torn velvet cushions and broken glass.

He searched the floor until he found what he was looking for: a laminated card about eight inches by six, the label from the display case. It showed a picture of the knife and what looked like a full jaguar pelt, complete with fanged skull and paws.

"It's an Olmec artefact," he said, reading from the card. "Olmec shamans worshipped the jaguar and wore its skin during their religious rituals. It was said that some shamans could use the pelts to become skinwalkers, manifestations of the Olmec jaguar god."

"Are you saying we're fighting a god?"

"You saw that thing. Bullets just bounced off it. So far the only thing able to hurt it has been a three-thousand-year-old ritual skinning knife. That thing is Ramirez!"

"God or not, we've hurt it. We need to get the fuck out of here before it comes back."

Naylor flexed his fist around the golden knife. He thought of all the good men lying dead on the villa's upper floors. He thought of all the evil Ramirez and his network of drug dealers had done. Yes, he had hurt it and it had felt good. He wanted to hurt it again. He wanted to go back and report mission accomplished. He wanted Ramirez's head on a plate. The jaguar pelt tingled in his hand. Maybe now they had the chance to do it.

* * *

They hurried out of the museum. There was no sign of the creature, but that didn't mean it had given up. The jaguar was a stealth predator. It hunted in silence, pouncing on its prey.

The night seemed lighter now. Naylor flipped up the night vision goggles and found he could see pretty well without them. They were getting close to the exit: he could smell the scent of the jungle wafting in through the shattered front door. It smelled like... like everything. He could smell the moisture in the air and tell you how long it had been since the rains. He could tell the season from the type of pollen on the breeze, he could smell the myriad creatures of the jungle night. If he listened closely, he thought he could hear them, hear their nocturnal burrowings and scurryings. He could almost taste them. The old dance again, but this time he was the hunter.

They made it outside. Naylor could see the path to the boathouse as clear as day. He could smell the sweat on his companions and hear the pulse of their beating hearts as McDowell helped the injured Lowe towards the boat.

And he could hear something else.

Something was stalking them. Ramirez had got out. He was here.

Naylor pulled the pin on an incendiary grenade and tossed it into the house. It exploded inside the building. Soon it would be engulfed in flame. Ramirez's millions in stashed cash, his priceless artefacts, Garcia and the bodies of Naylor's fallen squad mates would soon all be nothing but ash. The only trophies were the golden knife Naylor still clutched in his left hand and—

"Contact!" McDowell shouted.

Naylor saw it; saw the bulk of the skinwalker silhouetted against the sky as it slunk along the roof of the covered boat-house walkway.

"He's mine!" Naylor shouted and the words came out funny: deeper, with a rattle along the edge that was just short of a growl.

He flung off his helmet and MP5, tossing them into the burning house along with the rest of his grenades. He sprinted towards Ramirez, covering the ground with easy speed. He was aware of everything: the sounds of the night, the route to the boat and how long it would take his friends to get there. He felt like he could close his eyes and find Ramirez by scent alone. He had never felt so alive.

The Ramirez creature dropped in front of him but Naylor was ready for it. He swung the golden dagger up towards the creature's throat. His hand thudded into Ramirez's leathery paw as the creature blocked the knife with contemptuous ease. Its claws extended, slicing into Naylor's captured hand like five switchblades.

Naylor roared – a brutal animal roar of pain and rage ripped out from between his fangs and only then did the Ramirez creature notice the change.

Naylor swiped upward with his right hand, the hand bound in the fragment of the skinwalker pelt. Only it wasn't his hand now; it was a sleek, black javelin of sinew and claws. The one-armed Ramirez had no defence. Naylor's claws raked up his chest and tore out his throat.

Naylor tasted blood as the last beats of his prey's heart sprayed its lifeblood over him as it fell.

He lifted his head to the night sky and roared.

* * *

The motor launch chugged away down the river. Behind them, the compound blazed in a red and gold mirror of the sunrise that was just beginning to creep over the hills behind the house.

Naylor closed his left eye, the human one, and marvelled at the rich colours.

He looked over at Lowe who lay against the gunwale, swathed in bandages from the boat's first aid kit. "You look like hell," Naylor said.

Lowe looked back at him. "You can talk," he said.

Naylor smiled, feeling the unfamiliar length of the incisors on the right side of his mouth. He looked down at his paw: the black jaguar fur reached halfway up his bicep before giving way to human skin. But the changes didn't stop there. His right eye was bright yellow with a slitted pupil, his right ear was pointed and wouldn't keep still. It kept moving, searching out sounds on the riverbank.

"That was some mission," McDowell called back from the wheelhouse.

"Yep," Naylor replied. He hefted the rest of the skinwalker pelt he had taken from Ramirez's body. "But I reckon they're going to get a lot easier from now on."

SKADI'S WOLVES

Kirsten Cross

The English/Scottish border – 927AD

Dozens of unblinking eyes were watching every move Ælrik made. It was impossible to see the rest of their blue-stained faces in the shadows that clustered around the perimeter of the campfire. Only the whites of their eyes shone like malevolent stars in the darkness. The fire sent up greasy plumes of smoke, and every so often the resin that seeped out of the pine branches reached boiling point and erupted in a violent fizz and crack that sounded like condensed lightning. No matter how many times it happened, it never failed to make Ælrik flinch.

Flinching was something you didn't want to do in front of the 'Painted People'. These damn Picts saw any indication of fear as a sign of weakness – a sign that would instantly draw a violent and bloody response.

So the fact they were so frightened of what they called 'Skadi's Wolves' that they were even talking to Ælrik, a soldier and messenger of the hated King Æthelstan, without hacking him to pieces in the process was all the more astonishing.

The warlord and his priest squatted opposite Ælrik and his companion, a tousle-haired Dane named Jurgen. The lad was only in his nineteenth year, but already he had the mind of a far wiser and more experienced statesman on his young shoulders. If he lived, he'd go far. *If* he lived. His sword-arm was strong too, and in these times of turmoil that was probably much more useful than all the pretty words any silver-tongued envoy could pour onto the unimpressed heads of the Painted People – heads that bristled with lime-hardened spikes of white hair. To Ælrik's eyes they looked for all the world like hedgepigs that have rolled into a ball to defend themselves from the attentions of an over-curious wildcat.

The priest had spent the entire time muttering and drawing symbols into the dirt with a charred stick. His rotten teeth caused him to slur and stutter, but Jurgen could just about make out the guttural noises and interpret them into words. He translated the gibberish for Ælrik. "They come when the moon is full, he says."

"Who do?"

"Skadi's Wolves."

"Yes, I keep hearing this name. Who is this Skadi? Is he some kind of warlord?"

Jurgen shook his head. "Skadi is an ice giantess. She is one of the most feared of all the northern queens. She is the one who punished Loki for his crimes."

"Ah, right. So a myth, then."

Jurgen snorted. "As real to me as your mythical Fisher of Men is to you, my friend."

Ælrik rounded on the young Dane. "Blaspheme against the name of our Lord one more time and I'll kill you myself, understand?"

"*Your* lord, Ælrik, not mine. Anyway, I thought you Christians were supposed to forgive us simple Pagans?" Jurgen raised an eyebrow. "And perhaps this is a conversation for another time and not one we should indulge in now?" He gave an almost impercievable nod towards the Picts and lowered his voice. "They're nervous enough as it is of our presence, Ælrik. One wrong move and we could find ourselves skewered and roasting over this very fire. They eat people, you know. They really do."

Ælrik snorted. "No they don't, you young fool. But I agree that perhaps our spiritual debate can wait for another time. Continue."

Jurgen shifted uncomfortably. The Picts may be happy to squat for hours in front of a fire, but he had become used to the relative comforts of the Berwick garrison and, in particular, cushions. "According to the priest, Skadi's Wolves single out warriors. Anyone with a sword is fair game. They leave the villagers and farmers alone, unless, of course, they can't find any warriors. Then they'll feed on anyone they can run down."

"So what we actually have is a bunch of Norsemen raiders, dressed as wolves and led by a woman, and spoiling for a fight." Ælrik rolled his eyes. "Jurgen, you're a soldier. Do you honestly believe this nonsense about ice queens and men that shapeshift into wolves?"

"Says the man who asks some dickless monk to give him absolution every holy day, and then promptly goes out the next day killing and slaughtering. Be wary of what you make jests towards, my friend."

Ælrik stared open-mouthed at Jurgen. "You cannot possibly be telling me that you actually believe that some ice goddess–"

"Giantess."

"Whatever. Some ice giantess is hunting down soldiers with a pack of slathering, demonic wolves? Can't you see this is just a matter of simple campfire stories made up by a bunch of backward fools who still believe that painting their skin blue will make them invincible in battle?"

Jurgen shifted again. "*Hush*, man. Watch your tone. Our hosts may be ignorant, but they're smart enough to know when you're mocking them, even if it is in a language they don't understand." He twitched again, the merest of suggestions towards the warlord and his mumbling priest. The Picts scowled back. Ælrik held up an open hand in apology and indicated to the priest to continue.

Mumble, mutter, mumble. The priest scribbled in the dirt, the lines forming glyphs and symbols. Jurgen strained to see them and nodded. He pointed. "This one is Algiz – the rune of protection and concealment."

"And that means?"

"It means we are dealing with a hidden enemy. An enemy that uses the darkness to hunt its victims. But tonight it also means that we, too, are protected by the clouds that conceal the moon. Without bathing in her shining light, the beasts cannot take on their true form."

"So they can be killed when it's a bit cloudy? You jest, surely!"

"This is no jest, my friend. These are not ordinary wolves."

"Yes, I thought we'd already established that, Jurgen. These are not wolves at all! These are men *dressed* as wolves. And men, whether they wear the skin of a wolf, a bear or a flea-ridden alley-cat, I can kill." Ælrik stood and gave a stiff bow to the Pict warlord. "Jurgen, tell them we thank them for their hospitality and their information. I will inform our commander that we have a rogue band of Norsemen wandering around the countryside, and we'll hunt them down as we would a wild boar for a feast." He bowed stiffly again and turned to walk away from the fire.

A hand rested on his shoulder and he spun back, the warrior instinct immediately kicking in, his sword half drawn from his scabbard before he'd finished turning. He stared straight into the cracking blue woad and wild eyes of the priest. The smell of rotting meat rolled forward in blasts from the decrepit old man's mouth. Strands of putrid venison stuck between the stumps of his decayed teeth. The man's breath could have knocked down Hadrian's Wall itself.

"She comes. For you and your warriors. Her wolves come. They will *devour you all!*" The last words were snarled and filled with utter hatred. Damnation. The priest had understood every word, the foul little runt! Ælrik was tempted to draw his sword from the last half of the scabbard and run the disgusting little man through. But if he did, he knew he'd get no more than three steps before the entire tribe of blue-painted lunatics would be on him and tearing him apart. He had enough to worry about knowing there was some rogue Norse raiding party wandering the countryside between here and Berwick garrison, without having a horde of angry Picts chasing them through the badlands as well.

He sheathed his sword slowly, making damn sure the priest could hear the metal sliding back into the scabbard and know just how close he'd come to feeling the cold kiss of English steel in his belly. His eyes never left the wild, staring orbs of the priest. White foam collected in the corners of the Priest's mouth. The old man panted heavily, sending waves of foul breath washing over Ælrik. It was all the soldier could do to stop himself vomiting in the priest's face. He glanced at the taloned hand of the priest that still gripped his shoulder, and then back to the Pict. His eyes narrowed and he snarled at the vile little man. "Unhand me. *Now*." The authority in his voice – a voice used to giving orders – made the Pict retract his hand reluctantly and withdraw a pace. Ælrik could see him vibrating with anger, and sensed that the mood was spreading throughout the tribe. Angering a priest amongst these heathens was never a good move. The mood around the campfire was turning ugly. Time for a tactical withdrawal.

"Jurgen, the horses."

Jurgen sprang up, said a few hasty words of thanks to the warlord, assuring him they would be on the lookout for Skadi's Wolves as they journeyed back towards Berwick.

The warlord laughed. "You'll be looking for them? Northman, they already have your scent! You'll meet them soon enough!" He laughed again and, kicking dirt over the fire to extinguish the flames, barked a command at his followers. In a heartbeat they had melted back into the darkness. All except the priest.

The old man stood motionless by the smouldering embers and watched as Jurgen and Ælrik mounted their jittery horses. Ælrik gathered up his reins and, with one last dark look at the old priest, dug his heels into his mount's side. The horse leapt from standing start to flat gallop in just a few paces.

Jurgen paused, his hand on the pommel of his saddle. He turned and briefly bowed to the priest. The priest shook his head sadly. "You are a warrior. They will come for you too. I cannot give you protection. You have made your choice." The priest paused, and then picked up a pebble. With the burnt end of a stick, he scraped a shape onto the surface and held it up to the young man. "You are of the North. Perhaps Skadi will forgive you more readily than she will that Saxon dog. Take this." He thrust the pebble into Jurgen's hand, turned and vanished into the darkness.

Jurgen frowned, and glanced down at the stone. On its surface was a roughly shaped rune – Algiz. Protection. He pocketed the stone, looked around the deserted camp one last time, and spurred his nervous mount into following Ælrik. The horse needed little encouragement – it was keen to leave this place. It could smell them coming. It could sense them on the breeze...

* * *

Eyes, surrounded not by blue woad but by coarse, short hair, watched from the darkness. These weren't eyes full of fear, but shining golden orbs with elongated pupils. Eyes full of blood lust. The shadows twisted and writhed, as if the owners of those cold, gold eyes couldn't quite decide which form to take. The darkness rippled and contorted. A mouth twisted into a muzzle and curled back to reveal teeth that gleamed like polished walrus ivory. A low, throaty snarl rumbled slowly through the forest. It was joined by others, each one singing the same song, calling to their mistress to unleash them, to let them run the warriors down, to hunt, to chase, to *feed*.

"No. Not yet. We wait for the moon's light to shine upon you. Then you may hunt."

The darkness had a fractured, broken voice full of ice crystals and venom. A voice of the north, where the green, flickering lights of Asgard rippled and danced across the night sky. A voice that wrapped revenge in warm fur skins and set it loose across the frozen wastelands. The voice of a giantess with a heart that had no mercy for her enemies. Had she not challenged the gods themselves, and won? Had she not tormented Loki with the dripping toxin of a viper until he begged her to release him?

She knew no fear. And she knew no mercy, either. Mortal warriors like these two were nothing to her. They would lead her to a far greater bounty, a bounty that would generate more and more of her children until they grew into an army that would sweep the hated Saxons from this island – an island she claimed as her own. Then she would bring the ice, and a hundred winters and a hundred more...

* * *

Ælrik slowed his horse to a walk. A flat-out gallop through the darkness was foolish in the extreme. It would take just one tree root or one rabbit hole to send his horse crashing to the ground, screaming and snorting as its leg snapped. Then he'd be forced to either ride two-up on Jurgen's horse, or run the last few miles to Berwick garrison. And if they really did have a band of Norsemen, or demons, or whatever on their tail, then trying to outrun them would be just as foolish as galloping a horse along a trail in the dark. He'd never make it.

The horse puffed and blew, tossing its head up and down. Its ears flickered, flattening against its skull. It was spooked by something only it could see or smell. Ælrik patted its neck and made soothing, cooing noises. "Settle, shush, settle." He watched as Jurgen reined in his own horse and fell into step. His beast was just as nervous as Ælrik's, if not more so. The damn things scuttled and danced stiff-legged, rolling their eyes and snorting.

Something in the darkness was following them. Ælrik could feel the hairs on the back of his neck standing on end. Whatever it was – whether they were Norsemen or wolves – was keeping just out of sight, merging into the shadows and harrying them relentlessly. But just beyond the crest of the next moorland plateau was the warmth and safety of Berwick and the garrison. Thick stone walls encircled the town – a settlement that had been fought over for generations by Norsemen, Picts and Saxons alike. The Romans had regarded it as their most northerly frontier town. Even the women could wield a sword in this embattled place. The locals, bitter from years of bloodshed and violence, had faces as hard as the granite stone that formed the walls. They didn't like strangers, and they didn't like anyone or anything that hinted at Pagan filth and their degenerate beliefs. They knew the Lord looked after His own – and their swords would do the rest.

Once they were back in the safety of the garrison, Ælrik knew they could rest up, and then tell the commander of the potential threat in the morning. Then he and Jurgen could ride out with a company of cavalry and hunt these damn Norse wolfmen down. No fuss, no bother. A band of Norse warriors dressed in skins was nothing to worry about unduly. They'd need to be an army to go against the Berwick garrison, and from what the Picts said there was only a small band of these wolfskin-wearing bastards to deal with.

Ælrik wasn't concerned with anything except making it back to the garrison. Out here, and with only Jurgen for company, he was vulnerable. With his men behind him, he'd be invincible.

They reached the crest of the ridge and looked down into the valley. Ælrik could sense Jurgen behind him, growling rough commands at his increasingly nervous horse. He twisted in the saddle and looked at the young man. "You all right?"

Jurgen sawed at the reins and growled again at the skittish horse. "Aye. Just this damned animal. Never known it to be so unruly." Jurgen knew the horse was simply picking up on his own rising panic, and he inwardly chastised himself for his weakness. He was a soldier, damn it. Soldiers didn't get spooked by faerie tales and campfire exaggerations about men who could change into wolves, commanded by an ice giantess who could bring the very gods themselves to their knees. Without thinking, he slid his right hand into his pocket and curled his fingers around the runestone the Pict priest had given him. It wasn't much, but somehow its smooth, hard surface reassured him. He was careful not to rub it, though – doing so would remove the delicate charcoal symbol and turn it from a runestone into nothing more than, well, a stone, really. He let the runestone drop back into the depths of his pocket and focused on the here and now, rather than superstitions and magical talismans.

"Nearly there." Ælrik pointed to the horizon and the flickering lights of the garrison in the distance.

Jurgen managed to bring the prancing horse under control and shuffled alongside his friend. "You do know we're being followed."

"Yes. We have been ever since we left the Pict campsite. They're good, I'll give them that. No matter how many times I turn around, they're staying just out of sight."

"Isn't that strange, though?" Jurgen frowned. "Norse raiders would have been on us like a swarm of bees by now. Why are they holding back?"

"Perhaps they've taken one too many blows to the head." Ælrik laughed.

Jurgen wasn't convinced. "Or perhaps they're waiting for us to get to the garrison and the rush the gate when it opens?"

Ælrik's smile abruptly vanished. "And this is why I chose you as a companion, Jurgen. Not because you speak a dozen languages, but because you're a natural strategist." He patted the younger man on the shoulder. "Don't worry. They'll get a nasty surprise if that's their little plan. The garrison is fully manned right now."

"No, it isn't. I told you. The main company rode out for York yesterday. The King marches against the Norsemen. There's only a handful of men defending the place."

Ælrik spun around in his saddle. "What?"

"With so many Norsemen on the move, the King had to summon the entire garrison. That's why I was sent to call you back from Edinburgh. We were due to march with them, but our delay by the Picts means we'll have to defend Berwick with just a company of the walking wounded and a few peasants." Jurgen shrugged.

Ælrik cursed loudly, and backhanded the blond man across his mouth, knocking him from his saddle. "Damn you! When exactly were you going to tell me this?"

Jurgen pushed himself back to his feet and glowered at Ælrik. He spat a globule of spittle and blood onto the ground and wiped the red trickle that ran from the corner of his mouth. "Do that again, and I'll leave you to the mercy of my fellow Norsemen and their demons! I told you last night at the King of Alba's table! Or were you too befuddled by ale to understand the urgency of our return, you damn fool!" Jurgen grabbed his horse's reins and swung back into the saddle. "Perhaps it would be best to have the safety of the walls at our backs before we argue this out again, what say you?" With an angry shout, Jurgen spurred his horse towards the dim lights of Berwick.

Muttering profanities, Ælrik followed his friend, regretting his hasty reaction and determined to regain the Northman's trust and favour once they got back to the garrison. Jurgen was right. He had drunk too much ale the night before. It was his weakness. It helped to dull the blood-soaked memories and the dreams sent by the Devil himself to torment him.

As the prey cantered away, snuffling and snorting filled the ridge and a cluster of black forms shimmered into view, staying just below the skyline and hunched against the gorse and heather. One, its form indeterminate and fluctuating from man to beast and back again, came across the globule of blood. It sniffed at the blood and recoiled, pulling his lips back and baring fangs that were neither canine nor human. A shadowy form walked among them, and with every step frost spread out like a fungus, crackling and entombing every blade of grass, every leaf and every prickle, with ice. She looked down at the spittle and frowned. "This one carries the protection of the All Father. He is not to be harmed as long as he holds that mark. Even if he is a traitor to our people and rides at the enemy's side." Her ice blue eyes looked towards the distant lights of the garrison. "The Saxon and his kind, though, are yours." She turned her face to the sky, just as the last cloud slipped away and revealed the shimmering, silver disk of a full moon.

With a howl, the shapes finally settled on a single form. Bones cracked, broke and reformed, sending the morphing creatures into spasms of rage and agony. Thirteen men became thirteen raging, slavering wolves – bigger, faster and more vicious than any pack that ran through the wilds of the northern lands. These were Skadi's Wolves – feared not only by mortals and their mothers, but by the Gods themselves. The Christian Fisher King's mewing men would be no match for their fury.

Baying and howling, they looked to their mistress to release them. She smiled, petted the largest – a massive, black-furred, golden-eyed monster with a maw that would swallow a baby whole – and raised a glistening, frost-covered hand. She curled all but one finger into a fist, ice crystals dropping from her skin, and pointed at the garrison. "Feast, my children. *Feast!*"

With a final group howl, Skadi's Wolves were unleashed...

* * *

"What in God's name was that?" Ælrik skidded to a stop and spun around in his saddle.

"That was our doom calling us! Ride, you fool, *ride!*" Jurgen kicked his horse into a gallop, no longer concerned by possible tree roots or rabbit holes. They had just a mile to go before they reached the garrison. He knew his horse was almost at the end of its endurance – he could see the vein in its thick neck pulsing frantically. Damn it, the blasted creature's heart was close to exploding through sheer exhaustion and terror. "One mile, damn you, one mile!" He kicked the animal in the ribs, urging it on. If the wretched creature collapsed at the gates then it was of no matter. But they needed to get to safety before the Wolves descended upon them.

Ælrik scowled. "No man howls like that…"

The demonic, blood-curdling howling screamed defiance, vengeance and a lust for blood that only the beating heart of a terrified, dying man would slate.

"Lord God Almighty, protect us!" Ælrik kicked his heels against his horse's ribcage and the creature leapt into a gallop with no further encouragement.

One mile.

That's all.

Just *one mile…*

* * *

The garrison at Berwick was almost deserted. A few lame and injured soldiers, still beaten, bloodied and bruised from recent running skirmishes with the Norsemen, were all that were left. One cook, one stable boy and a couple of guards to protect the gate made up the company. It would be a pitifully weak defence against anything that may come from the north. But the Garrison walls were three feet thick in places, and the gates were made of solid English Oak that age had hardened to the strength of iron. Besides, all the problems were to the south, where York was now the focus of King Æthelstan's attentions.

Every man who could fight had marched with the King. All that was left in Berwick were those who would have simply slowed the column and become a burden to their comrades. Three monks had volunteered to stay and tend to the sick and the wounded, raining muttered benedictions and blessings on those who could not escape their pious mumbling. The monks did nothing except remind the dying soldiers of their impending mortality. Their poultices stank and stung, the bandages were merely sack cloth cut into strips, and the gruel they slopped into wooden bowls would not have sustained a child. Yet here they were, these monks with their tonsured heads, their filthy brown robes and their stinking, dirt-caked skin – and large, solid silver crosses swinging from their waists. The grubby, once-white cords that held their robes in place each carried a silver cross so large that, if melted down and beaten into coins, would feed and clothe a family for a year. Many of the soldiers, who were still struggling with their faith, felt a jarring at the juxtaposition of supposedly penitent monks displaying such ostentatious wealth so flagrantly. No wonder the men of the North constantly raided their shores, if they knew that such riches were on open display and there for the taking!

Many of the northern soldiers blamed the monks in no small measure for the violence that had plunged their land into such black and bloody turmoil. And now the sanctimonious bastards had the audacity to tell them to be grateful for God's bounty of watery gruel and stale bread? Damn them all! Damn them and their Fisher God…

The gate guards were roused into slothish movement by the sound of pounding hooves and shouting. "Open the gate! Open, in the name of God and the King!"

A screaming whinny indicated a horse that had finally given up and collapsed, its heart now just a flapping, bloody mess of torn muscle in its chest.

The gate guards rushed to the observation point to see who demanded entry at this hour. "Who goes there, calling by the name of the King?"

"Ælrik and Jurgen! For the love of God Almighty, man, let us in! We're under attack!"

The gate guard turned to his colleague. "Sound the alarm!" One guard nodded and sprinted off along the battlements towards the alarm bell, while his compatriot slid down the wooden ladder and ran to the gate. With a grunt, he heaved the heavy oak bar out of its resting place and hauled on the handle.

When there was just enough room to squeeze through, Ælrik stumbled his way in, spun, grabbed Jurgen by the scruff and hauled him through. "*Shut it! Shut it now!*" The guard slammed the gate shut and Jurgen helped him lift the oak beam and slot it back into position.

The clanging alarm bell brought the few mobile occupants of the Garrison scurrying out into the courtyard. Limping soldiers on crutches, those with bandages around their heads or with their arm in a sling, stood bleary-eyed and confused. The three monks scurried out like brown rats, twitching their noses and scuffling their sandals through the horse-shit and mud. "What's this? What's this?" The eldest of the tonsured fools scuttled up to Ælrik. "Are we under attack?"

"Why do you think my men have sounded the alarm, you dolt? Of course we're under attack! And by something unholy too, Father. So we may have need of your skills and machinations before this night is through!" Ælrik glowered at the monk, his instinct to backhand the damn fool battling with his reverence for the supposed authority of a priest.

The oak gates shook violently as a force slammed into them from the outside. The beam held. Just. Another violent judder shook the entire gate. Small flakes of stone and mortar floated down. From the other side of the gates came snuffling and growling – deep, guttural and primeval. Claws scrabbled and dug at the wood, scraping and scratching into the oak planks.

Ælrik, Jurgen, the guards and those men that could stand and move stepped slowly back, drawing their swords and readying themselves. The gates were strong, but would they be strong enough? Another shudder shook the gates as the beasts on the other side threw their weight at the oak.

"What manner of attack is this?" The oldest of the monks stared at the shaking gates and crossed himself frantically.

"Demons, Father. Demons with big teeth and a taste for Christian blood!" Ælrik snarled at the monk. "Vile hounds from the north. They delight in the name of Skadi's Wolves."

"God preserve us!" The monk wailed. "Not here, not again!"

Before Ælrik had a chance to ask the monk what he meant by 'not again', the gate juddered violently. A sliver of wood broke away from one of the planks, and a single golden eye filled with menace and evil peered through. The owner of the eye snarled and growled, a long, low rumbling that lasted several heart-beats. Taloned fingers, part human, part animal, curled through the small gap and started to worry and scrabble at the planking.

Before Ælrik or any of his men could respond, a monk leapt forward. The silver cross that usually hung from his grubby, knotted cord was in his hand and pointing straight at the beast's golden eye. The monk, yelling for the power of God to protect him, plunged the long shaft of the cross deep into the wolf's orb.

The screaming was horrific. The beast disappeared from view and continued to howl in agony, the silver cross still embedded in its eye. Thrashing and snarling came from beyond the damaged gate, as the injured beast yelped again and again like a kicked puppy. The smell of burning flesh filtered through the gap in the wood; an odd, acrid smell that stung the back of the men's throats.

Above the animal sounds rose a scream of absolute fury that stopped every living creature – man and beast – in its tracks. The sound of a furious ice giantess. *"NO! You dare defile my children? You dare? Kill them! Kill them all! Spare no one!"*

The gate shook violently as the beasts launched a barrage of attacks. The sound of splintering wood sent the men back further. Ælrik had a nasty feeling that English steel, while it may have been good for skewering Pictish priests, would be no match for these hellish creatures and their furious mistress. "Priest! How is it that your man's cross had such an effect?"

"As much as I'd like to say it's the power of our Lord God Almighty that smites them, it is the silver. They cannot bear its touch. That and the touch of the sun's rays." The monk held up the cross that dangled at his waist. "See this?" He indicated to the main shaft that tapered down into a point. "Have you never wondered why our crosses are shaped so? It is because we know of these beasts."

"Then you know how to fight them."

"Normally? Yes. But they're too great an enemy for us to fight, soldier. We must flee."

"You do and I'll cut you down myself!" Ælrik snarled. "We have just an hour until dawn. We hold them off. We *fight!*"

The monk shrugged. "Then we'll die. I suppose it is God's will that we die alongside you and your men."

Ælrik shook his head. "No. Leave the fighting to us. The three of you get the wounded to the keep. If they breach the outer gate, that will be our only chance. *Move!"*

The monks scuttled away, leaving the soldiers to face the gates and the hellish creatures that lay beyond them. Time and again the beasts threw themselves with renewed vigour at the oak, and time and again it managed to repel them. But slowly, surely, the wood was starting to weaken.

"Ælrik! Look!" Jurgen pointed to the top of the gates. White frost was starting to creep slowly down the surface of the wood. Deep, penetrating fingers of ice crackled and snapped, plunging deep into the timber and pushing its fibres apart. The ice giantess' touch was sending permafrost deep into the solid oak, splitting it like a woodsman's axe would go through soft pine.

"Damn it!" Ælrik could see they had moments before the gates fell. "Fall back! Fall back to the keep!" The soldiers turned and ran, the more able supporting their wounded colleagues.

Jurgen stood motionless, watching the frost creep down the wood, mesmerised by the glistening patterns. His Norse blood pulsed. He knew he was in the presence of one who had seen the halls of Asgard, who had stared into the eye of the All Father himself. One who had defied the gods and chosen her own path. Could he deny his heritage any longer? Could he sit and listen to the burbling of the Fisher King's priests, knowing now what stood before him just beyond that gate?

He had abandoned his people. His kin. He had turned traitor and ridden at the side of the enemy. He deserved Skadi's wrath. His sword clattered from his hands and he dropped to his knees, bowing his head, waiting for the wolves.

"Jurgen! What in God's name are you doing! Run, man! *Run!*" Ælrik started to move towards his friend.

The gates gave way, exploding in a shower of ice crystals and deadly splinters. The thirteen beasts stood snarling and slathering at the threshold. Slowly, Jurgen looked up and opened his arms, welcoming the wolves at the door, inviting them in. In his right hand was a small, round pebble. It was just possible to see the mark of Algiz – the rune of protection. Smudged. Smeared. *Incomplete...*

A wolf, massive, muscular and with one ruined and bloody eye socket that still seeped sticky vitreous fluid, moved forward slowly. He stood in front of the prostate man. The lips of his muzzle were pulled back to reveal two rows of gleaming, savagely sharp teeth – teeth designed for tearing flesh and crushing bones. He reached out and batted the worthless pebble out of Jurgen's hand, a low, rumbling growl vibrating in its massive throat.

The pebble clattered onto the cobbles and rolled away. Jurgen looked into the golden eye of the beast. A single tear rolled down his cheek. "Take me. Spare the others. I am your kin. Take me."

The beast studied the prostate man for a moment, its hot breath blasting onto Jurgen's cheek. Then it turned, looking back over its shoulder and waiting for permission from its mistress to begin the carnage by feasting with the one who had carried the mark of the All Father. The one who now kneeled, defenceless and unprotected, believing foolishly that his sacrifice would protect the others.

It wouldn't.

In the darkness a figure, massive and imposing, nodded once. The beast turned back to Jurgen and its muzzle wrinkled in a savage snarl. The massive maw opened and with a roar the beast fell on the blond man. The others, taking their cue from their leader, swarmed through the ruined gates and, snapping and snarling at each other, tore Jurgen to pieces.

"*NO!*" Ælrik screamed defiance and rage at the savage slaughter of his friend. "You foul demons! No!" Screaming in fury with every step, he charged towards the beasts as they ripped into the flesh of his comrade. He could see Jurgen's leg protruding from the melee of writhing bodies, twitching and jumping as every savage bite tore another lump of flesh from his body. The poor man was still alive. The beasts were prolonging the agony. Finally, Jurgen's screaming was cut short as one wolf tore off his face, ripping the skin from his skull as one would peel the fur coat from a coney.

His men saw the savagery of the beasts, and despite their injuries the warrior instinct filled every single one of them. With a roar, they charged towards the beasts, determined to cut them down and avenge Jurgen's horrific death, or die like soldiers in the attempt.

The silver light of the moon dimmed.

In mid-feast, Skadi's Wolves stopped and looked up as a cloud slid across the face of the moon, shielding her rays and plunging the courtyard into gloom. The moon vanished and the beasts howled in unison. The men of the garrison watched in horror as their enemy struggled to find a form.

"Now! While they're weakest! Attack now!" Ælrik charged forward, hacking at the writhing bodies with his sword. His men followed suit, stabbing and slashing at anything that moved.

The cobbles became slick underfoot. Blood and guts mixed with shit and the slippery ice crystals from the shattered door. Yelping and howling filled the night – the roar of an unholy battle between ancient demons and terrified, enraged men.

Men died. Badly. The beasts, torn between the agony of transformation and the injuries the soldiers were inflicting on them, still fought with a ferocity that was matched only by the fury of the soldiers they tried to slaughter. It was a vile, bloody stalemate.

In the darkness, a huge figure stood and watched impassively, a cold smile playing around thin, hard lips. What the mortals seemed to forget was that clouds were transient. They drifted like snow on the wind. Skadi looked up. A twinkle of a frosty star and the silver edge of the moon's glow indicated the cloud was passing. She looked back at the melee. The mortals believed they were winning as her twisting, writhing children howled and bayed, falling back under a barrage of sword strikes.

Then the cloud drifted on.

The moon blazed forth in all her glory.

Skadi threw her head back and let out a roar that was heard in Valhalla itself.

Ælrik watched as the beasts writhed and twisted back into demonic hounds full of golden-eyed fury and snarling rage.

"Oh, God, *no...*"

SEMPER GUMBY

Steve Coate

Robert Neidermeyer grabbed hold of the straps securing him in the back of the C-130 Hercules. He felt a jolting impact with each turbulent shudder of the aircraft's hull. Around him, the other members of his squad paid no heed to the rough and tumble ride. Neidermeyer straightened in his seat and willed his hands to release the straps holding him in place. It was his first active-duty mission and he wanted to impress the others in his squad.

Lieutenant Ron Bradley strode from the forward cabin, bellowing to be heard above the roar of the plane's four powerful engines. "Okay, ladies! The pilot has informed me we are at cruising altitude, so feel free to remove your restraints. We've got another couple hours before we reach the drop zone in Tikrit, so make sure your tactical gear and chutes are ready and then feel free to natter on about the latest dress your favorite celebrity is wearing, or hold a knitting circle, or whatever it is you ladies do best during your down time!"

A chorus of "Hoo-ah!" filled the cabin and the lieutenant – the LT – showed them his back before returning to the forward cabin.

Neidermeyer unlatched his safety straps, reached for his M16, and performed a quick check of the weapon then the rest of his gear. When he had made sure that all was in working order and in its place, Neidermeyer looked across to where Jack Howling Wolf sat opposite him. The big Indian held a combat knife in one hand, his eyes fixed on its silvery blade.

Neidermeyer leaned to his right and elbowed Joe Leeds. "Hey, what's Tonto's deal?" he whispered, tilting his head toward Wolf.

"Don't let him hear you call him that, man," whispered Leeds. "Wolfman's full-blooded Navajo and he don't take any shit about it. Watch what you say, or he'll kick your ass, newbie or not."

"I didn't know." Neidermeyer held up a pair of placating hands, leaning close to Leeds. "But what's the deal with him and the knife? It's giving me the willies."

Leeds grinned, his pearly whites a stark contrast to his ebony skin. "You're new, so you haven't heard the story yet." He turned toward Jack. "Hey, Wolfman! Newbiemeyer wants to hear the story about your blade. What do you say?"

Wolf raised his gaze from the keen edge of the silver blade to look first at Leeds then to Neidermeyer. With his eyes never leaving the new soldier's face, Wolf flipped the knife into the air where it spun end-over-end until it fell prey to gravity and continued its descent, the flat of the blade slapping into Wolf's outstretched palm. "Cuts Like a Knife. 1983. Bryan Adams. The album was released to great commercial success and few singles of the day sold nearly as well as the title track, particularly from Canadian artists such as Adams, who was made popular by love songs."

"Wolfman Jack, baby!" Leeds thrust a forefinger through the air. "Dropping musical knowledge left and right."

Wolf balanced the knife by the tip on the pad of one out-stretched finger. "This knife saved my life in Mosul. I keep it with me for luck. And protection." A slight movement of the finger caused the knife to topple to one side, where Wolf caught the hilt in his other hand. "Before I transferred to this unit, I was part of an eight-man squad tasked with what was supposed to be a simple rescue mission."

"They never are," Leeds interjected.

Neidermeyer looked to the man and saw that others in the unit were crowding close to hear the story.

Wolf looked at the lean, dark-skinned soldier. "Who's telling this story, Leeds?"

Leeds bowed his head and his voice dropped an octave. "You are. Sorry."

Wolf nodded. Whether in forgiveness or agreement, only he knew. "We'd just been dropped into the shit. It was 0200 hours when we hit the ground. We figured we'd catch the enemy napping, hustle our guys, a pilot and a journalist out of there and be done with it. Little did we know the shitstorm we were walking into. It was a complete eleven up, three down, eight up situation."

* * *

Jack Howling Wolf and Lieutenant Rudy 'Hawk' Hawkins hustled to the next available cover, keeping their weapons trained on a fixed point ahead, ready to fire if the enemy should present themselves before the unit could reach their destination. The next fire team, comprising Jester, Hulk, and the only female soldier, 'Swerve' Raiborne, moved past Wolf and Hawk to the next vantage point, where they covered and waited for the third and final team – Slim, Doc, and Preacher, who moved forward to the next point.

Wolf and the LT advanced once more, but when they reached the first fire team, Hawk signaled for a squad-column movement. The fire team followed behind Wolf and the LT, who repeated the hand signal when they reached the second fire team. Moving ahead in this manner, they eventually came to a halt a few hundred meters from the camp.

Hawk turned to the rest of the unit and signaled no gunfire until absolutely necessary, or until fired upon. He was met with grim nods as several of the unit withdrew knives, their blades dulled with camo so the weapons didn't shine in the moonlight.

Hawk switched off his night-vision goggles and slipped them up to his forehead. The others in the unit followed his example to avoid being blinded by the fire that burned in the center of the camp. The LT waited thirty seconds for their eyes to adjust to the darkness then signaled for one fire team to head east around the perimeter of the camp, and another to the west. Wolf and the LT would take the more direct route.

As the two soldiers crept closer to the encampment, Wolf spotted a lone enemy moving along the far perimeter of the camp. Two more soldiers stood sentry outside what Wolf guessed to be a command tent. While Wolf looked on, Swerve emerged from the shadows across the camp, snaked one hand around the perimeter guard's mouth, and drove the blade of her Ka-bar into one of the man's lungs, stealing his ability to scream an alarm. Swerve dragged the twitching body into the darkness and Wolf lost sight of them both.

Wolf and the LT stayed out of the line-of-sight of the command-tent sentries and crept into the nearest tent, where four of the enemy slept, unaware. They went to work with their knives, moving from one sleeping enemy to the next. When they had done, the desert sand drank the blood the marines had spilled.

As they exited the tent, Wolf noticed the command-tent sentries were no longer at their posts. Swerve stood outside the tent nearest and when she saw Wolf and the LT, pointed at the command tent, raised two fingers and then drew another across her neck. Jester and Hulk emerged from the tent at which Swerve stood lookout, and read her hand signals. They looked to the LT who motioned for them to clear the perimeter then converge on the command tent.

Wolf and the LT made another bloody visit to the next tent as the other fire teams finished up the rest. Once this was done, the three teams converged on the command tent. Still no prisoners, which Wolf knew meant one of two things: they were either inside the command tent, or they were already dead and disposed of. The LT signaled breach orders then Hawk unclipped a flashbang, pulled the pin and lobbed the grenade inside.

The flashbang did its work. Screams of alarm followed the explosive light and sound. The LT and Wolf rushed inside, moving around the edge to the tent's rear. The other fire teams followed, one moving left and the other taking up a position near the entry point. At the back of the tent, two bound and hooded figures knelt on the sand, one with his wrists in gleaming shackles. The restraints lacked the dull, weathered hue of iron, or the gunmetal grey of solid steel. They could only be made of silver. There was no time to ponder this oddity. Standing behind the hostages, reeling from the effects of the flashbang, stood two enemy soldiers. One held an AK47, the other a knife. Wolf took aim at the latter and squeezed the trigger of his M16, placing three rounds in his center mass. The enemy dropped his weapon and toppled to the ground next to his ally, whom Hawk had already dispatched with his own three-round burst. Ordered chaos erupted as gunfire took out the remaining targets. One of the two prisoners found his feet and rushed toward the tent flap.

"Watch your fire," Hawk yelled.

Against all probability, the hooded prisoner made it out of the tent without being killed by friendly fire. The LT nodded toward the tent flap. "Wolf, Swerve, go get him."

Both marines exited the tent. Wolf caught up as Swerve took hold of one of the fleeing prisoner's arms. Wolf nabbed the hood by one corner and yanked it free of the man's head. "Take it easy, pal. We're going to get you home."

The man's head snapped around, fear alight in his eyes as he faced the marine. The man wore a disheveled Air Force uniform. "No. You don't understand. We have to get out of here *now*."

"You're spooked," Wolf said as Swerve cut the ropes that bound the pilot's wrists behind his back. "It's understandable. You've been held captive and mistreated. Don't worry. It's over now."

The Air Force pilot's blue eyes widened as he looked from Wolf to Swerve. "We have to go, *now*. The other one, he's not like us." The pilot stared over his shoulder toward the command-tent entrance.

"Hey," Wolf said. "Just be glad we showed up to save your ass. We'll get out of here just as soon as we regroup with the others." He tugged the pilot toward the tent.

The pilot wrested his arm free of Wolf and held his ground. "You're not listening."

"Stay with him," Wolf told Swerve. "I'll get the others." He moved toward the tent but the bellow of a great beast stopped him in his tracks. He had been around the world, set foot on four continents, yet this … sound was foreign to him. The hairs on the back of Wolf's neck stood to attention as the beast's eerie cry resounded through the marrow of his bones. Wolf faltered, then steeled himself. He motioned for Swerve to stay put then advanced on the tent. Gunfire erupted. Not the disciplined 'one burst, one kill' shooting he was accustomed to from his unit, either. This was wild, panic-stricken fire, the kind often heard from enemy troops when caught unaware.

Wolf readied his M16, and entered through the tent flap just in time to see Preacher impaled upon the claws of a great furred beast, the man's weapon aimed skyward and firing, indiscriminately ripping holes through the top of the tent. Wolf froze as he took in the tableau of blood, entrails and viscera that had once made up the members of his unit. The interior of the tent was covered with bodies and gore. It must have also been from the enemy soldiers they had put down – there was just too much of it.

Hawk, Jester, Doc, and the others had been ripped apart by this beast that stood on two legs like some horrific mockery of a man. Wolf did not see the body of the second prisoner as he raised his gun toward the beast. It was naked except for a pair of tattered slacks and the remnants of boots that clung to the sides of its clawed, three-toed feet. A strip of cloth clung to one side of its neck. Beneath a pair of inset eyes that burned an unnatural amber, an elongated snout thrust forward. Jaws housed ferocious fangs sharp enough to rend flesh and bone. The blood of Wolf's comrades staining the beast's fangs seemed to back that theory.

Near its feet lay a pair of open silver shackles.

The beast tossed Preacher's mangled body aside and whirled to face Wolf. Crouched on its haunches, it roared its disapproval at the intruder. Wolf thumbed his M16 to full auto and squeezed the trigger, backing out of the tent as he fired. "Die, motherfucker!"

Once outside, Wolf stepped sideways, out of sight of the doorway. "Get him out of here," he called to Swerve, as he swapped out his empty mag for a fresh one.

"I told you. I fuckin' told you!" Wolf heard the pilot say, panic rife in his voice.

With a sound between a bellow and a growl, the beast charged through the tent flap. "Holy shit!" yelled Swerve as she unloaded on the creature. Wolf saw the chickenshit pilot run for the perimeter while Swerve defended his hasty retreat. The beast seemed at least eight feet tall and despite the fusillade of bullets, it kept coming. Swerve goggled. The inertia of the impacts pushed the beast back and she even managed to make it bleed. But not for long. Where the creature's flesh had been pockmarked with bullets, the damage repaired itself almost immediately. "It's healing faster than I can hurt it," Swerve yelled.

With a swipe of one arm, the creature batted away Swerve's M16. She had barely managed to draw her Ka-bar by the time the beast's claws sliced her throat on its backswing.

Swerve's eyes widened in shock. Blood spurted. She fell to one side, maintaining a death grip on the blade. The beast raised its head to the sky and howled. It then loped after the fleeing pilot. With the tools at hand, there was no saving the pilot, Wolf knew, but if he moved quickly perhaps he might be able to do something about that.

He ducked back inside the command tent, making sure to breathe through his mouth so the stench of death within wouldn't overwhelm his senses. He moved to the back of the tent, where the prisoners had knelt when he had first entered the tent. There, he found the silver shackles and the knife – also fashioned from silver – the enemy soldier guarding the prisoners had been wielding. Wolf slung the shackles around his neck then grabbed the silver-bladed knife.

A blood curdling scream pierced the night. It was soon cut short before it could give full voice to the depth of its pain. A howl. The pilot was dead. With the knife in one hand and the M16 cradled in his other arm, Wolf exited the tent.

The creature loped toward him, red-stained tongue dangling from its mouth. If not for its intimidating size, menacing fangs and claws, and the death and destruction the marine had witnessed this morning, Wolf might have thought it wanted to play. He took aim and unloaded into the advancing beast. As soon as he was out of bullets, he tossed the rifle aside and pulled the shackles free where he began whirling them through the air like a lasso. In his other hand he gripped the silver knife, blade outward. "Bring it, you bastard," he said through clenched teeth.

The great beast halted before Wolf and began pacing back and forth on all fours. It growled at the marine, then raised its snout to the sky and sent forth one long howl. The two locked eyes; neither the trained military man, nor the preternatural creature willing to show a sign of weakness. It gave a ferocious growl and leapt.

Wolf slashed at the beast with the knife and was rewarded with a yelp of pain as he ducked a swipe of its claws. The two faced-off again. The beast paced before him, blood oozing from a gash that ran from its left shoulder down across its pectoral muscles. The beast growled, deep and guttural.

The silver shackle whistled through the air at Wolf's side. "Rethinking your strategy, now, aren't you, you furry fuck?"

The beast feigned a leap then slashed at Wolf with one clawed paw. Wolf anticipated the strike, sidestepping as he looped the shackle's chain around the beast's arm. Wolf yanked on the ends of the shackles, ensnaring the creature. It howled in pain as its flesh began to smoke beneath the silver. The creature swiped wildly with its free paw, but Wolf dodged the careless strikes easily.

In a desperate move, the creature pulled its trapped arm inward. The silver chain bit through the flesh, severing it midway between elbow and wrist. The beast howled in agony as Wolf took a step back. This time, the force of the creature's soul-shattering wail nearly knocked Wolf off his feet. His breathing was labored. "That was for Swerve, you piece of shit."

When the beast dived at him again, Wolf timed his own jump perfectly, flying over the creature and latching onto its back. He drove the blade into its eye, holding tight to its neck as it bucked and swayed. Grasping the blade and using it as a pinion, Wolf swung the silver shackle around the creature's neck like a metal collar, before releasing his hold on the knife handle and grasping the other end of silver links.

Like a garrotte, he applied pressure. The beast bucked and writhed, the stink of burning fur fouling the air, but Wolf held on, desperately sawing the chain through the flesh.

Wolf yanked the chain toward him, then threw his head back and roared all of his rage and loss and pain into the sky, finally understanding why the creature howled at the heavens. But he felt no sympathy for the freak of Nature. With each sawing motion, Wolf called out the name of each squad member felled by the beast. With one final roar, he wrenched the chain back, beheading the creature. The lifeless body thumped to the ground, Wolf riding it down. He pushed to his feet then spat on the corpse.

He bent, yanked the knife from the dead thing's eye then went about the maudlin task of retrieving dog tags from the dead. Once done, he moved the bodies of Swerve and the pilot into the command tent and stepped outside, holding a fragmentation grenade at the ready. "You were good soldiers," he said, pulling the pin. "I hope this Viking funeral does you enough honor." He lobbed the grenade into the tent and hustled away.

The explosion ripped the tent asunder. Flames leapt high into the air, consuming everything within. Wolf bowed his head, then turned and began to trudge his way to the extraction point.

* * *

"Holy shit," Neidermeyer said. "You're fucking with me, right? Having fun with the new guy?"

Wolfman contemplated his knife. "Adapt and overcome in any situation, soldier."

"Right, I paid attention at Basic," said Neidermeyer. "But seriously… a werewolf?"

Wolfman shrugged. "You asked."

Neidermeyer blew air out his nose. "Yeah, I guess I did." The others in the unit began to disperse now the tale had reached an end. Neidermeyer admired the tips of his boots. "I realize you feel you have to put the new guy through his paces, but you should know I'm less naïve than the average FNG."

"Good to know," Wolfman said.

"So with all due respect," he looked to the weathered soldier. "Don't bullshit a bullshitter."

"Wouldn't dream of it, son." One side of Wolfman's lips raised in a lopsided smile revealing yellowed teeth and an unnaturally long canine that gleamed almost as bright and sharp as the knife the soldier had been toying with.

ANCIENT RUINS

John W. Dennehy

The Amtrack amphibious assault vehicle grumbled over rubble during another hot summer night. Lance Corporal Simmons breathed the stale air and adjusted his flak vest, wondering when the Marine Corps would get around to issuing the Kevlar body armor he'd heard about. Packed in tight with twelve other marines, he jostled on the bench seat as the tracked transport creaked over crumpled buildings.

They were on routine patrol through the outskirts of the ancient city. Simmons had been on numerous others without incident. His helmet was set on the deck at his boots; the steelpot similar to those issued in the last big wars. His M16-A1 rifle barrel was pointed down with the pistol grip turned away. Simmons held the stock tightly, even though he didn't expect to use the weapon. As the Amtrack came to an abrupt halt, his stomach turned and his pulse quickened. The intercom crackled with static as his staff sergeant attempted to communicate with the Amtrack crew.

"What's the hold up?" asked Staff Sergeant Watson.

"There's a dog or something blocking the way," the driver responded. "Some kind of animal."

"What?" Watson snapped.

"All set. It ran off."

The Amtrack lurched forward then came to another jerky stop. Watson swayed forward and back. As he reached for the intercom button ready to chew some ass, the fifty-caliber machine gun let rip.

Simmons felt the turret shifting to the left, then another volley of rounds.

"What the hell is going on out there?" Watson barked.

"We're taking fire," the driver responded. "We're taking fire!"

Watson turned toward his marines. "Seems it may be the Palestinians. Our orders are to fire only when necessary."

Simmons and the others stared at their staff sergeant blankly.

Watson looked back at them sternly. "You got that?" he demanded.

"Yes, Staff Sergeant!" they called out.

"So, what are we doing?" This from Corporal Anderson. "We're just sitting here waiting to get nuked?"

Automatic weapons rattled away outside the Amtrack. A few dings sounded from the armor-plated vehicle. The fifty cal roared from the turret overhead. Between the blasts of the turret gun, Simmons tried to place the enemy position. The shooting sounded faint through the dense armor, likely off in the distance to their left.

The Palestinians were surely entrenched in a hillside. They were probably engaged in a firefight with ground troops, maybe the French. His routine patrol merely happened upon the conflict. Simmons doubted it would amount to much more than the Amtrack providing support for the Multinational Force.

"What are we doing just sitting here?" Anderson griped.

Staff Sergeant Watson waved him off. "Just hold tight. We've got rules of engagement, and we really don't know what's going on out there."

Never expecting to disembark from the Amtrack, Simmons leaned back and took a deep breath. He thought about his new bride living back at the base. Then he saw Watson picking up the field phone.

* * *

Watson hung up the phone. "Listen up!" he barked.

Everyone's eyes were glued to the staff sergeant.

"The captain has authorized us to engage the enemy. Palestinians are firing at friendlies from a nearby hill." Watson looked them over. "We're going to disembark from the assault vehicle with Marine Corps precision. You got that?"

The young marines looked up at him, baffled. *Finally engaging the enemy?*

Watson towered over them with both hands on his hips. Simmons had gone out on numerous patrols, and even heard the fifty cal light up a few times, but they hadn't been authorized to engage. Ever.

"Do you hear me?" Watson screamed. "Because I certainly can't hear you!"

"Yes, Staff Sergeant!" they yelled. "Understood, Staff Sergeant!"

"Now lock and load," Watson barked. "And don't let me catch any of you using full auto."

Simmons and the others pulled out ammo clips and slammed them into the receivers. They pulled back the charging handles. When they were released, the chargers snapped back, chambering rounds with an ominous *clang* that rang out in unison. Privates Collison and Harmon were to his left and Private First Class Wells sat to the right.

Staff Sergeant Watson eyeballed them fiercely. "And make sure your moonbeam lenses are set to red," he snapped.

They all reached for their flak vests and checked the flashlights. Peering at the lens, Simmons saw that his was red.

Simmons strapped on his helmet, then reached around and grasped the M-16 pistol grip. He thumbed the selector switch, confirming it was on safety. From countless exercises beginning on Parris Island, Simmons knew his rifle must be pointed down until he stepped from the transport.

"The first two fire teams will set up outside the ramp," Watson instructed. "The second two will alight and set the perimeter. Then the first two will head for cover."

"Understood, Staff Sergeant!"

"The ramp is coming down," Watson said. "Ooh-rah!"

"*Ooh-rah!*" they all yelled. "Let's kill!"

Simmons could feel the intensity in his own yelling, his adrenalin pumping. As the ramp lowered, Watson hollered: "Welcome to Beirut! Now, move!"

* * *

As the second marine down the ramp, Simmons swung his rifle into place and dropped to a knee at the rear of the Amtrack. Collison and Harmon rushed out of the transport and took up positions nearby.

As the last marines out set the perimeter, Simmons glanced around and saw machine gun fire emanating from a distant hillside. Muzzle flashes lit up the night. There was a pile of rubble about twenty paces from him, and he waited for the fifty cal to rattle away then ran hunched over toward the heap of debris with PFC Wells in tow.

Simmons slammed his back into the jutting blocks of broken concrete, the flak vest absorbing most of the impact. As other marines joined him, Simmons peered over the top of the mound. Gunfire erupted from the distant hill again. The enemy fire didn't seem directed at them. The PLO might not even know the marines had hit the ground.

A few marines had their moonbeams out, red lights bobbing as a fire team flanked to the right. The flashlights would be noticeable to anyone watching, but minimal fire came their way. "Anderson," Simmons yelled. "I'll take my team left. You head up the middle with yours."

Anderson grinned. "Roger that, Lance Corporal." Anderson led, and the central fire team hustled after him, weaving through massive heaps of crumbled buildings. Simmons took his team to the left, crawling along open ground until they got to protective cover.

Glancing toward the hillside, Simmons realized they were closer to the city than he'd expected. Vacant buildings lingered in the backdrop of the battlefield.

Simmons further marked the enemy position by the hunter's moon. It cast beams of light through the abandoned dwellings, illuminating the combat zone.

Rifle fire erupted from the hillside. Numerous rounds ricocheted off the broken concrete. "Get down!" Simmons yelled to his team. The shooting was erratic. *Panic fire.* It was mainly directed towards Anderson's team, but Simmons ordered his squad to take cover in case of stray bullets.

When the shooting settled, he peeked around a collapsed concrete stanchion considering the scene. Only the Amtrack's turret gun had returned PLO fire. The French were taking the rules of engagement to an extreme, if they were even out there in the vestiges of the embattled city.

Simmons strained his eyes to discern if anyone else was on the battlefield. No sign of entrenched allies. In fact, the enemy fire was so sporadic it didn't appear to be honed in on any one location.

Scanning the heaps of rubble, he tried to spot marines closing on the Palestinian position. He expected his comrades to flank the enemy hill from the right, and plainly saw the red glow of moonbeams bobbing along.

Then he noticed movement down the middle. Despite Watson's instructions, a couple of marines had forgotten to change their flashlight lens covers over to red. Simmons clearly saw the yellow glow of two moonbeams from Anderson's fire team. They were huddled close together, likely hunkering down from the last barrage of machine gun fire.

After cutting back toward the center, and moving his fire team closer to the enemy position, Simmons and his troopers held up behind a mass of debris at least fifteen-feet tall, providing enough cover to get a bearing on the other teams.

After the fifty cal had settled down, there was a lull in the firefight. The night turned silent. *Had the PLO just given up?* The marines would have to abort the foot patrol if the enemy was no longer engaging but Simmons wanted to be sure that was the case before they withdrew. The Palestinians could merely be getting a better bearing on Multinational Force positions.

"You guys hunker down here," Simmons said to PFC Wells. "I'll worm forward and get a better handle on what's going on."

Wells nodded his understanding.

"Don't get lax and let someone flank you. They could advance from that position."

"We'll move around to get a better visual," Wells replied.

Simmons smacked Wells on the helmet and then stepped to the edge of the heap. There was a line of broken blocks running for about fifty yards, followed by a couple more mounds. He ran hunched toward the halfway point.

Glancing over the protective rubble, his squad had maneuvered close to the enemy hill. The ancient city loomed large behind them. All remained quiet, but the Palestinians had not called it off. He could hear them chattering nervously in the distance.

Simmons suspected they had sent a younger fighter to scout the rubble. The night was eerily still. A slight chill crept over the desert, bringing with it a sense of dread that caused him to shiver.

A scream.

Loud and fearful. Agonized.

And nearby.

The screaming was accompanied by growling and the macabre sound of... ripping; it was a terrifying noise – shredding clothing and tearing meat. Anxiety turned his stomach.

The growling seemed to multiply. The screams faded to a loathsome wailing. Then pitiful moans. Then ceased altogether. The tearing and chewing continued. The snap of bone pierced through the ruins. Something was feasting upon a soldier in the debris.

The carnage was occurring close to his position, just beyond a massive bank of rubble. The frenzy seemed to be winding down...

A shudder ran through him. *I'm being watched*. The rest of the squad was behind him. He glanced ahead at the top of the heap. A menacing set of yellow eyes stared directly at him. In the moonlight, the creature resembled a timber wolf: covered in thick fur, with a long snout and pointed ears, but larger than any wolf he'd ever seen. The neck was muscled and its torso extended into long hind legs, almost... humanlike. *But that can't be.*

On all fours, massive hand-like claws crimped the rubble.

The wolf snarled. Long fangs dripped with saliva. And blood. This was the creature who'd been feasting. A surreal apparition having no place on a battlefield, the ominous wolf seemed wrought from hell. Despite the M-16 in his hands, Simmons was horrified by the beast. Panic raced through him.

The wolf tensed, muscles rippling, ready to pounce but it snapped its focus to something down to the left.

A yell. Rifle fire. The unmistakable sound of M-16s. Corporal Anderson's team had engaged the enemy. The muzzle flashes didn't seem directed at the hillside. Firing was erratic. The wolf let out a long, bellowing howl that filled Simmons with dread.

The beast scurried down the rubble, rushing toward the fray. It was joining its pack, and Simmons needed to do the same.

He broke toward the melee. Glancing at the opposing hillside, he expected to see an outbreak of gunfire, but nothing came from the enemy position. The Palestinians were retreating to the desolate city.

Weaving through the rubble, he realized the fifty cal was quiet. The Amtrack crew probably didn't want to risk hitting the marines with friendly fire. This conflict was small arms versus... beasts. *Could the M-16s could take down the wolves, like a .30-06 drops a deer?*

Entering the gauntlet, carnage greeted Simmons. His pulse quickened. Adrenalin pumped up his spine. *It wouldn't be that easy.* A marine lay torn to shreds. Blood and gunpowder tainted the air. Another marine was firing his rifle directly at a charging wolf. Two more wolves had another marine pinned to the ground, clawing his flak vest and tearing at his neck – the marine was toast.

Rounds zinged about the narrow passageway, ricocheting off the debris. Simmons rushed toward the marine firing at the charging wolf. The creature took direct hits but didn't slow. It closed the distance. Fast. When it was about ten feet away, the marine switched to full auto.

The magazine emptied into the creature. A yelp and it dropped to the ground, squirming. A stray bullet skimmed through Simmons' cammies grazing a thigh as his comrade tried frantically to reload. Another wolf pounced. Knocked to the ground, the marine wrestled viciously with the beast.

Dropping to a knee, Simmons took aim and fired. The round had little impact. The fallen marine pulled his fighting knife and drove it into the creature's belly. Simmons squeezed off two more rounds. The animal pulled away then scampered off.

Yet another wolf stalked towards a fourth marine whose rifle appeared to be empty. The marine pulled his sidearm – *Anderson*.

The wolf sprang at the fire-team leader. Anderson fired, stepping aside to avoid the lunging wolf.

Simmons rushed into the fracas and took aim, adding fire to the wolf attacking Anderson. The marine's forty-five elicited a yelp from the animal. It turned and swiftly climbed the broken blocks of a decimated building. Simmons fired two rounds into its side, but the wolf leapt nimbly into the darkness.

The scene stilled. From the sounds Simmons heard during the first attack, he'd anticipated two or three wolves, but now it was apparent a pack was roving the ruins of the ancient city. Most of them were a little smaller than the one he'd initially spotted.

The alpha wolf hadn't been among those wounded in the fray.

Simmons rushed to assist the knife-wielding marine; kneeling beside him, Simmons pressed a hand to the throat wound and noticed a huge wolf stalking them. It showed no fear, intent only on finishing off the prostate victim.

Simmons slung his rifle over a shoulder and yanked a canister from his belt. Pulling the pin, he counted two seconds then lobbed it near the animal.

He snatched the marine's flak vest and furiously back-pedaled, dragging his fallen comrade with him.

The incendiary grenade exploded, igniting the wolf.

The creature tore off into the darkness, ablaze. Ears ringing from the blast, Simmons watched the creature burn; its agonized yowling pierced the shrill of battle. Soon it was gone.

The injured marine's Colt .45 lay in the dirt and Simmons pocketed the pistol then turned.

Anderson was missing. The injured attack wolf was gone. Simmons unslung his rifle and raced down the corridor of wreckage. He glanced back at the injured marine – no wolves lurked.

Weapon raised, Simmons turned a corner and spotted the alpha wolf trotting away, its muzzle clenched around Anderson's neck, dragging the man behind like a rag doll. A wounded wolf limped alongside them. There was no sign of struggle from Anderson, and taking a shot now would just attract attention.

Simmons returned to the fallen marine.

The young man was groggy but alive. Adrenaline was beginning to power down. Simmons took a deep breath and wiped the sweat from his brow. The kid looked familiar. He was from their infantry unit – the 1/8 out of Camp Lejeune, North Carolina. A quiet guy; Simmons didn't know his name.

Simmons checked him over carefully; no sign of bullet entries, but there was a nasty gash to his neck, leaking blood fast.

Blood also oozed from the graze on Simmons' leg; a bullet fragment from a ricochet, but that didn't stop it from hurting like a son-of-a-bitch. As the battle settled down, his adrenaline rush subsided. Aches and pains resonated all over his body.

Simmons removed the web-belt from his trousers and fastened it around his leg, then used his K-bar fighting knife to cut a piece of green t-shirt. He pulled a field first-aid kit from a cargo pocket, and dressed the wound, then tied it off with the strip of cloth. He checked the kid's dog tags: Daniel Grimes, PVT.

It was only when he was done patching up Grimes that Simmons noticed how quiet it had become. A deafening silence.

The lull was interrupted by voices from his right. Mumbled French. The Allies had been here after all. He expected the marine fire teams would join with the French to collect the wounded–

A burst of machine-gun fire disrupted the night.

Scanning the battlefield, a Thysasen Henschel UR-416 had rolled into position. The antiquated German assault vehicle appeared like a relic from The Great War. It was merely an old Mercedes truck frame loaded with armor-plates; the nose of the vehicle protruded, resembling an aardvark.

A Browning thirty-caliber machine gun was mounted on top manned by a freedom fighter. He sprayed Multinational Force units with round after round. There was a horde of ground troops rattling off AK-47s as they swarmed through the ruins.

The Amtrack returned fire as the marine rifle squads advanced. The French flanked in support of the marines. This was going to play out for a few more hours.

Simmons hoisted Grimes off the deck, carefully loading the injured Marine into a fireman's carry as he held his rifle at port arms. Although the fire teams were engaged, Simmons planned to double-back and catch up with his unit.

Turning on his heel, the way was impeded by a set of glowing yellow eyes.

His pulse raced. The wolf was marking them, waiting to make its move. Simmons reached for his M-16 slung under his shoulder.

Swinging the rifle into place, he fired off a round while holding onto Grimes. It struck the injured wolf in the shoulder. A lucky shot. Before Simmons could get off another round, the wolf dodged behind the rubble. The beast was quick.

Considering options, the deserted buildings were closer than the Amtrack, and Simmons was uncertain if the battle cut them off from the transport.

He made his way toward the burnt-out dwellings. Under Grimes' weight, each step caused a jolt of pain from his wounded leg. The moonlight guided his way, but a surge of dread crept up his spine as he waited for the wolf to bring them down from behind.

Peering over his shoulder, Simmons searched for the creature. Nothing. Then he saw it. Lingering in the shadows – a hunter tracking its prey. The beast was wounded and alone. It would likely wait for the right moment to pounce... or wait until the pack could join it.

Although the nearest dwelling was now only about a hundred and fifty yards away, the distance seemed vast. Simmons pushed on; striving to save himself and Grimes from Anderson's fate.

* * *

Inside a vacant building, he placed Grimes on the deck, and found an iron bar to brace the door shut. Simmons scanned the room; the place was vulnerable. Numerous broken windows and a bombed-out roof provided access. The place was anything but secure.

Maybe the fighting had whittled down the size of the pack and worn away its resolve, but the injured wolf could easily track them to their refuge. He had to prepare against an attack.

Simmons found a corner walled in by a concrete block and moved Grimes into the niche. Dragging an old iron engine block, discarded filing cabinets and a table, he fortified the marine's position then sat with his back against the wall, his M-16 held tight, a new clip in the receiver. A stack of fully loaded magazines rested on the deck beside him.

The pistol lay ready as well. If they could hold out until daylight, they'd get through this. Moonlight shone through broken windows in the upper stories, cascading through bombed-out flooring that opened for three levels. If the wolves came that way, they'd be exposed, but a shot would be difficult. The creatures held the advantage.

Simmons thumbed his wedding band, thinking about his young wife. *Marion.* Their wedding had been back home in Vermont, outside on warm spring day. A full contingency of marines assembled along the aisle with crossed swords. He kept thoughts of Marion close as he hunkered inside the building for close to an hour. He hoped the worse was behind them.

A wolf howled from the ruins outside. *Sounds like it's summoning the others.* Simmons feared a conflict. The wolves could easily access the building. He wanted to engage the enemy, close-with and destroy, but the creatures seemed impervious to their weapons. They seemed to be more than mere wolves. *What were they doing here in Beirut? And what could they actually do to him?* Waiting in the ruins for an almost certain demise, Simmons preferred the engagement of the earlier firefight.

Sitting in the shadows, his mind raced with dreadful thoughts. He'd witnessed wolves take fire and keep coming. They'd ruthlessly torn apart his comrades. The fight would be futile. These creatures weren't ordinary animals. Some small part of him merely wanted to give up; but there wasn't any other place to flee, and going outside again would mean certain death. *We are marines, dammit! Have to protect Grimes.* Simmons scanned the dilapidated dwelling; the lower floor had been a machine shop or garage. He was hunkered down in the old office, but the engine told of its utility. Taking stock, he found what was needed to pull the plan together. He would fight; he would have vengeance.

It was that part of him that began devising a plan.

* * *

Simmons reached for the K-bar strapped upside down to the shoulder of his flak vest. He withdrew the fighting knife then removed the clip from his Colt .45, 1911. He popped two rounds from the magazine then whittled the bullets down meticulously to fashion an effective weapon, Marion once again in this thoughts – he would make it home to her.

Reaching into the breast pocket of his utilities, he pulled out a cigar and his Zippo. The chrome lighter had been a gift from Marion; the Marine Corps emblem embossed on the front.

He bit off the end of the cigar and lit the damn thing. If this was going to be his reckoning, then Simmons was going out on his own terms, like a man, a marine. Puffing the stogie, he prepared himself mentally for the showdown.

The alpha wolf was the linchpin for the entire pack. Wounded and weary from battle, most of them would scamper if he could take their leader down.

He sipped from his canteen cup; thinking about his wife again… Simmons glanced at his wedding ring then removed the sterling-silver band. Perusing the ring, it was a reminder that Marion would be waiting for him whenever he returned from a deployment, whether walking the flight deck or in a pine box.

He wheeled an acetylene torch over to the iron engine block, praying the damn thing still worked. He quickly checked Grimes; the man was still out. Simmons breathed a sigh of relief when the torch lit, then heated the empty basin of a combustion chamber. Once the iron was hot, he kissed the silver ring then dropped it into the chamber with a metallic clang. The torch heated the iron quickly, but the ring sat there unchanged. *Fuck!* Just as Simmons began to doubt whether the plan would work, the unmistakable thud of a large four-legged creature landed on remnants of the top floor.

Moments later, two other sets of paws padded around the vestiges of the third floor. They must have crossed from an adjacent rooftop. Two sets of glowing yellow eyes peered through the aperture of the bombed-out flooring.

The wolves circled their perch, staring down, stalking their prey. The alpha was leading two others.

Simmons glanced down into the engine chamber; the ring was now liquid silver. He turned off the blow torch, and reached slowly for a .45 caliber round. No need to alert the things. Dipping the bullet into the silver, he quickly coated the tip then retracted it from the chamber and dipped it into the canteen cup, sizzling.

There was a thump onto the second floor. Their treading grew more frenzied. An attack was imminent.

He hastily dipped the other round into the silver then cooled it off. A small amount of the liquid remained in the combustion chamber. Simmons grabbed his K-bar and coated the tip. As he worked the silver over the blade, the wolves descended to his level.

All three beasts trotted back and forth just beyond his make-shift barricade. They began to growl and snap. Long white fangs reflected in the scattered moonlight. A couple of the beasts shook their heads, whipping saliva about.

Simmons trembled, breathing deeply – these weren't ordinary creatures. Dread of losing the battle with the wolves morphed from utter fear to a momentary paralysis. But the thought of failure, even death wasn't as daunting as not pressing forward. Giving in wasn't the Marine Corps way. Like all young marines, he was indoctrinated in the heroics of marines pushing forward against insurmountable odds: the Chosen Reservoir, Tarawa and Iwo Jima. He shook off fear and doubt. Simmons began to feel numb to the thought of death, as the hard mettle of his months on the *island* solidified. He was a *marine. Ooh-rah!*

Simmons loaded the magazine with the silver bullets. He placed them halfway down the clip, allowing him to fire a couple of shots before and after releasing the deadly rounds. *Lull the bastards into a false sense of security*

A wolf edged its way toward the barricade like a scout searching for the weakness in a fortress.

The alpha remained in the background. Simmons couldn't dispense with the silver ammunition on the lower-echelon beasts before getting a crack at the leader. Another wolf limped slowly forward.

Simmons raised the M-16 and thumbed the selector switch to semi-automatic. He shouldered the rifle, held his breath and eased the trigger. The rifle fired a volley, striking the lame creature in the right front shoulder. It scampered like a dog being struck with a newspaper. Although the shot struck home, it didn't have a lasting effect.

The two wolves cowered slightly at the sound of the rifle blast.

PVT Grimes flinched at the sound of the M-16 firing, his breathing heavy. The man was still alive, and Simmons intended to keep it that way.

The wolf checking the perimeter lifted its nose over a filing cabinet.

Simmons aimed and fired two rounds in rapid succession. It ducked below the barricade and whimpered. The creature was sniffing out signs of weakness, allowing a sense of confidence to grow. The alpha howled, loud and ferocious in the confined space, and the other two wolves turned and rushed the barricade, jumping over the table and filing cabinet. Simmons let loose with the pistol shooting three rounds at the lead wolf. It dropped in its tracks, but the other kept coming.

Simmons took up the rifle and flipped the M-16 to full-automatic and emptied the clip into the advancing beast. It squealed but continued its charge.

The wolf lunged at his throat. Simmons held up an arm to ward off the ravaging beast but it knocked his arm aside. He grabbed it tightly with both hands by the scruff of the neck, struggling to lock his elbows and keep the wolf at bay. Spittle and phlegm splattered Simmons' face as the beast thrashed and tore at his flak vest.

Simmons wrestled with the wolf as it flailed and shred his utilities. *Can't let this thing bite me.* He feared death less than the alternative. In his gut, he knew what they really were.

Everything slowed. Simmons felt the heat of the werewolf's breath on his face. He locked his elbows, holding the beast back by its neck. Saliva dripped from its elongated fangs. Numbness from shock began to set in. Pressed into the concrete floor, there wasn't any place else to go.

He expected the wolf to lunge at his throat, finish him off, but it paused for a moment. *It's making way for the alpha.*

Peering beyond the bloodied, matted coat of the wolf bestride him, the alpha approached.

Do or die. Simmons unsheathed the K-bar and plunged it into the beast standing over him. It howled. Simmons instinctively retracted the fighting knife, pushing the beast aside. He dropped the K-bar on the deck and drew his pistol.

The alpha leapt.

Descending, the wolf bared its fangs, extended its claws.

Ready for the kill.

Simmons fired the .45 into the wolf's chest. A jolting yelp of pain resounded like a shriek within the room, but pain seemed to drive it. The alpha landed on Simmons biting at his throat. Its claws cleaved into Simmons' arms and legs.

He emptied the clip into the alpha. It howled again, but kept at him. Simmons grasped for the K-bar on the deck, fumbling for the knife. The alpha's yellow eyes shone bright with hate. The last bit of its life seemed directed at annihilating Simmons – retribution for killing members of the pack.

The beast's muzzle reeled about and snapped. As it closed in for the kill, Simmons found the leather handle of the K-bar. With a shout, he plunged it deep into the alpha. Right to the hilt.

The werewolf snarled, writhed in his arms. The warrior beast locked glances with Simmons. They stared into each other's eyes. The proud wolf battled for its pack and the marine fought for his comrades. A somber moment between two enemies in combat.

As life slipped from the wolf's eyes, it collapsed onto Simmons' chest. For a moment Simmons felt sorry for the loss of a worthy adversary. He took a deep breath and tossed the creature aside. Lying on the deck, muscles weak, he took another deep breath. He sat up then scrambled back on his rear as the dead wolves began changing form.

Bones snapped. The bodies quivered and contorted. A crunching echoed through the building as the jaws and cheek-bones diminished. Gas released from the corpses, fouling the air. Legs trembled as their haunches twisted and pulled straight. The tearing of flesh turned Simmons' stomach as the claws retracted. Then the shaggy hair slowly receded, exposing human forms.

Dead men, naked, wounded and broken, lay sprawled upon the cold floor. The affliction had been indiscriminate. A tanned Palestinian lay not far from a dark-haired Frenchman with a long prominent nose. The well-muscled build of the alpha was covered in tattoos; the words inked in Slavic.

Howling broke the silence. Simmons pushed to his feet and peered out the window. Under the moonlight, the remaining pack circled the top of a distant heap of rubble.

Standing at the center, a man thrashed and clawed at the sky. *Anderson. Almost Anderson.* Huge clumps of hair protruded from the tears in Anderson's cammos; his jaw and cheeks seemed... bigger. Ferocious.

Alone in the shadows, Simmons watched the proud wolves as intermittent light cascaded into the broken building. His heart raced.

With a trembling hand, he reached for the window and splayed his fingers against the glass, drawn to the moonlight and his howling pack.

THE FENRIR PROJECT

David W. Amendola

Got a mission for you, Moses."

Second Lieutenant Moses Cole raised a black eyebrow. "Thought we were going back to Germany, sir."

"We are. But something's come up," said Captain Hogue, his company commander. "G2 heard rumors of diehard Nazis holed up near Teufelsdorf." He turned to a map tacked to the wall of the command post and pointed to the location. "Probably nothing, but the brass wants it checked out anyway. That area always seems to be cloudy and foggy, so aerial reconnaissance is useless. Someone needs to reconnoiter on the ground."

Cole rubbed his mustache with a brown finger as he studied the map. "Not familiar with that town. Don't think there was any fighting there."

"No, but don't expect any help from the locals. It's the home town of SS-Major Rudolf Krebs, a wanted war criminal."

"We'll take care of it, sir."

"Special Agent Rosenthal from CIC will be going with you." Hogue gestured at a spare, attentive white man standing quietly off to the side.

Like all members of the Army Counter Intelligence Corps, Rosenthal wore no rank on his uniform, just an officer's U.S. collar insignia. Spectacles perched on a thin nose, and a smoldering cigarette dangled from pale lips. He did not offer to shake hands, but simply gave a curt nod.

CIC detachments gathered tactical intelligence during the war. Now they hunted for wanted Nazis and investigated illegal activities and possible Nazi resistance groups.

Hogue turned around. "Rumors also said they might have a *Jagdpanther*, so be careful. Any questions?"

Cole saluted. "No, sir."

* * *

Private Lewis shifted uncomfortably in the assistant driver's seat in the cramped front hull of the M4A3(76) Sherman medium tank. "What's a *Jagdpanther*?" he asked.

"Means hunting panther in German," said Cole over the intercom, standing behind and above in the open turret hatch. "Tank destroyer built on the chassis of the Panther tank. No turret so it can hold a bigger gun."

"Yeah, same eighty-eight millimeter as the King Tiger," said Corporal Kinkaid, the driver, seated to Lewis' left. "Slices through these tin cans like butter."

"Oh." Lewis fell silent.

The five green Shermans emblazoned with white U.S. stars clanked and rumbled along the macadam road spouting blue-white exhaust as they wended through verdant hills sprinkled with blue and yellow flowers. Far in the distance towered white-capped mountains. They drove in march column at the prescribed seventeen miles per hour, thirty-five yards between each tank, with Cole's machine in the lead. Trailing at the end were two Willys jeeps: one – prominently marked with the Red Cross – driven by two medics from the battalion medical detachment, the other driven by Rosenthal.

It was a bright spring day, but inside the tank it was noisy, smelly, and claustrophobic.

"How'd we get stuck with this job?" asked Technician Fifth Grade Robinson, the gunner.

"Y'all know why we got it," said Private First Class Youngblood, the loader, sitting next to him in the turret basket.

The crew was black, as were all the enlisted men and most of the officers of the 761st Tank Battalion. During World War II, the U.S. Army kept black soldiers in segregated units. As usual there were doubts about their abilities, despite the fact they had fought honorably in every major war going back to the American Revolution. Every generation had to spill its blood to disprove the same old stereotypes. The 761st 'Black Panthers' had racked up an impressive record battling across Europe, finally halting when they met the Red Army in Austria.

The battalion, part of General Patton's Third Army, was not permanently assigned to any particular division. An independent unit, it was attached to whoever needed armor support.

Now the war in Europe was over and the 761st, posted at the city of Steyr, was preparing to leave Austria and move to Germany for occupation duty.

The weather abruptly changed as the platoon neared Teufelsdorf. The clear blue sky clouded over and turned somber gray. The fresh breeze died. Mist veiled the landscape and it began drizzling. No flowers grew on the murky meadows; not even a bird song brightened the dismal atmosphere. The mist thickened as the road cut through an oak and beech grove.

"Can't see shit," said Kinkaid.

As the column emerged from the trees and rumbled around a curve the quiet was shattered by the scream and crash of a shell, followed by the deep boom of a cannon.

The urgent voice of Sergeant Waters, one of the other tank commanders, came over the transceiver mounted in the back of the turret. "Taking fire!"

Cole grabbed the microphone. "Get into town! We're out in the open here!"

Kinkaid accelerated as quickly as the 450-horsepower engine could push the tank's thirty-plus tons.

"Able Two Three is hit, sir," said another tank commander, Staff Sergeant Brown, the platoon sergeant. "Crew's bailing out."

"Cover 'em with smoke."

The view from inside using slit periscopes was restricted, so Cole stayed in the open turret hatch, exposing himself so he could oversee everything. He had not earned a Silver Star and a battlefield commission by being timid.

Behind him Able Two Three - Sergeant Lindsey's tank - sat smoking on the road. The other tanks laid down a screen around it with their 2-inch smoke mortars. Cole prayed Lindsey made it out. Wet ammunition stowage had lessened the Sherman's infamous propensity for catching fire, but not eliminated it.

As another shell screeched overhead he tried to glimpse a

red muzzle flash or green tracer trail so he could pinpoint the enemy position. He saw nothing.

They barreled into Teufelsdorf, engine bellowing, tracks clattering on the cobblestones. Civilians glared at the Americans and sullenly withdrew into their homes and shops, banging doors and shutters shut.

The narrow, crooked streets – now deserted – intersected at a square. Cole halted behind an inn. Like most of the buildings, it was a solid structure of white, plastered stone and brick with a red tile roof. Teufelsdorf had been of no importance during the war so it had survived unscathed. Cole wrinkled his nose at the familiar manure smell of a farm town.

He felt the tanker's unease of close terrain where his machine was vulnerable to hidden foes armed with *panzerfausts* – German shoulder-fired anti-tank rockets. He watched as the other three Shermans and both jeeps entered the square and spread out, seeking cover behind nearby shops. Finally Lindsey and his crew straggled in on foot, one clutching a wounded arm, another limping heavily. All five had escaped. He beckoned to Lindsey.

"Sounded like an eighty-eight," said Cole. "Where'd it come from?"

Lindsey stared at him with a dazed expression, blood trickling from his nose and ears. The concussion of the shell had stunned him. His gunner answered for him.

"North, sir. We got hit in the right side as we rounded the bend. Shell tore right through us and knocked out the engine."

"Guess the rumors were true."

"No way he could see us, sir."

Cole pondered the matter. "Heard a report about a new gun sight the Krauts invented to see at night. Uses infrared light. They equipped a few Panthers with it and there were rumors they also put it on some *Jagdpanthers*."

The shaken crew limped over to the curb so the medics could administer first aid.

Cole got on the radio to the rest of the platoon. Interference forced him to raise his voice. "Anybody see anything? Over. Over!" He finally received a crackling series of negative replies.

Cole stood in the hatch and looked around. Oddly, the village lacked a church, normally a ubiquitous feature even in the smallest European hamlet. At two stories, the inn was the tallest building. He clambered out and got onto the roof. From here he scanned the area with binoculars. Nothing. The fog was just too dense.

Returning to his tank, he tried contacting Captain Hogue, but the company and battalion command channels were drowned out by torrents of static. Youngblood adjusted dials and double-checked the equipment, but was unable to clear it up.

"Where's this interference coming from?" asked Cole.

"Don't know, sir. Maybe we're being jammed."

He was still able to talk on the platoon channel so he called, "All TCs come to my tank."

He jumped to the ground as the other tank commanders clustered around. Digging a cigar from a pocket of his olive drab overalls, he chewed on it thoughtfully as he unfolded a map and spread it out on the engine deck.

"Radio net's jammed so we can't reach anybody," he said. "Krauts know we're here and if we sit here they'll move to another position and start picking us off – or use the fog to slip away."

"So we're on our own," said Waters.

"Looks that way."

This prompted head-shaking and muttered profanity from the others.

"No use complaining about it. Let's just get the job done. They're somewhere on this ridge." Cole tapped the map. "Hill 207. We know it's an eighty-eight so we'll have to assume it's a *Jagdpanther*. They may have night-vision sights."

"So if we try to move they'll nail us," said Sergeant Jackson.

"Well, if we all move at the same time and go at full speed in different directions they'll have multiple targets to deal with. And we'll fire smoke as we go."

"If they can see through fog, won't they see us anyway?"

"WP burns hot so maybe it'll blind them. And the fumes could make them bail out."

The others exchanged skeptical looks. Brown voiced the others' concerns when he said, "Sir, if it really is a *Jagdpanther* its armor's thicker than ours and sloped. Our shells will just bounce off."

"We'll charge the ridge from both ends and outflank it. It doesn't have a turret so they can only swing their gun back and forth so far. Beyond that they have to turn the whole vehicle around to aim. If we knock off a track they'll be stuck and then we can circle around and hit them from the side or rear where the armor's thinner. Lindsey's crew will stay here in town. So will the medics and the CIC guy until we have the hills secured." Cole folded up the map. "Any questions?" He raked dark eyes over resigned faces. "We roll in five minutes."

Everyone returned to brief their crews, then 'buttoned-up' – closed hatches – and put steel helmet shells over their fiberboard tanker helmets. Loaders pulled shells off ready racks. The 761st had the Sherman with the 76-millimeter gun, inadequate against the heavy armor of late-war German tanks like the Panther and Tiger. It had to get close to penetrate and the fearsome panzers had long high-velocity guns capable of destroying it before it could get within effective range. It did have a hydraulic traverse and gyrostabilizer, allowing the crew to rotate the turret quicker and even fire with some accuracy while moving, but that did little good if they were out of range. High-velocity armor-piercing rounds had greater penetration, but HVAP was scarce and the platoon only carried standard APC.

Cole's bass voice boomed over the radio. "Move out!"

The platoon burst from Teufelsdorf, the two tanks under Cole and Jackson heading northeast and the two under Brown and Waters going northwest, all charging full speed across fallow farm fields, smashing through hedges and fences. Their cannons hurled a salvo of phosphorous shells up into the heights above and white pillars of smoke immediately rose.

Cole stood in the turret, unlit cigar still clenched between his teeth. A loud clang deafened him as he felt the hot rush of a passing shell. It had grazed the top of the turret, barely missing him and tearing off the 50-caliber anti-aircraft machine gun. He hissed profanity. Despite the fog and smoke, the enemy could still see them.

Kinkaid shifted into high gear and worked the steering levers, trying to zigzag and make the tank as difficult a target as possible. A second shell gouged a crater in the earth just behind them, throwing up a geyser of dirt and smoke.

Finally they reached the foot of Hill 207 and drove into the protection of a draw. Kinkaid downshifted and followed by Jackson's tank they slowly crawled uphill.

The mist thinned somewhat as they ascended, but this was countered by dark, melancholy stands of pine and fir covering the slopes. At the top of the draw they halted. The forest was dense and the only way through was a dirt trail snaking along the crest. Brown and Waters radioed that they had reached the other end of the ridge unscathed. Cole ordered them to stay put for the moment. Cannons were reloaded with armor-piercing shells.

"Got a bad feeling about this, sir," said Kinkaid.

Cole grunted agreement. "For sure he turned around and is aiming right down that trail, just waiting for us. Youngblood, grab your grease gun and come with me."

They climbed out, Youngblood holding an M3 submachine gun. He paused to snap in a 30-round magazine, pull back the bolt, and flip open the dust cover. Then the two crept through the wet brush alongside the trail, silently cursing the bramble thorns tugging at them. Water dripping from the needled branches pattered on their helmets. The trees stood like ghostly sentinels in the murk, silent and watchful.

Youngblood pointed. Brush had been crushed and earth churned up by the passage of a heavy vehicle, bigger than a Sherman, with wide tracks. Cole nodded. They continued on.

Cole abruptly froze, listening intently. Up ahead he heard the low, throbbing growl of a powerful engine, like the breath of a monstrous, mechanical beast.

The stillness was shattered by a stuttering roar he recognized as an MG34, a machine gun commonly used on German armored vehicles. 7.92 millimeter bullets slashed through the foliage, punching through tree trunks, clipping off branches, and sending splinters flying like shrapnel asthe pair flung themselves into a muddy depression and hugged the ground. They hastily squirmed behind a fallen pine as a second burst whipped overhead.

"No tracers," hissed Youngblood. "Can't see where he is."

"We know which way he's pointing and that's enough. Let's go!" Keeping the windfall between them and the enemy, they crawled back down the trail until they were far enough to safely get to their feet and run the rest of the way back to their tank.

Cole jumped inside and grabbed the microphone. "Able Two Two and Two Five, move in! He's pointing away from y'all!"

"Wilco!" Soon Cole heard roaring engines and crashing guns.

Brown's triumphant voice came over the radio. "He's tracked! Got the son of a bitch as he tried turning back toward us. His gun's stuck pointing away from all of us now!"

"Step on it, Kinkaid!" said Cole. "Able Two Four, follow me!"

The Sherman swung down the trail, followed by Jackson's tank. Cole discerned a vague, menacing bulk ahead. It was the sleek casemate of a *Jagdpanther*, armored skirts protecting its interleaved road wheels, the long barrel of an 88-millimeter jutting from its angled front armor. Painted in splotches of green, brown, and tan, evergreen branches further camouflaged it. The left drive sprocket had been hit, blowing off the track and immobilizing the 45-ton vehicle.

Cole ordered Kinkaid to veer off the trail to provide a clear field of fire for Jackson. Both Shermans lurched to a halt; gunners lined up sights and stomped firing pedals. The tanks rocked from the recoil. Shells punched through the *Jagdpanther*'s flank, ripping deep into its metal insides. The others mercilessly pounded it from the opposite side. Black smoke poured from grilles; orange flames licked out. A series of sharp explosions blew it open as ammunition overheated and exploded. The *Jagdpanther* sat there gutted, reduced to a burning wreck.

The tanks trained their machine guns on it to shoot down the crew as they tried to escape. Fog and drifting smoke made it difficult to see. At length the fire died down.

"Didn't see anyone," said Kinkaid. "Reckon they're all dead,"

"Check to make sure," said Cole.

The crew dismounted, fingers on submachine gun triggers as they warily approached. The reek of cordite and burning rubber and oil hung thick in the air. As they got closer they could see the *Jagdpanther*'s top and rear hatches were open.

Cole, holding a grenade, peeked inside through a shell hole, bracing himself for the sickening sight and stench of human beings torn apart or burned alive. The compartment was roomy compared to a Sherman – and the five seats surrounding the gun breech were empty.

"They're gone!" he said.

"Must've bailed out just before it blew up," said Youngblood.

One of the medics drove up in his jeep, followed by Rosenthal in his.

Cole scowled and stepped back as he stared at the wreck, arms akimbo. "There's no infrared apparatus. How the hell could they see us?" He looked inside again and saw charred remnants of uniforms, socks, field caps, boots, even underwear. "They left their uniforms behind."

"So what the hell are they wearing?" asked Robinson.

"Don't know. Left their guns behind too. I can see a Schmeisser and four pistols, They had to bail out so fast they didn't have a chance to grab them,Good, that means they're unarmed. And there's no sign of any other Germans so those five are it." Cole turned to face the others. "All right, let's track them down. Jackson, bring your crew with me. Waters, Brown, stay here."

The two crews fanned out into the forest. Those left with the tanks relaxed a bit, slinging weapons over their shoulders. The Shermans were parked in a circle, facing outwards.

Rosenthal lit a cigarette and circled the *Jagdpanther*. It bore the black-and-white German cross on the sides, the white tactical number 101 on the sides and rear, and the white tactical symbol for a tank destroyer unit on the glacis plate. Next to it was a yellow wolf's hook, a heraldic symbol he recognized as the unit insignia of the 2nd SS Panzer Division.

The wreck was still smoldering, so he fetched a fire extinguisher from his jeep and put out the remaining flames. Then he gingerly climbed onto the hot, mangled engine deck and swung inside, eyes watering in the smoke. He examined scorched seats and hatchways minutely with a magnifying glass, picking off samples he placed in an envelope.

He inspected the burned uniforms. Tank destroyers were considered artillery in the German Army, so their crews wore panzer uniforms of field gray instead of black. The jackets bore the collar runes and sleeve eagle of the Waffen-SS, but no unit cuff title. For security reasons SS soldiers had been ordered to remove these. A General Assault Badge was pinned on the left breast indicating combat experience. These were veterans. He searched for paybooks, wallets, or letters, finding nothing.

Climbing out, he studied the muddy ground nearby, kneeling to take a closer look.

Finally he returned to his jeep. He drew his Colt M1911 automatic from its shoulder holster, ejected the magazine, and loaded one of the special magazines he had brought with him. Then he picked up a Thompson M1 submachine gun and swapped its magazine too. He cocked both weapons.

Brown looked at him, curiosity written on his face. "What's up?"

Rosenthal flicked away his cigarette. "I don't think these are normal Germans. I have to find the lieutenant – and I'd suggest getting back in your tanks." He hurried off into the woods.

At length he found Lewis, who directed him to Cole.

"Sir, pull your men back," said Rosenthal.

"Why? What's wrong?"

They were interrupted by the harsh chatter of automatic fire, followed by yells. It came from back where the tanks were. The two crews dashed back up the slope.

Near the top they stumbled over Waters. His throat had been ripped out.

As the tanks came into uncertain view Rosenthal spotted a dark, shaggy figure on top of Brown, trying to wrench away the man's M3. Rosenthal saw Brown hold down the trigger and pour 45-caliber slugs into the belly of his attacker – with seemingly no effect.

Rosenthal whipped up his Thompson and squeezed off a burst. This time the figure let out a shrill howl and toppled over. A twig snapped; he ducked behind a Sherman as bullets ricocheted off the steel. Rosenthal leaned out and fired back, blindly spraying the tangled vegetation. He was rewarded with a yelp of pain and heard brush crash as someone ran away. Then silence.

They searched the area for more lurking foes, but there was no sign of anyone.

Rosenthal and Cole ran over to Brown. Dark blood spilled from a severed jugular vein. There was nothing they could do as Brown gave a final gasp and slumped lifeless in Cole's arms.

Corpses were strewn all over the bivouac. They had literally been torn apart – dismembered, disemboweled, or decapitated. Heads and limbs and entrails lay scattered on ground that was red and soaked with blood.

The only survivor was Brown's driver, Jones, who stood dazed, holding a bleeding arm. Kinkaid opened a first aid kit, dusted the wound with sulfa powder, and began bandaging it.

"What the hell happened here, Jonesy?" he asked.

"It bit me."

"What bit you?"

"I don't know." Jones swayed and slumped against the tree. He was sweating profusely and breathing heavily. "I don't feel so good."

"You're gonna be all right, man, just hang in there."

Rosenthal examined the enemy he had killed. The dark shaggy figure was actually a blond white man riddled with dozens of gunshot wounds. He was totally nude. Rosenthal lifted the body's left arm, revealing a black letter tattooed on the underside.

"SS blood group tattoo," said Cole.

Hanging from a cord around the dead German's neck was an identity disc, the Wehrmacht equivalent of dog tags. Made of zinc alloy, it was stamped with the wearer's replacement unit, personnel number, and blood type. Rosenthal opened a notebook, compared the information with a list, and grunted confirmation. He scribbled a few notes with a metal mechanical pencil he drew from his pocket.

"Why's he buck naked?" asked Cole.

Behind them a clamor rose. Jones writhed on the ground, gripped by violent convulsions. Kinkaid and two crewmen struggled to restrain him. With a shout he hurled them back and sprang to his feet. His eyes were wild and distended, saliva dripping from his gaping mouth, his face contorted. His overalls began bursting at the seams as his body bulged with pulsing muscles. Horrified, the others recoiled.

Rosenthal switched his Thompson to semi-automatic and stepped forward. Without a word he raised it and shot Jones once in the forehead.

"What the hell you do that for?" asked Jackson, snatching the Thompson away. His crew seized the CIC agent, jamming their gun muzzles against him.

"I had no choice," said Rosenthal calmly. "He was turning into one of them."

"One of them what?"

"Werewolves."

Jackson stared at him in stunned disbelief. "Are you serious?"

"Dead serious."

Angry protests came from the others. "You're saying that dead Kraut's a werewolf?" said Jackson. "Bullshit!"

"Look around. You'll find wolf tracks all over the place."

"Yeah, it's a forest."

Rosenthal shrugged free of the tankers holding him. "The last wolves in this part of Austria were killed almost a century ago. I found wolf hair in the *Jagdpanther*. The dead man's dog tags match a list I have. And look what happened to your buddies.

How could unarmed men tear them to pieces? Why were your guns useless?"

"You were able to kill him," said Cole, pacing around looking at the carnage.

"My guns are loaded with silver bullets. They're severely allergic to silver. It sends them into anaphylactic shock."

"Why isn't he a wolf now? And why's he naked?"

"When they die they revert back to human form. They have to undress before shape-shifting or the transformation tears apart their clothes. That's what was happening to Jones. If their saliva gets in your bloodstream you get infected. He'd have tried to kill us." Rosenthal sighed with exasperation. "We've got to get out of here. They didn't capture our tanks, but they'll try again. We have to get clear of this radio interference and call for reinforcements."

"Goddammit, I ain't running away," said Jackson. "I want payback." A vengeful chorus of agreement echoed from the others.

Cole stopped pacing. "You got more of those silver bullets?" he asked Rosenthal.

"About a hundred rounds."

"That's not enough – and they've got some of our guns now." He turned to the others. "We're pulling out. We'll pick up Lindsey on the way."

The tankers reluctantly obeyed. The dog tags of the dead were collected; there was no time to bury them. Waters' and Brown's tanks and both jeeps would have to be abandoned so their engines, radios, and armament were disabled. Small arms and ammunition were retrieved. Rosenthal brought two boxes of .45 ACP from his jeep and passed them out so each crew could load at least one magazine with silver bullets.

"Only use them at close range," he said. "Silver bullets don't shoot straight."

Thunder rumbled in the distance. Wind moaned like a lost soul and rain drummed on the tanks as the survivors drove back down Hill 207 towards Teufelsdorf.

Cole tried radioing Hogue again, but the channels still had too much interference. "Dammit. Who's jamming us? I still can't get through."

"I don't think that's jamming," said Rosenthal, who was riding in the tank with him. "Atmospheric conditions aren't normal around here. Lots of creepy rumors about the locals – stories of devil worship and so forth. Teufelsdorf means Devils Town in German. People from neighboring villages shun this place."

Cole hung up the microphone. "You know a helluva lot more than you've been letting on about. Start talking. Where did these werewolves come from?"

"Remember that SS-Major your captain told you about? Rudolf Krebs, the one wanted for war crimes?"

"Yeah, so?"

"Krebs is Austrian, but received doctorates in anthropology and medicine from the University of Munich. He became a research assistant at the Kaiser Wilhelm Institute in Berlin. He was obsessed with medieval alchemy, and while a student had been a member of the Thule Society, the occult group that founded the Nazi Party. Joined the Party and the SS and volunteered as a doctor at Mauthausen concentration camp, where he conducted experiments on prisoners. His work came to the attention of Heinrich Himmler, who expanded it into a secret program called the Fenrir Project, named after the giant wolf of Norse mythology. Krebs was appointed project director. He destroyed his records before fleeing at end of the war, but his reports to Himmler were found in captured SS archives." Rosenthal shifted in his seat, trying in vain to get comfortable.

"Krebs' study of medieval manuscripts uncovered a potion for lycanthropy," said Rosenthal. "Prisoners he first tested it on developed horrific deformities and died. But he eventually perfected the formula for a serum that alters the genetic makeup. When injected into a select group of SS volunteers, the test subjects gained the ability to transform at will into a hybrid wolf-man with increased strength and enhanced senses. In either form they have incredible regenerative powers, recovering from injuries in minutes or hours. Werewolves are true supermen, almost unstoppable soldiers."

Cole looked stupefied, shaking his head.

Rosenthal continued. "To test their combat effectiveness, they were formed into a heavy tank destroyer platoon assigned to the 2nd SS Panzer Division. They fought ferociously at Budapest and Vienna, but were too few to make any difference and were practically annihilated – even their regenerative powers were no match for heavy Russian guns. During the German retreat problems started with the survivors."

"What happened?" asked Cole.

"They became increasingly violent and uncontrollable – apparently a side effect of the serum. Military police who tried to restore order were mauled. The werewolves deserted."

Cole had their cannon reloaded with high explosive, ammunition used against fortifications, infantry, and unarmored vehicles. Unfortunately the 76-millimeter HE shells only had half the explosive of the old 75-millimeter used by earlier Shermans, making them less effective.

"Lead might not kill the bastards," said Cole, "but it'll be damn hard to regenerate if they're blown to bits."

They reached the bottom of the ridge and the trees started thinning out. Lightning flashed.

Four feral figures jumped down from the branches above. Each was black and furry like a wolf, but lacking a tail, and moved on two legs. Clawed hands gripped captured submachine guns. They dropped onto the backs of the tanks.

Kinkaid floored the accelerator; one of the creatures fell off the Sherman as it surged ahead. Then Kinkaid abruptly stopped, shifted into reverse, and backed up hard. The unexpected movement caught the beast by surprise and Kinkaid heard an agonized howl as the tracks rolled over him.

A second flung open the turret hatch. A snarling, shaggy head with a black canine snout, slavering yellow fangs, and glowing red eyes thrust inside. Cole grabbed the gaping jaws, struggling to keep from being bitten. He gagged on the brute's hot, foul breath. Rosenthal snatched out his Colt. He quickly fired three times, the shots deafening inside the tank. Warm blood spattered Cole's face and the monstrosity fell back out.

He reached up to close the hatch and saw that Jackson's tank had abruptly stopped, the hatches open. Screams and a flurry of shots came from inside. Then silence.

Cole got on the radio. "Able Two Four, come in. Jackson. Jackson! Over!"

No reply. His blood froze as the turret began rotating towards him.

Cole issued terse orders. Youngblood swung the breech open and replaced the high explosive shell with armor-piercing; Robinson stomped the firing pedal. The cannon boomed. The turret of Jackson's tank stopped, jammed in place by a damaged traverse. Unless the whole vehicle moved around it could not fire at them. Robinson's second round blew off a track and immobilized it. Cole stood in the cupola, submachine gun ready.

A werewolf scrambled out the turret hatch. Cole peppered the creature with silver slugs and watched coldly as it tumbled to the ground, twitching. Cole waited for the last werewolf to emerge, but no one appeared.

"C'mon, Rosenthal, let's make sure the bastards are dead."

They climbed out. Thunder crashed; rain hissed down in sheets, soaking them to the skin.

The werewolf which had tried to get into Cole's tank was found stone dead; the carcass had turned back into human form again.

The one Kinkaid had run over was still alive and in the guise of a wolf, dragging crushed legs as it crawled towards a dropped submachine gun. Already the bleeding had stopped; mangled bones and muscles were knitting back together at an astonishing rate.

Cole kicked the weapon away before the werewolf could reach it.

It glared up at Cole, fangs bared in a defiant snarl. "Heil Hitler," it growled – and lunged for him.

Cole shot it, and the beast collapsed at his feet. Cole's M3 was empty now, so Rosenthal handed him the Thompson and drew his pistol.

The pair cautiously moved up to Jackson's tank, smelling death and cordite. Blood was splattered all over the white walls inside. Jackson and his crew had been ripped apart by the two werewolves before they commandeered the Sherman and tried to use it against Cole. The second werewolf was gone: the floor escape hatch lay open.

Rosenthal cautiously circled the tank and pointed. Wolf tracks led away. They followed.

As they passed an outcropping of mossy boulders the werewolf charged out of the gloom and smashed Cole across the head with a clawed hand, knocking his helmet off. Stunned, Cole reeled back, slipped on the sodden grass, and fell. His wet hands lost their grip on the Thompson and it skittered down a gully out of reach.

Wheeling, the beast pounced on Rosenthal, throwing him down and dashing the pistol from his hand. Broken spectacles fell off. The monster dove for his throat; he tried to block it and cried out as jaws clamped like a vise on his forearm. They grappled.

Rosenthal frantically fumbled for anything he could use as a weapon. Desperate fingers found the mechanical pencil. He stabbed the werewolf in the eye as hard as he could.

The creature howled and recoiled. It tried yanking the pencil out, but let go sharply as if just touching the pencil burned. It staggered a few steps before its knees buckled and it fell headlong.

Cole came to. He gaped at the dead werewolf and gave Rosenthal a questioning look.

"Sterling silver," said Rosenthal.

They watched the matted fur fade away. Claws, triangular ears, and the canine snout retracted, muscles shrank to normal proportions, and the carcass slowly became human again.

Rosenthal stared numbly at the bite marks on his trembling arm. He felt dizzy and nauseous. He looked at Cole. "You know what to do."

Cole nodded grimly and got to his feet. He picked up the Colt and made sure a round was in the chamber. Then he aimed at Rosenthal and pulled the trigger.

Project Lupine

Brian W. Taylor

An alarm blared – the nasal tone repeating over and over like a hammer beating nails into Rolf Alfredsson's head. He heard but pretended like he didn't.

"Yo, Red, get your ass up, man."

Rolf groaned before opening his eyes. "How many times do I have to tell you not to call me Red?"

Lou 'Sully' Sullivan smiled, his teeth like headlights cutting through the darkness. "Shit, man, I can't help your ginger complexion, or that the name's already stuck."

A light clicked on reflecting harshly off the white of the floor and walls. Everything was white in TriGenex's classified laboratory, the actual labs, the living quarters, and even the bathrooms.

"C'mon though, for real. Dot will have our asses if we're last to respond." Sully rummaged around his footlocker and pulled out a fresh uniform – classic, black BDUs, with the TriGenex logo on the breast and back.

"Fuck Dot. And fuck you." Rolf looked at the clock; he had only slept two hours. They weren't paying him enough for this shit. Well, maybe they were, but that was beside the point. This job was supposed to be his ticket to early retirement.

A multitude of footsteps rushed along the hallways of the living quarters as scientists, technicians, and security personnel scrambled like ants summoned by their queen toward their duty stations. In this case, their queen was project lead Doctor Cecily Sturgess, a woman who was about as joyful as a dip in a frozen lake. She cared about her experiments and little else.

Something had to have gone wrong with the latest experiment if the queen had put out the call.

Rolf was beginning to think taking the security job at

TriGenex had been a mistake. In truth he had only been employed a little over a month but in that short amount of time he had seen some ungodly shit – shit that already had him pondering early termination of his contract. Grunts like him weren't supposed to ask questions or pay attention. In fact, they were paid to do the opposite. Rolf had always asked too many questions during his time in the United States Army; they had politely suggested he take his talents elsewhere despite his exemplary service record. His time at TriGen was turning out to be the sequel to a movie he wished he had never auditioned for in the first place.

Both he and Sully were suited, booted, and strapped in two minutes. They hurried from their quarters and followed the green line along the floor until reaching Lab One.

Consisting of five floors built into the heart of the Adirondack Mountains, the complex was shaped like a giant hourglass. Only the offices of the top floor were visible, while recreational, exercise, and cafeteria facilities dominated the second. The third and fourth floors housed the labs and associated personnel. Nobody ever talked about what lay below on five. Rumor had it that's where they kept the test subjects.

Up until today, Rolf had considered himself lucky to have been assigned to the genetics half of the facility. He mostly stood around and watched over the scientists while they conducted their experiments on witless death-row inmates. Those same fool inmates had signed their lives over to science and their families received a nice sum of money. It seemed harmless enough until Rolf had seen what was left of the last batch of experiments. He guessed it would be better than waiting around in a cage to die though.

Nearing the lab, the two ex-soldiers heard shouts. Through the observation window they saw a guy in an orange jumpsuit strapped to a table shudder under his restraints. Dr Sturgess shouted orders at two technicians while preparing a syringe. Two other technicians ran around like chickens with their heads cut off, scrambling from station to station pressing buttons on various machines and monitoring vital signs.

"We've got a situation." Their squad leader, Dot, looked from Sully to Rolf, her normally calm demeanor shattered. A line of sweat trickled down her forehead and rolled past her eye. Rolf appraised her reaction and surmised she probably had never seen any real combat. Her eyes lacked that hard edge he saw in the rest of his squad.

The inmate strapped to the table cried out, sweat pouring from every nook and cranny. As the rest of Rolf's team lined up, the inmate shot up, tearing through the straps and ripping free from the metal clamps holding him to the table. Dr Sturgess shouted at the window but her words were lost as everyone watched in rapt horror as the inmate's orange jumpsuit split, coils of muscle bubbling up through the material. Bones stretched, limbs lengthened in ways that went against nature or God, depending on what you believed. Hair rose in thick clusters all along its skin. Teeth clattered along the floor as fangs forced their way through.

What had been a man a few moments ago morphed into something...*else*.

"Oh my God," someone, Rolf wasn't sure who, murmured.

The creature stood upright, towering over the scientists. It snarled, saliva dribbling from its snout to chest. Dr Sturgess looked up, eyes wide. She scrambled to get away but a hairy arm connected with her chest. The air was forced from her lungs, her needle bouncing away. She landed on the floor in a heap and didn't rise. The thing in the other room turned and looked at the window and growled – an imposing hulk of fur and muscle.

If Rolf hadn't seen it with his own eyes, he would have never believed it. He had watched enough movies to know what he was looking at. And yet, he refused to think the word. Things like that weren't supposed to exist.

"Holy... shit," Sully said, giving voice to everyone else's thoughts.

One of the technicians screamed.

The experiment was across the room in a flash. It lunged at the closest technician, opened its toothy maw and latched onto her throat. The thing shook its head from side to side like a predator would with its prey, blood spraying in wild arcs. Screams filled the room as the remaining technicians watched on in horror. One of them made a mad dash for the door while the remaining technician attended to the fallen doctor.

"Open the outer door. Now." Rolf readied his HK416.

Dot didn't move. She stood transfixed by the scene beyond the window. Her mouth moved but no words came out.

"Dot! Open the goddamned door!"

Dot jumped. With her eyes still fixed on the experiment, she slid a card through a magnetic reader beside the large window. A small light went from red to green. The outer door slid open with a hiss.

It looked like their squad leader checked out. Considering the circumstances, Rolf couldn't blame her. He had commanded and fought with plenty of good men and women in both Afghanistan and Iraq and thought he had seen just about everything. After seeing that *thing* in the other room, he knew he was wrong.

"Sully and I will break right," Rolf said patting his roommate on the shoulder. "Peretti, you and Kang break left. Cruz, get those people out of there. Everyone clear?"

Peretti and Kang nodded.

"You got it," Cruz said pulling his Desert Eagle from its holster.

"Dot, keep that outer door clear."

Their squad leader nodded, still unable to draw her gaze from the window.

Rolf entered the small hallway between the outer and inner doors, the rest of his squad close behind. The only thing keeping the experiment contained was a few inches of reinforced steel of the inner door. Once he pressed the large red button they'd be face to face with a savage beast who had already tasted human blood. He took a breath and jammed on the button. The scent of blood and wet dog lay heavy on the air. The experiment had finished with the first technician and had another cornered. The skinny guy slid down the wall, sniveling, snot bubbling from a nostril.

Cruz cradled a hysterical technician in his arms, running from the lab. They disappeared through the inner doorway unharmed.

The experiment leaned in and sniffed. The skinny technician shielded his head with his arms. Bloody drool dribbled down the experiment's face. It reared back and howled. Just like a wolf.

Rolf motioned to Peretti. He and Kang moved like smoke through the lab, easy and silent. They came to a stop a few feet from the experiment, flanking the creature, rifles at the ready.

Rolf and Sully made their way from cover to cover until reaching the downed doctor. A trickle of blood ran from the top of her head. "Is she breathing?" he asked the technician attending her.

The technician—her badge identified her as Mara Leitch—nodded.

"Cover us," Rolf said to Sully.

Sully cocked his shotgun as Rolf slung the unconscious doctor over his shoulder. He hustled for the inner door; the experiment paid him no attention.

"P-please," the skinny technician stammered from across the room. He held out a hand toward Peretti, pleading.

The experiment let a clawed hand fly. With a sickening crunch, the cowering technician's neck twisted sharply, three long lacerations running the length of his face. He slumped to the floor a moment later staring through unblinking eyes.

Peretti and Kang opened fire.

A hail of automatic gunfire filled the experiment with holes. The thing turned, seemingly more annoyed than injured. It dove over Peretti and Kang, cleared a work station, and was halfway across the room. As Kang turned, he barely had time to react as the creature closed in from behind. It clubbed him in the chest, swatting him aside as if he were a child. With a wheeze, Kang slammed into the wall before sliding down to the floor.

Peretti strafed sideways as he fired, moving toward the exit. Sully fired from across the room hoping to draw the thing's attention. It didn't work.

In a blur of hair and teeth, the experiment closed in on Peretti much faster than anything any of the ex-soldiers had ever seen. Peretti barely managed to avoid the chomp, teeth as sharp as knives snapping shut where a moment ago his head had been. Another inch and he would have seen the inside of the experiment's mouth up close and personal. Peretti rolled aside and squeezed off another three shots. The experiment staggered back, crimson lines running from multiple wounds along its arms and torso. Anything else would have died ten times over.

Still, the thing advanced.

Rolf could only watch from the observation window as Peretti grabbed Kang by the BDU top and pulled. They didn't make it very far before a claw punched a hole clean through Peretti's chest. Still unconscious, Kang remained oblivious to the shower of gore.

From the doorway, Sully peppered the experiment with another shot. It focused on him with yellowed eyes, little trace of the human it had once been. Sully looked from the experiment to Kang. The thing raised its head, issuing another howl.

Dot pounded on the window.

Rolf slammed a fist on the red button and wasted precious seconds waiting for the door to fully open. He charged into the lab guns blazing, coming to a stop by the table where the experiment had been strapped. Sully seized the opportunity and hurried toward Kang.

The experiment growled, flexing its clawed hands. In an impressive display of strength, it ripped an entire workstation out of the floor and hefted it across the room. Instead of retreating, Rolf dove forward. He landed on his stomach and carefully aimed at the one spot he knew would hurt any male. Three bullets hit the thing between the legs. It dropped to its knees, clutching at its bloody meat.

Sully had Kang at the door. Dot was there helping to pull the wounded guard through the hallway and outer door to safety.

Rolf got to a knee and emptied his clip in the thing's head. Fifteen bullets made fifteen new holes. It finally dropped. After a raspy gurgle, the thing stayed silent.

Even though he didn't want to, Rolf knew he had to confirm the experiment was dead. After a quick reload, he approached with caution, stopping an arm's length away. His gun remained fixed on the body, finger tensed over the trigger.

The experiment's chest didn't rise.

Rolf inched closer, sweat chilling his brow. He nudged the thing with his foot. It didn't react. He eased a hand down and felt for a pulse. "Clear!" he shouted over a shoulder.

Even though the thing was dead, Rolf backed out of the lab without taking his eyes from it – he couldn't shake the feeling the thing would get up. A hand on his shoulder made him jump. "Stand down. We're clear." Dot's voice was composed, more like her normal, efficient self.

Rolf took a moment and exhaled a long breath. He wiped the sweat from his brow on a sleeve. "Anybody injured?"

"Dr Sturgess has a bump on her head. Nothing serious as far as I can tell," Cruz said.

"Dot, get on the horn and see if you can get Doc Brogan up here to take a look at Kang and Dr Sturgess." Rolf leaned against the wall and relaxed despite the jolt of adrenaline spiking through his body. "Somebody want to tell me what the fuck just happened in there?"

"I second that," Sully said, looking at the two technicians and their unconscious leader.

"Genetic splicing." Mara folded her lab coat and placed it under Dr Sturgess' head. She looked over at Rolf; her green eyes would have pierced a hole through lesser men. "That," she said motioning toward the lab, "was Project Lupine. We've been attempting to pair human genes with various animals. Until recently, we hadn't had much luck."

"You call that luck?" Sully grumbled. "Remind me not to invite you to Atlantic City."

"They'll never understand, dear." Dr Sturgess pushed up to a sitting position. She rubbed at a spot on her head and grimaced. A splotch of crimson streaked her mostly silver hair. "What we do here is for the benefit of all mankind. Think of all the disease and sickness that decimate humanity but not animals. If we could only find a way to combine some of their DNA with our own, the results would be miraculous. Diseases like Alzheimer's, Ebola, or AIDS could be eradicated at the genetic level. At least, that was our intent."

"Look, no offense Doc, but I don't give two shits about your intent. All I care about is getting the rest of our happy asses out of here alive." Rolf motioned around the small group around him.

She shook her head. "You don't understand. Once the alarm sounded, a quarantine protocol went into effect. Only the project leads and TriGen brass, seven of us in total, were to be evacuated along with our research." Dr Sturgess held up a flash drive attached to a nylon strap from around her neck. She looked at her assistant, an expression of pain on her face.

"How could you?" Mara said backing away, betrayal lighting those green eyes. She sat next to the other rescued technician; they leaned on one another.

"Mara, Bernice, I'm sorry. TriGen wouldn't have let us work if we didn't agree to their demands. You must understand."

"What about the rest of us? What about the facility?"

Dr Sturgess looked down. She licked her lips but said nothing.

"Answer the question," Bernice said.

"An explosion would wipe out the facility and any evidence of our experiments. It's supposed to look like an accident. Your families would all have been paid handsomely." The calm, even tone in Dr Sturgess' voice turned Rolf's stomach.

"We're all expendable." Rolf shook his head, slowly letting the anger fall away. "I guess I should have suspected as much. Typical executive bullshit."

"I hear that," Sully said with a nod.

The alarm blared on. A few people in lab coats ran past seemingly uninterested in anything else but where they were going.

"I thought we were clear? Why didn't they cut the alarm?" Dot asked.

"Each of the labs tried the same experiment at the same time. The only difference being the subject. Lab Two reported their subject expired shortly after the initial injection. Lab Three's subject didn't survive the transformation," Dr Sturgess said.

"What about Lab four?"

"No one has had contact with them since the experiment began." The doc looked down at her watch. "It's been just over an hour now." She pulled a handheld radio from her lab coat and handed it to Rolf. After trying to get ahold of anyone but only getting static, he handed it back.

"We simply didn't know what effects, if any, the splice would have. That was Leroy 'Pig Sticker' Addison."

"The cop killer?" Sully whistled. "That's one bad dude lying dead in there. He killed a dozen cops with a Rambo knife or something."

Dr Sturgess nodded. "It would seem the splice took to the more violent subjects – the more violent the better the splice. If only I had more time to discover why."

Rolf grabbed the old bird by the lab coat and pulled her close. Through clenched teeth he asked, "Who was on four?"

"Richard Dean Novak."

Rolf let the doc go. She took a step back and smoothed out her lab coat.

"You've got to be kidding me," Cruz said. "The serial killer?"

Dr Sturgess only nodded.

Mara rose and moved closer to Rolf. "You lied to us, manipulated us. And you were prepared to throw us away like trash. For what?" She slammed a fist into the window. "So you could play God with your genetic experiments?"

"Out of everyone here, I expected more from you, Mara," spat the doctor. "This could be the next step in human evolution. Ten years from now the world will be full of human and wolf hybrids. Think of the possibilities!"

Rolf could tell by the gleam in the doctor's eyes there would be no reasoning with her. He saw complete dedication there. There was no telling how far she would go if push came to shove. He'd have to assume she'd do whatever it took to ensure her work survived, even if it meant stabbing each of them in the back. Unfortunately, right now, they needed each other–

Everything went dark.

The lab, hallway, and every other room lost power. A moment later the emergency generator came on. Yellow lights did little to illuminate the hallway. Visibility was poor at best.

"That's just great." Cruz stood and started for the door marked 'stairwell' when a scream echoed from somewhere below.

All eyes went to Dot as the small radio clipped to her shoulder crackled and popped. More than one of them jumped. A moment later a garbled voice came through. "...request immediate assistance. I repeat...all security forces are dead. The experiment...loose..."

"That sounded like Dr Dillard," Mara said.

"Yeah, but what's he doing on the security forces' frequency?" Dot asked.

As if in response, the radio crackled and the blood freezing sound of a wolf howling vibrated the small speaker. Dot's eyes went wide.

"We can't worry about any of that right now," Rolf said. "All we can do is get the doc here to her rendezvous point and persuade the powers that be it would be in their best interest to let us come along for the ride." Rolf glared. "Have I made myself clear, Doctor?" He extended a hand and helped her to her feet.

"Yes, very clear." She smoothed out her lab coat. "Allow me to make myself clear. The only hope you have of getting out of here is escorting me down to the fifth level. There's a ventilation shaft that leads directly to the surface. A helicopter will be waiting."

"Fine. But we play by my rules. I say stop, you stop. I say go, and you go."

Sturgess nodded.

"Any objections?" Rolf asked looking from person to person.

"What about everyone else?" Bernice asked. "Are we just going to leave them?"

"They're already dead," Dr Sturgess said. Rolf could almost see her breath from the iciness of her words.

Another scream preceded running footsteps, the sound coming from the stairwell.

Cruz moved closer to the wall and raised his Desert Eagle. Rolf motioned Sully over to support him. "Cover our six," he whispered to Dot. She moved a few paces away from the group, her rifle pointing off into the gloom.

A guy in a blood streaked lab coat burst through the stairwell door and tumbled over Cruz. The guy came to a stop a few paces from the door as it closed behind him. Heavy breathing could be heard from the stairwell. Someone, or something, was coming after him.

The guy's face blanched. "It's right behind me. We have to get out of here!" He clutched a shredded arm to his chest, blood staining the polished white floor below. "They all started changing. Costello. Beck. Coates. Don't you see? They're all infected!"

"Whoa, take it easy, buddy." Sully moved toward him but the guy inched back.

"Don't come any closer!" He looked down at his wound and grunted.

"Dot, get them in the lab," Rolf ordered, seizing command. "Keep your heads down and don't move until I give the signal."

Without a word Dot gathered up the scientists and did as instructed. The wounded scientist refused to budge.

Cruz backed away from the door as a pair of feet slapped to a stop on the other side. They all heard something sniff the air the way a dog would.

"Oh, God, she found me." The wounded scientist leaned against the wall and staggered a few steps down the hallway leaving a bloody trail. After another two steps he fell, sweat pouring from his body.

The door burst open.

The slender hybrid stood silhouetted in the doorway, a confused look on its face. It sniffed at the air as Cruz retreated. A tattered lab coat clung to her shoulders. The badge identified it as Ashley Costello. In her little photo she had much less hair and smiled. With one giant stride, the thing that had been Ashley was at the puddle of blood, lapping it up.

"Holy mother of God," Cruz mumbled.

Sully eased up behind her, and double-tapped the beast. Ashley's body slumped to the floor adding to the crimson puddle.

Rolf ran past the carnage and stepped into the stairwell. Gunfire from below. Someone was still alive down there. As he turned to head for the lab, the injured scientist jumped up to his feet, his body changing from normal to hybrid in about a minute. Cruz turned just in time to catch a claw to the jaw. He tried to scream but only a garbled whimper escaped. The hybrid was on him and biting as Sully opened fire. Two shotgun blasts tore chunks out of the thing's back. It stumbled forward trying to stand, but fell.

Rolf hurried to his fallen comrade. Cruz was a mess of shredded flesh. Blood poured from his ruined mouth. He clasped Rolf's hand and choked. Rolf squeezed back knowing it wouldn't be long. "Hang in there, Cruz."

With another shotgun blast, the infected scientist was no more.

"Sully, get one of those scientists over here. Now!"

By the time Mara ran over, Cruz was gone. Rolf handed her the Desert Eagle. "I hope you know how to use it."

"I don't understand," she said, a frown creasing her brow. "He wasn't part of the experiment. How did he change?"

Dot and the others turned to Sturgess.

"We don't know," the doctors finally replied. "It happened shortly after the first successful splice. One of the technicians got too close while recording a hybrid's vital signs."

Realization washed over Mara's face. "Oh my God, Natalie."

Dr Sturgess nodded. "Yes. We covered it; said she had a family emergency."

Mara slapped Sturgess, snapping the older woman's head

sideways. "You son-of-a-bitch! You knew. All this time you knew what could happen to us and you said nothing!"

Sturgess responded with a smirk then moved to within an inch of her assistant. "Don't be so naïve, Mara. You knew the risks when you agreed to work for TriGen. We all did. What happened to all that talk of changing the world? The first sign of trouble and you're ready to throw in the towel. You're pathetic and weak."

Rolf pulled Mara back as she lunged. "Easy now. We need the good doctor in one piece."

Mara yanked free and pushed past to the stairwell. Rolf motioned for Sully to follow.

"I want details," Rolf said to Sturgess. "What makes people change?"

Sturgess hesitated a moment. "As far as I can tell it's the scratches and bites. Unfortunately, we haven't had much time to discover why. I'm afraid that's all the information I can provide."

"Things just keep getting better." Rolf looked into the doctor's eyes but wasn't sure if she was lying or not. The old gal had a pretty good poker face. He supposed she had to in order to keep so many secrets from her staff.

Kang stood there scratching his head, taking in the scene. All eyes went to him.

"What? Why's everybody looking at me like that?" He took a step back and raised his hands. "Take a look. My shirt isn't ripped. No scratches."

"Check him," Rolf said to Bernice.

She jumped up and inspected Kang. "He's clean."

"Good. We need you." Rolf handed Kang his weapon. "You and Sully have point. We move easy and slow down to five."

Kang nodded and hurried to the stairwell.

"Let's go, ladies. Time to leave." Rolf herded Dot and the two scientists to the stairwell. When he saw that Kang and Sully were in position, he waved them down.

They made it down to four without incident. As they neared the door to five, a chorus of howls sounded from above and below. Sully gave the sign to stop and Rolf made his way to the front. "We've got company," Sully said.

"We've got to clear that door," Kang whispered.

Rolf nodded. He put an ear up to the metal and listened. Another howl cut through the gloom. There was no telling how many of those things were on the other side. Kang stood off to the left, weapon ready. Sully stood a step behind Rolf who was in position to turn the knob. When he did, Sully would be the first through with his shotgun immobilizing any immediate threat, Kang right on his heels.

Rolf held up three fingers. He brought one down.

Sweat trickled down Kang's freshly buzzed head. Each infected person he had observed thus far started off sweating. Could Kang have ingested some blood earlier? Would it be enough to cause an infection? In the end he decided to trust his squad mate and Bernice's evaluation. Still, he'd have to keep an eye on the guy.

Another finger fell. Rolf's muscles tensed.

As the final finger fell, the door to the fourth floor crashed open above them. All eyes turned toward the sound.

Five hybrids poured into the stairwell.

"Go!" Dot yelled. She opened fire, spraying all five creatures as they closed the distance.

Rolf opened the door to the fifth floor and prayed it would be clear enough to make a stand. What he saw looked like a slaughterhouse. Blood and gore painted the walls and floor. Two hybrids ripped at a corpse fifteen feet away. The sound of them smacking and chewing was audible over the firefight in the hallway behind them. Three others fought over what looked like an arm a short distance away. More creatures stirred in the darkness beyond.

Sully and Kang advanced down the hallway. Bernice and Dr Sturgess were close behind. Mara looked from the doorway back to Dot unsure.

Rolf turned back.

One of the hybrids was down and moaning. Another limped. The biggest – a black haired beast towering over seven feet tall

– advanced on Dot. A growl rumbled through its chest, fangs gleaming white through the gloom. She raised her gun. "Suck on this, Fido," she said before pulling the trigger.

A click was the only thing that escaped the gun; her clip empty.

"Shit."

The beast took to the air, its claws poised to strike.

Rolf squeezed off four sets of three-round bursts, hitting the hybrid in the eye, neck, chest, and abdomen in quick succession. It whimpered as the bullets tore into it. Dot dove aside as it landed with a thud. She fumbled for a fresh clip. Rolf slammed a boot on the hybrid's neck holding it in place. Another three round burst ended its life.

Gunfire sounded from beyond the door. As Rolf looked over, a howl echoed through the stairwell from above. Dot shoved him aside just as a grey and black-haired hybrid swung at him. Rolf hit the wall and spun toward the door. The remaining two hybrids had Dot pinned down. She struggled beneath their weight. A brown-haired hybrid reared back and tore out her throat.

"NO!"

"C'mon," Mara said, pulling Rolf by the sleeve. She led him through the door and straight into a pile of Bernice's entrails. There was a blood stain on the wall above what was left of her.

Rolf expelled his empty clip and traded it for a full one. He turned toward the door expecting the hybrids to follow. They didn't. *Probably too busy snacking on Dot.*

A shotgun blast sounded from somewhere in the distance.

"Where's Dr Sturgess?"

Mara shrugged.

"Nine o'clock!" Sully shouted from somewhere ahead.

Gunfire sounded soon after.

Mara and Rolf hurried toward the sound. A door off to the side opened as they passed. It was too dark to see how many hybrids emerged from the room beyond.

Kang and Sully advanced slowly, Dr Sturgess close behind. She directed them toward an unfinished section of the complex.

Sully turned and dropped a hybrid in a tattered black uniform, its rifle still slung over a shoulder. The doctor knelt and retrieved it. Yellow light reflected in the sweat covering each of them.

"Whatever you're going to do, you better do it fast," Rolf yelled from behind. He and Mara sprinted to catch up, numerous hybrids bounding after them.

Dr Sturgess pointed at a door. Kang opened it. The five of them hurried through, howls following them.

They found themselves in a spacious and mostly empty room. A pile of dead bodies had been stacked in a corner. Various medical supplies lined metal shelves on the other side of the room. Pipes and ducts lined the walls and ceiling. It looked as if the contractors ran out of supplies and left this section as bare as possible.

"Failed experiments," Sturgess said moving past the rancid pile of corpses. She ran to the back corner and a door marked 'ventilation access'.

Rolf and Mara pulled a metal shelf lined with disposable gloves toward the door. They slammed it in place just as it started to open.

"This isn't going to hold long!" Rolf yelled.

The shelf rattled as the hybrids pushed and pounded on the door. Rolf and Mara pushed back but both knew they weren't strong enough to hold back a pack of genetically-altered hybrids. The shelf was forced back a little with each blow – the gap between the door and wall widening.

Dr Sturgess slid a keycard through a slot then punched in a five digit code. A clicking noise preceded the door opening.

"Go," Rolf said to Mara. She sprinted across the room and skidded to a stop as Dr Sturgess opened fire.

Kang took most of the barrage. He dropped to his knees, a look of disbelief on his face. He fell a moment later. Sully returned fire, hitting Sturgess in the leg before she disappeared through the door.

A hairy claw punched through the door. Rolf pushed back with everything he could muster, the tread of his boots squeaking as he fought for every inch. A multitude of howls sounded from the stairwell, hunger bleeding into their frenzied cries.

"What I wouldn't give for a grenade."

"Hey," Mara said.

Rolf turned and she tossed him a fire extinguisher. "I could kiss you right now."

She cracked a smile before helping Sully limp toward the ventilation room door.

The door flung open, the metal rack swept aside. Several sets of glowing eyes peered from the half-light beyond. Rolf tossed the fire extinguisher. It hit the first hybrid in the chest and clanged to the floor. Pistol in hand, he squeezed the trigger.

The hybrid squealed as the extinguisher exploded in a white cloud.

Rolf ran across the room to find Mara and Sully pounding on the ventilation room door. "What's the hold up?"

"Door's locked." Mara said.

Rolf took Sully's shotgun and obliterated the keypad and door handle. The wires fizzled as the first hybrid entered.

A howl resounded around the room.

A multitude of howls answered back.

The ventilation room door opened.

Mara helped Sully through. Rolf followed the bloody trail. He slammed the door shut and leaned on it. Much of the space in the small room was taken up by different machinery and a trio of air ducts. A trail of blood led to the rear of the room and the furthest air duct. A metal grate had been tossed aside.

Mara stuck her head in. "There's a ladder."

The air coming from the vent was noticeably cooler.

Sully limped over and slid down the door next to Rolf.

"Get over there and start climbing."

"Not this time." Sully moved an arm. Blood leaked through a hole in his chest. He flashed a toothy smile. "I survived the werewolves, but not the old lady." A bitter laugh escaped him. "Fucking werewolves, man. Can you believe it?"

Rolf handed him his gun.

Sully nodded, much spoken between the two in that one action.

Rolf slid through the opening in the vent and started climbing. He didn't look back when he heard gunshots, or Sully's screams before a single shot echoed through the vent.

The crisp mountain air felt good on Rolf's sweat covered skin. He emerged from the shaft to a setting sun that normally would have taken his breath away. A light dusting of snow covered the rocky ground beneath them. Mara shivered, clinging to the side of the mountain. She slammed the heavy grate closed behind them. Neither of them thought the hybrids would be able to fit in the shaft. Still...

They followed the trail of blood to a helicopter pad and made it just in time to see a helicopter whir away.

"Looks like we missed our ride." Mara's head followed the helicopter as it sped away.

"We better get moving. The temperature's going to drop as soon as the sun sets."

They moved past the landing pad and found a narrow path leading down. "Thanks, you know, for getting me out of there," Mara said.

Rolf looked down and noticed a few drops of blood. "We're not out of the woods yet." A few steps later they found a discarded gun. "It looks like the good doctor missed her ride too."

"We might be able to catch her if we hurry."

A few steps later they found a tattered lab coat and the same flash drive Dr Sturgess showed them earlier.

Beside the flash drive were footprints. Hybrid footprints.

"Damn," Rolf said.

Mara came closer. "What is it?"

Rolf pointed down.

"At least we got her research. Maybe we can help stop it." Mara slipped the flash drive into her pocket.

A howl sounded in the distance and bounced around the peak of the mountain.

WERWOLF!

W.D. Gagliani & David Benton

A hybrid excerpt from W.D. Gagliani's Wolf's Edge

1

Northern Italy
1944

Giovanni Lupo walked fast, hands in his pockets, one wrapped around the tubular lead weight he carried in case he needed a little more oomph behind his considerable right hook.

It wouldn't help against a German patrol, but a single adversary would pay the price if his jaw got between Giovanni and his escape route. It might be all the advantage he needed. He walked fast, hoping to beat the rapidly approaching darkness as well as the random patrols.

For as dusk arrived, so would the Allied bombers.

They came every night, almost as soon as the sirens went off and the spotlights went on, trying to catch their silhouettes like bugs on a glass.

Giovanni Lupo lived with his family on the outskirts of Genova, the huge port city whose importance to the German war machine was incalculable. Its factories had turned to slave labor to churn out goods for the war effort, but it was Germany's war effort – no longer Italy's. In September 1943, the Italian monarchy and its political backers signed a secret armistice with the Allies. As soon as it became known that Italy had surrendered, the German ally's resident forces had become an outright occupation. Everyone knew the war was lost except the mad German leadership, and few Italians saw the benefit of that, but the die was cast.

But those factories were a fat prize for the Allied bombardiers. As was the German high command, located somewhere near the harbor.

Now heading home on foot from his meager employment in a local foundry that had miraculously avoided nationalization by the Germans, Giovanni Lupo kept a cautious watch for German patrols, his greatest fear. They would sometimes sweep up able-bodied Italian men to fill gaps in factory assembly lines.

A typical tactic was for a covered truck to drive to a public square or market, pull up, and disperse a platoon of Wehrmacht infantrymen who would then round up bystanders and passersby and hold them at gunpoint until a cattle van could cart away the victims.

Giovanni watched for the rumbling covered trucks.

He was convinced his ears were sensitive. The moment he heard the unforgettable gear-grinding sound of one of those vehicles, he would melt into one of the narrow lanes that lined the street. He had mapped numerous routes home to avoid this very danger. He walked briskly, avoiding the glances of strangers, hoping he could make it home without trouble. His fellow pedestrians surely thought the same and went their way, avoiding him.

He looked straight ahead, ears attuned to the infrequent roar of a motor vehicle or the grinding of trucks.

Maria, I'm coming home. Don't worry too much.

He hoped his son had found his way home from school by now. A month ago, a teacher had disappeared – presumably in a street sweep. The children had been dismissed until a substitute could be coaxed from another school farther away. Hardly anyone wanted to work so close to a German high command, for it was an Allied high-priority target.

Giovanni had worked a full day for the first time in months, eagerly accepting the opportunity to earn a few extra *lire*. Maybe there would be eggs and some lard in the kitchen tomorrow because of it.

Again Giovanni thought of his son's long walk home from school. Some of it was through rural lanes and secondary streets, but he should be safe if he walked straight home without any distractions. Unfortunately, Franco was the kind of boy for whom *everything* was a distraction. If not for this damnable, senseless war – and its resulting occupation by the goddamned Germans – his son would have been at the top of his class in studies. But the school slowdown had stunted the book learning, and Giovanni was beginning to fear his boy was getting too much of a street education. He spent half his days running in the streets.

But it was the thought of extra food, especially eggs and meat and oil, all of which he could almost taste – though he suspected that soon the Germans would begin to run out of oil as well, if the rumors of their losses in the South were true – that distracted Giovanni from his single-minded route home.

And distracted him from two very important things.

One was the approaching command car, which was crawling along scouting the streets ahead of its "collection" squad.

The other was the exact moment at which dusk would become evening.

Giovanni turned the corner and found himself facing the command car, which swerved toward him with a squeal of tires. Two burly German soldiers leapt from the rear before the vehicle had even come to a full stop.

Taken by surprise, Giovanni shrank back against the wall behind him, having forgotten it was there. He lost precious time trying to decide whether he should pull his lead-heavy hand from his pocket and fight, or flee the way he'd come. Unfortunately, the momentary indecision tied up both options, for his weighted hand caught in his clothes and at the same time he couldn't reorient his legs and feet in order to allow for a sprint away from the uniformed thugs who were upon him.

Merda!

His fist was trapped.

His feet tripped over themselves and he went down sideways even as the two Germans caught him and yanked him off the sidewalk as if he were a child, their guttural orders and commands just a jagged jumble of sounds in his ears.

Oh no, Maria! This wasn't what I wanted!

He struggled in their grasp. The two were larger than average, two bruisers who knew the ropes. They suspected his hand held a weapon and made sure it couldn't clear his damned pocket, and by keeping his feet off the ground he was off-balance as well and found it impossible to gather enough leverage for a kick.

"Nooooo!" he shouted in frustration. Tears wet the corners of his eyes.

The two uniformed goons manhandled him, their faces grim with determination and single-minded purpose. Perhaps their well-being in the barracks depended on how they performed their duty.

He struggled in their iron grip even as they dragged him, sweating and screaming, past the waiting command car to where a covered truck was just now pulling up.

His legs swinging empty kicks at his attackers' shins, his mouth keeping up a steady stream of curses that would have made his wife blush, he found himself being tossed face-first like a sack of spongy rotten potatoes over the rear gate and into the back of the truck.

His face stopped its painful slide on the rough planks by smashing into the muddy boots of another German soldier who thrust the muzzle of his submachine gun into Giovanni's skull.

He couldn't look up, but what was in his range of vision deflated his spirit and took the fight out of him. Boots all around him, and at the front of the truck bed, scuffed shoes and even bare feet – other conscripted unfortunates.

A stream of guttural syllables followed him onto the truck bed. One of the two burly thugs telling the other troopers he was probably armed.

Hands reached out for his arms on both sides and dug his fist out of his pocket as the gun muzzle threatened to burrow straight through his skull and into his brain. Rivulets of blood seeped down his forehead and into his eyes as he felt the gun metal scraping his cranium like a crowbar. His fist was forcibly removed from his pocket, the fabric tearing loudly, and the lead weight was pried from his fingers with inexorable strength.

My Maria! My son!

Beyond the pain in his head, the only thought he had was of his family and the fact that he would never see them again.

And almost exactly the next moment, the Allied bombers came.

Grinding up to a screaming wail, the nearest air-raid sirens signaled the arrival of the first wave of the night's bombers. Not every night, not yet, but often enough to keep the German occupiers – and the innocent populace – guessing. Tonight the raid was slightly early, with a tendril of daylight left across the darkening sky, but there it was. The rumble of airplane engines slowly crawled over the land, and in seconds the *crump-crump-crump* of anti-aircraft fire joined in the cacophony as gunners began to lay down a barrage that would knock a percentage of the Liberators and Fortresses out of the sky before the raid was over.

Waves of American and English long-distance bombers targeted the harbor, the suspected high command, and the factories arrayed in long blocks between them. Typically, the first strings of ordnance fell short and landed in civilian neighborhoods.

Like this one.

The truck's driver gunned the motor and squealed away from the cobbled curb.

The thugs who had thrown Giovanni onto the back of the truck leapt for the command car in their haste to escape the open street. They were in the crosshairs for a direct hit, or burial under rubble if the Allied bomb strings found a nearby building.

The soldiers who'd been frisking Giovanni and driving the gun muzzle into his cranium were thrown clear to the side as the driver swerved.

Giovanni took his opportunity, ignoring the pain in his head and face, he leapt up to dive off the rear of the truck. The soldier with the submachine gun regained his balance and managed to partially block Giovanni's access to the open gate. Behind them, the cobblestones fled past as the vehicle gained speed. A series of explosions rocked the ground and the truck careened to the right-hand side.

Without even thinking, Giovanni's hands wrapped around the barrel of the German's submachine gun as if of their own volition and he snatched it away. Once in his grasp, he turned it around.

The short burst cut the soldier in half and threw him against his fellows in a heap.

As completely instinctively as the shooting had been, Giovanni made his split-second decision and dove from the rear of the vehicle. He hit the cobblestones hard, knocking the air from his lungs even as he rolled toward the gutter.

He still held the gun.

Down the street, a building collapsed after an Allied bomb struck its roof and ripped out its guts. The cloud of dust and debris obscured the street and pelted Giovanni's back as he lay on the cobblestones trying to draw a breath.

He glanced over the debris and saw the truck teeter momentarily on two wheels, strike the opposite curb and overturn, spilling its human cargo like sacks of trash.

Giovanni struggled to his feet, submachine gun still in his hands.

Three soldiers spilled from the truck and one pointed at him.

Giovanni's hands were bruised, his arms ached. But his right index finger twitched on the trigger as if he'd lost control, causing the Schmeisser MP40 to stutter in his grip. The breech ejected a stream of hot brass casings as the gun spoke in its own guttural dialect.

The soldiers flopped around in a gruesome dance as the 9mm slugs tore through them in ragged, bloody lines. The muzzle went silent when the magazine was empty, the bolt stuck in the open position.

Giovanni's hands opened and the smoking gun dropped to the bricks.

He stared at the carnage he had wrought.

More soldiers were crawling from the truck's sideways cab, one reaching for a sidearm. Yet another emerged from the covered rear, struggling to bring a Mauser rifle to bear.

Giovanni closed his eyes, waiting for the feel of the slugs tearing out his chest.

Instead, gunfire erupted all around him.

The Germans' bodies fell twitching to the gore-slick road. Masked gunmen, sprinting from the cover of dark doorways and narrow lanes, ran to the wounded or dead Germans and shot them repeatedly in the head. Several motioned other civilian men from the rear of the truck, one of whom had been wounded in the gunfire and had to be carried. When the gunmen had made sure all the German soldiers were dead, they stripped the bodies of weapons and ammunition.

A gangly young man in a rakish beret walked up to Giovanni, who stood still stunned by what he had done, grasped his hand and pumped it enthusiastically.

"Grazie, signore. Lei e' un eroe!"

You are a hero!

"No!" Giovanni spat at him, breaking into a racking cough as the dust swirled around them. "No," he repeated softly in disgust at what he had done.

"Si, certamente." The young man was clearly in command of the rag-tag group of gunmen. He wore a tweed coat crossed by bandoliers – shotgun shells – and in his hands he held a fine Beretta hunting shotgun. He had a German Luger pistol holstered on his hip. He smiled broadly under a thin moustache. "I am Corrado Garzanti, field commander of the local brigade."

"Partigiani?" *Partisans?*

"Of course." He gestured at his men. "We were about to ambush the collection patrol when you took matters into your own hands, eh? Very nicely done." He pointed at the bleeding bodies.

"How? How did you know? To be here, right now?"

Corrado waved the question away. "We have sources. People

who listen and report. We expected them. We did not expect *you*, however."

Giovanni's head spun a little and he stumbled sideways, almost losing his footing. Ragged bursts of gunfire and screams came from farther down the street and he whirled, apprehensive.

"It's just my men taking care of the command car. Those dirty German bastards are never going home." Corrado reached out and steadied Giovanni before he could collapse.

"I think you had better come with us. It won't be safe here very soon. We survived the bombing, but the bastards will be out looking for revenge. Damned bad idea to be out on the street then." He waved at one of his men. "Dario, come here. I want you to escort our hero home to pack his things."

"No, no, it's not necessary."

"Oh, it is. If they find you, they will hang you with metal wire from a lamppost. It's what they're doing these days. Among other things. Come with us. We have a safe haven. It's not a palace, but it's a good home. And they don't know where it is."

"No, you don't understand, I have a wife and a child. I have a family! I can't go away with you. What happens to them?" Giovanni swayed and the partisan leader steadied him again.

"Clearly, you cannot just go home. *Va bene*, we take you there and you take your family with you. We have enough space. Most of us have lost our families, but there are a few."

"Corrado," said Dario, pointing at his watch. "It's almost time for the *lupi*."

"I know—"

The air raid siren ground to life again, its insistent wail gathering strength as the rumbling of invisible aircraft reached them.

"*Arrivano ancora!*" Corrado shouted. *Second wave!* His men knew what to do. And suddenly Corrado's fist jabbed out and caught Giovanni's jaw, snapping his head back and dropping him like a broken doll.

"You and you," Corrado pointed at the strapping Dario and another man. "Take him between you. He's coming to the sanctuary. He has no choice now."

Giovanni moaned as hands grabbed him.

Maria.

He lost the light at the same moment the first string of bombs stitched their way toward the harbor, taking down a block of tenements and shops in a cluster of explosions, jetting gas fires, and a spreading cloud of dust and debris.

Giovanni welcomed the darkness.

2

He opened his eyes and immediately closed them. His vision was a blur of indistinct shapes – darkness broken only by flickering blobs of light. *A church?* He smelled candles. He tried to move his head and stopped when it seemed his jaw would break.

Somebody had hit him. There had been an air raid. There were guns and a shooting.

Santa Maria, he thought, *I was doing the shooting.*

Bit by bit the memory came nosing back and he started to put the pieces together. He realized he was shivering.

Where was he?

His moan brought one of the blobs suddenly closer. A cool touch on his forehead triggered memories and thoughts, but blinking brought forth only tears and pain.

"Sono io, Giovanni," a calm but shaky voice spoke in his ear. "Sono io. Stai tranquillo."

Maria! Thank God!

His hand gripped hers and brought it to his chest. He still couldn't see very well, but the simple gesture slowed his heart from its onrushing pace and brought the tranquility she'd wished upon him. He started to rise but she pushed him back firmly.

"No, you might be hurt. And we have to stay silent."

"What?"

"Shhhhhh." Her hand caressed his face. "Trust me."

He noticed movement behind her, more blurs making jagged little gestures. He smelled sweat and bodies. "What– Where are we? Where is–?"

Suddenly he was seized by the thought of what he hadn't heard or yet felt. His son.

"Where is Franco?" he groaned, his voice rough.

"I don't know," she said, crying. "He was–"

Somebody stepped closer and whispered in a clipped voice, "Be silent or you'll get us all killed!"

Giovanni felt Maria's hand caress his face and softly cover

his lips. He kissed her cool skin, but his mind reeled. His son wasn't here, wherever *here* was. Maria was here, and these others, but not Franco.

His memory slotted into place and he remembered the firefight in the street. How he had ended up with a machine gun, and turned it on the hated German.

The bombing raid. The partisans.

Corrado Garzanti was the rogue's name.

Corrado had hit him.

The bastard.

Giovanni's legs trembled as he tried to stand. He reached for Maria.

Sounds – crashing, smashing sounds – from above and nearby reached them and his heart started to race again.

Corrado materialized beside him – a blob with glasses pinching his nose. "Listen to me," he hissed into Giovanni's ear, "they're close to finding one of our secret entrances, and if they do we are all fucked in the ass. You understand? We have to slip out and fight them, kill them all before they can report. Are you up to it?"

"Up to it?"

Killing people?

Who was this idiot, asking him to kill…

Corrado's band of partisans was gathering just behind, preparing by checking guns and knives, facing a wall that until now Giovanni had thought solid. But there was a vertical slit, a sort of narrow sloping passage, and the men were slipping through one by one.

"We'll need you. Here." Corrado handed Giovanni an old revolver, which he took but loosely. Corrado plucked it from his hand and tucked into Giovanni's belt for him, where it felt alien. Then someone else handed him a Beretta submachine gun on a sling. He took it, reluctantly. It also felt strange in his hands, heavy and awkward, but not very different from the German gun he'd used to good effect earlier. This one was heavier, the stock wood and the barrel shrouded with extra metal. He looked back at Maria – but a tall man behind him was crowding him toward the passage.

It appeared he would have to pay his way.

The tall man and another fell in behind him, and all he could do was nod and try to smile at Maria before she disappeared behind them, but he had lost sight of her. And then he was stumbling into the passage. It was a ruined staircase, brick and mortar debris underfoot. Boots and shoes scraped in front of him, climbing, so he followed instinctively even though he could barely see.

They climbed single-file, seemingly endlessly until they reached a collapsed corridor. Then Giovanni smelled the evening air. They were outside, emerging from a hidden fissure between leaning stone walls. The short column of men snaked around the corner and he realized they were attempting to flank the German patrol before the shelter was sniffed out.

He gripped the Beretta's stock tightly, his mind a jumble of fears.

They were nearly around the ruined building's front corner when someone's shoe kicked over a pile of debris, which groaned and came tumbling to the ground in a clatter of stone and wood, raising a cloud of dust.

An angry shout in German, and then another, and then there was a submachine gun burst and Giovanni realized the partisans, not yet in position, had been forced to open fire without cover. They were outlined against the wall.

"All'attacco, ragazzi!" Corrado shouted, urging his men on the attack, their intended surprise flanking shattered by the shouting and the gunfire. "Per la patria!" *For the homeland!*

The enemy was a series of indistinct shapes, like ghosts shimmering in the dark.

A man went down on Giovanni's left, his chest split open by a fusillade of slugs.

Giovanni screamed in fear and anger and squeezed the Beretta's trigger, letting loose a burst. Recoil tugged the barrel upward and to the left and he saw his rounds shatter a window too high up to catch any of the enemy. Another man went down on his right, a bullet in the head silencing him forever. Giovanni held the Beretta barrel down and sprayed lead until his breech locked open, the magazine empty. Someone shoved another magazine at him and he reloaded, somehow catching on instinctively. He shot at the ghosts again, and this time one of the shapes threw up his arms and collapsed, broken, against the bricks.

Gunfire raged around him and for a moment he thought the partisans were holding the enemy back, their bursts exacting a terrible toll.

A series of loud snarls broke through the gunfire, followed immediately by an unearthly howling. Giovanni stopped short, a shiver shooting down his spine. Despite the gun battle, this sound was viscerally more terrifying.

"*Lupi!*" someone shouted. Then the man's voice turned to a gurgle as a dark, muscular shape lunged from the shadows and ripped out his throat.

Whatever it was, it snarled and shook its long snout and Giovanni heard a slaughterhouse ripping of bone and flesh and the dead man's head came rolling to a stop at his feet.

Dio mio!

Giovanni couldn't help staring for a split-second down into the dead man's terrified eyes, already glazing, and then he stumbled aside until he couldn't see the head and the jagged piece of spine protruding from its torn neck.

All around him he heard men screaming as more four-footed shapes materialized. For the first time he saw that they were giant dogs—

No, they were wolves.

And they were large… very large…

They lunged at men who shot at them over and over without any effect, their jaws snapping and tearing necks and limbs. *Here* was a partisan going down under a slashing, biting jaw full of fangs. *There* was a man with a wolf's snarling snout buried in his belly, tearing out loops of bloody intestines as he screamed his last.

Out of the corner of his eye Giovanni saw one man shoot a wolf and the animal went down, screaming in rage, trying to reach around its back and bite the smoking wound. The tall man who had been behind him on the staircase leaped onto the wolf's back, a silver blade flashing, and stabbed it twice in the neck before slitting the animal's throat.

It all happened in mere seconds, but Giovanni swore he saw the wolf catch fire and squeal in agony as its blood seemed to boil. And then its body blurred, and impossibly, became a naked man, a human, whose greasy hair the tall partisan grabbed with a fist and pulled up, using the glowing blade to sever the head. The partisan tossed it aside with a shout of fury and victory.

Giovanni opened his mouth to scream, but no sound came out. What he had seen, it was not possible...

The battle had degenerated into single shots and snarls, screams of terror and pain, and gurgling sounds of bloody death.

And he heard the tearing of bone and tissue, the howling of victorious wolves.

How many are there?

He turned in time to see a giant wolf leaping for his throat. With no time to sidestep, he brought up the Beretta's barrel and let loose a burst.

The bullets stitched across the wolf's body and head and should have cut him to pieces, but Giovanni was horrified to see that the deadly lead barely knocked the animal off its stride. Its weight smashed into him and slammed him to the ground, jaws snapping at his neck.

The Beretta flew out of his grasp, and he threw up his hands to avert the wolf's continuous attacks. Giovanni risked one hand and scrabbled for the revolver tucked in his belt, the other hand desperately fending off the wolf's fangs. Its raging eyes seemed red in the near-darkness.

He brought up the pistol by feel and shoved the barrel under the wolf's jaws. Those red blazing eyes seemed to roll crazily, and held his as the wolf gathered for a final push. Giovanni pulled the trigger once, twice, three times. The bullets ripped through the fur, bone, and skull.

Giovanni sucked in air and started to throw off the dead animal's weight.

In the moonlight, the wounds caused by his bullets began to close up and disappear. The wolf's red eyes found his and it seemed to smile at his shock and terror.

Then he was awash in a gush of gore as an anonymous hand bearing a flashing silver blade slit the wolf's throat just before it could press its advantage and bite off Giovanni's face.

It was the tall man from the tunnel who'd done it, a grim smile on his face as he nodded and then jumped to the aid of another partisan locked in a struggle for his life with yet another impossible animal. The tall man's blade slashed, opening the wolf's throat. The animal's shriek of pain and rage as the blade burned through its flesh and tendons would haunt Giovanni to the moment of his death. And so would the sight of this dead wolf blurring into a dead human. To his right, where his lupine attacker had been, now sprawled a dead man. The tall partisan severed both heads with grim efficiency.

"Must make sure, eh?" he said gruffly.

Giovanni got to his knees unsteadily. The battle was over, won apparently, by Corrado and his men, but at a terrible cost. A half-dozen partisans lay dead, their bodies scattered near the side of the building, grotesquely disemboweled. Five naked, decapitated men marked where the wolves had died. Several uniformed German soldiers also lay dead, their bodies riddled with bullets.

Corrado was alive, his coat covered with splattered blood.

"Thank you, Turco," he said, clapping a hand on the tall man's shoulder. "Without you, I don't know–" He stopped, his haunted eyes finding Giovanni's. "You fought well. You're one of us now. We saved the shelter, this time. But now you must not watch. Turco, I don't envy you this job."

The tall man shrugged. He moved to each of the dead partisans and stabbed them in the heart before sawing off their heads.

Giovanni thought he had been horrified by everything up to now. But this was too much!

He was too hoarse to shout, but almost did. "What sacrilege are you–?"

"It's necessary, believe me," Corrado said, making a half-hearted sign of the cross. "We must be sure they are dead, and that they were killed *with that blade.* Otherwise there's a possibility…"

Turco was finished with his task. The two rallied the surviving partisans around them. Wounds were inspected. Most were minor, and Giovanni noticed that Turco remained nearby, the unsheathed silver blade touching every survivor – including himself.

Corrado noticed Giovanni's questioning look. "We have learned to look after ourselves," he explained, but it was no real explanation as far as Giovanni was concerned.

Exhausted, his body aching and his mind still reeling at all he had seen, all he wanted to do was climb down those stairs and see his wife.

And then he would go find his son.

Se Dio vuole, he thought. God willing.

3

Corrado had shucked his bloody coat and now wore a thin, once-white dress shirt. He shivered in the night's chill, present even here in the shelter.

"Now you know what we are up against," he told Giovanni. "Since late last year, the Germans have sent those things against us, night after night."

"But… what *are* they?"

"Do you not remember the stories your parents told you when you were young? They are wolf-men, just like the legends."

"It's just too… It's impossible."

"You saw it with your own eyes. But for Turco, one would have torn you apart. We know what they are, but they are almost impossible to kill. The Germans are retreating, but they have deployed a rear guard made up, partly, of this *Werwolf Division* of theirs. The monsters have done their worst in the hills and used to stay out of the cities, mostly, but now they are being used against us here as well."

"You said you can't kill them? But they did die."

Corrado snorted quietly. "Sure, but at what cost. They can be killed, but it takes special…" He leaned over and whispered even more quietly. "That man there, hunched in the corner?"

Giovanni saw a man whose look was haunted. His eyes seemed feverish, his skin pale. He hadn't been part of the gun battle.

"He's a priest. He has fought with us. He is a Jesuit. You know what that means?"

Giovanni shrugged. He knew who Jesuits were, of course, but…

"He has done exorcisms. He has faced evil before and survived. And he has brought us more than just his own fighting spirit. From Rome, he has brought us a weapon."

"Rome?"

"From the Vatican." Corrado scratched his stubble. "You

want to talk with him? Will it make you feel better about what you have seen?"

Giovanni's eyes unfocused as he stared at the priest. Then he nodded.

"Hey, Babbo, this guy wants to talk to you," Corrado called out across the room.

The priest stood and moved as if uncertain of his footing. As if his feet were submerged. He looked to have been muscular and then run to fat, but now the fat had dissipated and his skin was sallow and bag-like.

He came to a stop near Giovanni and Corrado. His priest's collar was long gone. His eyes were glazed by lack of sleep or war-weariness. Both.

"You're that new one," he said. "You have a pretty wife."

Giovanni nodded. "Yes, and a son. But I don't know what happened to him. I wanted him here with me, but he's missing. And now I'm not sure I want him here. I don't know what I want. Except... I want to know that what I saw out there cannot exist."

The priest sighed and sat stiffly near them.

He pointed at Corrado and said: "He calls me Babbo, *dad*, because he's not very religious." His expression was more sympathetic now. "I see how much you fear for your son. What happened?"

Corrado moved away, checking on his men.

"I was out working when the Germans picked me up for one of their damned slave-labor details. I didn't intend— I... found myself fighting even though it was the last thing I wanted. My son was out with his friend Pietro, playing, as he does every day since their school was closed. That was when Corrado's men grabbed my wife too, but my son wasn't home. I'm grateful, they may have saved her, but now I want to find Franco and they won't let me go."

"My name is Father Tranelli. I will have a word with Corrado. He's a good man, but he feels responsible for his fighters, and he cannot separate his hate for Germans from his responsibilities. But you saw what the Germans use against us..."

"What are they, Father?" The tremble in Giovanni's voice betrayed how haunted he was by the horror.

"They are men who have the ability to turn into wolves. You must remember the legends? The Middle Ages were full of sightings, convictions, and executions of so-called wolf-men. Mothers still terrify their unruly children with tales of the *uomolupo*, the wolf-man, or the *lupo mannaro* – the werewolf. We have always had the legends, especially in the hill villages. But after the Germans became our occupiers and the war seemed already lost, they brought in the Werwolf Division as a rear guard. You know the damned Nazis, they like all that occult stuff. Nobody paid any more attention than to anything else they do. They have already a reputation for shooting civilians and imprisoning anyone they deem dangerous. But as Corrado will tell you, partisan units began coming into contact with groups of these wolves. First our fighters found their sentries killed, torn apart and disemboweled. Men on lonely outposts were killed by mysterious animals. But then the attacks became brazen, and now sometimes several werewolves will attack a patrol or even a safehouse."

"But why can't you kill them?" Giovanni slapped his hand on the table. "I saw your men shoot them at point-blank range and yet the wolves survived and still reached them."

"Werewolves are magical beings, young man. I have no other explanation. They are of the devil, perhaps. They cannot be killed by normal means."

"Then if there are many of them, we'll all die…"

"These monsters *are* vulnerable to one thing. You saw yourself. They are averse to silver. Any weapon made of silver will have an effect on them, and bullets cast from pure silver can kill them. It acts like liquid fire inside their bodies. We have dispatched quite a few, recently. And tonight. But we are still susceptible to their attacks."

"Why not make silver bullets by the thousands then?"

"My friend, because there is not so much silver to go around. The people used it for money in the early days of the war, when they needed to buy food for their families. Whatever they hoarded is not nearly enough. We use whatever we can get, but we have to make it count. Whenever new people join us, we ask for their silver. It is still not enough."

"How can you still have your faith after seeing... after seeing *that*?"

"Who says I still have faith?" The priest rubbed his tired features with a claw-like hand. "Well, I do, even if it's not like before. I know things have changed in my mind. But I'm a Jesuit, and I can persevere through anything, as Jesus himself was able to do."

Corrado had returned and heard the last part. "Have you told him yet? The worst part?"

"No, but I will now." He sighed a long sigh and Giovanni thought he heard the rasp of disease coming from him. "We learned that it's much better to be killed by the beasts than merely bitten. *A man bitten but not killed will inevitably turn into a monster on the next full moon.*"

Father Tranelli shook his head. His brown eyes were watery.

"Dio mio." Giovanni crossed himself. Startled, he realized he hadn't done so in years. "This is why even the corpses were... stabbed and..."

"God forgive us, yes. *Beheaded*. We believe it's the only way to make sure."

Giovanni was reminded of what Corrado had said. "You spoke of the weapon. It was the blade? Something about the Vatican?"

Tranelli glared at Corrado for a second. "I was in Rome a year ago," he said, finally nodding and rubbing his thinning hair, "but originally I'm from a small village about fifty kilometers from here. It... it *was* a village. Now it's a butcher shop that has been closed a long time. The people there, they were my family and my flock, and this damned Werwolf Division went there and slaughtered all of them because of one shot a boy took at a German soldier. These hellish things, they were let loose in the town square and by the time they were finished, there were thirty-eight butchered corpses. It was worse than what they usually do, line people up and shoot them. This time they… they hunted them down and tore them to pieces, all for the sake of vengeance. When I heard, it was too late to save anyone from my family. The people I grew up with. Everyone was gone. All I could do was pray over what was left of their corpses, and hire men from the next town to dig a long line of graves. It was all I could do, you see?" His skin seemed feverish. The priest clawed through his thinning hair again, a habit by now. "But it wasn't all I could do. I made a visit to the Vatican library. The Prefect is a friend of mine, and he has the keys to the secret archives which almost no one is allowed to see."

He paused again. "Corrado, do you have wine?"

"No more for you, Babbo," said the wiry partisan leader. "I need you almost sober."

Tranelli licked his dry lips. The priest seemed used up, dried out.

"Va` bene, figlio mio."

"You were saying," Giovanni prodded. "About the materials stored in the secret archives."

Father Tranelli hunched over the rough table. "Yes, there are many secrets in the catacombs below the Vatican," he whispered, perhaps afraid the Germans would hear. Perhaps afraid something else would hear. "You see, the archives are located beneath a modern building, but there is an area at the rear of the newer section where walls were breached and the archives now include a long portion of the maze that makes up the fabled Roman catacombs. This area is under lock and key and watched over by armed guards, for the Vatican has acquired many books and other items in its history about which the world would be amazed and surprised to learn."

Like an omen, air raid sirens started their frightening wail. Tranelli closed his mouth. Moments later the rumble of Allied engines reached them just before the rattle of anti-aircraft batteries and the rolling thunder of bomb drops.

Tranelli shrugged. "And so it continues. Where was I? Ah

yes, the silver weapons. When I spoke to my friend, the Prefect of the Archives, and we discussed these cursed wolves and their aversion to silver, he showed me an old book – medieval, at the least – in which a mystic theorized that silver was a symbol of purity from time immemorial. And, as we all know, thirty silver coins were the payment Judas received for his betrayal of Christ.

"But the Prefect went even further than that, my young friend. You see, he told me that another book on his secret shelves contained the description of a pair of weapons fashioned from relics of the crucifixion. Someone was charged with smelting the thirty coins and using the silver to plate two daggers fashioned from a metal spear-point. It was no simple spear, however, but the spear of Longinus, the centurion who inflicted the fatal wound on Christ while he languished on the cross. Normally death comes to the crucified by asphyxiation. The Roman soldier later realized his spear had been blessed by its contact with the holy flesh and repented, even though his act had been merciful."

The priest paused here, wiped his dry mouth, and clearly wished for wine. "I don't know exactly how it came about, but the silver-plated blades were specially intended to kill were-wolves, which up to that point had been invulnerable to any weapon. Since then, it is said, all silver is abhorrent to wolves. The silver-plated weapons were matched with wood from either the Longinus spear, or from the true cross – or from both, the book was imprecise, as old tomes often are – which was fashioned into scabbards for the daggers."

"What's the value of that?" Giovanni asked, interested despite his meager belief. In the distance, Allied planes pounded the harbor. He hoped this time, at least, they had found their target. Giovanni also hoped the German warships anchored there were taking a beating.

The priest explained: "One thing, the sanctified wood seems to veil the silver's presence, so a werewolf cannot quickly sense the imminent danger of a formidable opponent, making it easier to take one by surprise. The mystic I spoke of further theorized that the holy weapon might be used by one man afflicted with the werewolf disease to fight and vanquish another, because he would be able to keep the blade close to his body without himself suffering the excruciating burns the silver would have caused him otherwise. The mystic called the dagger *the werewolf's werewolf killer.*"

"Well, all this knowledge is fine and good, and your friend was certainly helpful, but what good has it done here?"

"After showing me the book, the Prefect went to a locked cabinet in this most secret of places and from it he removed a wooden case which held both daggers. He gave them to me, my friend, and I have brought them to Corrado."

"My God."

"Yes, perhaps it is God giving us an advantage. Perhaps it is something older than God. I am certain I do not know."

"What does your friend think is the origin of these monsters?"

"My friend recounted the famous legend of Romulus and Remus, the babes who founded Rome – but more importantly, who were abandoned and later suckled by a she-wolf. Every schoolchild has heard this one, but there is an older, lesser-known legend in which the two male babes were not rescued, but were the offspring of the she-wolf, the result of copulation with a human. In this version, the babes Romulus and Remus were the first shapeshifters, and they passed on the gene to their own offspring. Perhaps the full moon's influence on the night of conception has something to do with it. No one knows. But nothing could kill the cursed wolf-men until the Christ's death led to the fashioning of the daggers."

Giovanni digested the priest's words.

"Now I want wine, Corrado, damn you."

Outside, the all-clear sounded and the city came crawling out of its holes.

4

Giovanni blinked as they led him out of the air raid shelter they called Sanctuary.

It was dark, but even so it was brighter than the candle-lit cavern below.

After the all-clear, Corrado had assigned two men to accompany Giovanni to his apartment, where he hoped to find Franco.

Giovanni followed the tall, strangely nicknamed werewolf-killer Turco (who didn't appear in the least Turkish) and a taciturn hulking giant of a man named Manfredo. They had given him a newer German P38 pistol he had again tucked into his belt, a commando-style knife, and in his hands he carried another Beretta submachine gun.

Just like that, it seemed, Giovanni had become a partisan.

Porca fortuna!

He was content to know Maria was as safe as she could be in the shelter, which was extensive and well-stocked, but his son's safety was on his mind. And, if he were honest with himself, his own safety was as well – now, if he were stopped by the Germans, he would be summarily executed.

They crept through the ruined street, hoping that when they reached Giovanni's there would be buildings left standing. No bombing could be completely accurate, but the amount of civilian devastation ringing the port was incredible. Parts of buildings spilled out debris and belongings, some still smoldering from this last Allied bombing run, which had mostly missed the harbor after all.

Here and there Giovanni saw a bloody arm or leg protruding from piles of brick and cement rubble. Confused survivors stumbled over the broken remainders of their lives, searching for loved ones, or memories to salvage.

Dazed, Giovanni followed Turco and Manfredo as they led him in redundant zig-zags down the street.

Turco held up a hand and they stopped, crouching low behind the remains of a brick wall. The thin, bearded academic didn't look like a seasoned partisan, but Corrado had called him one of the best.

Giovanni couldn't see what had caused Turco to stop them so suddenly.

Then a match flared only a couple meters away on the other side of the broken wall, and Giovanni made out a reflection on a German coal-shuttle helmet and the glint of a long bayonet fitted to the muzzle of a Mauser rifle.

Posted to catch us, Giovanni thought, his throat seizing and his heart racing.

Turco pressed his index finger on his lips, then waved Manfredo closer. His hand told Giovanni to wait there, under cover.

The two partisans crawled silently along their side of the wall until they reached a demolished corner. Shattered bricks lay all about. Giovanni could barely see, but these men had lived as outlaws for so long he assumed they'd developed night vision. They were now positioned immediately behind the unsuspecting sentry, as far as he could tell.

Suddenly there was a rattle of equipment, clothes, and debris as Turco went in high and dragged the German backward, his hand clasped tightly over the unfortunate's face to keep him from shouting.

Manfredo lunged in from the side with the silver-bladed knife, ruthlessly plunging its length into the German's side a half-dozen times. While Turco pulled the dying soldier back over the wall, Manfredo finished the job by slitting his throat with one savage motion.

They laid the bleeding, dying soldier on a bed of shattered bricks and raided his pockets and belt pouches for ammunition and food. A few moments later, a spasm took him and he sighed his last. Manfredo spat on him.

Turco nodded at Giovanni and they were on their way.

Giovanni gritted his teeth.

The whole encounter had taken less than a minute.

They continued, carefully avoiding the flickering light of fires that marked where gas lines had erupted, and any movement by crossing from shadow to shadow, occasionally hearing screams of pain and fear from people trapped in the ruins of their buildings. Giovanni's heart cried, but Turco motioned them on, indicating they had to ignore the victims or they would themselves be sacrificed.

"We stop, we die," he whispered.

Soon they left the devastated section behind with only a glow from the fires to mark what they had seen. As they approached Giovanni's neighborhood, he was grateful to see that his building still stood – a seven-storey stucco-sided tenement with solid marble floors and heavy clay tile roof. It looked unharmed and his heart swelled at the thought of finding Franco at home.

"Watch out!" Turco cried, and lunged past.

Giovanni saw the glint of silver.

And heard snarling behind him.

5

By the time Giovanni managed to whirl around, the wolf was on him.

But Turco had also lunged at the attacking beast and intercepted the muscular body in mid-air. They both crashed into Giovanni and the three went down in a tangle of arms, claws, and fangs.

Giovanni dropped the Beretta and tried to wrestle the wolf with his bare hands, while Turco attempted to bring his magical blade to bear and still avoid the slashing teeth and claws. The wolf was damnably quick, out-maneuvering both men and making the three a blur that the giant Manfredo could do nothing about.

Giovanni kept the jaws away from his throat by pushing the red-eyed head away. Turco struggled with the sheathed dagger. If the Jesuit had been right, then the wood scabbard was shielding the wolf from the silver blade. Giovanni tried to shift the balance of the three squirming bodies to give Turco a chance to draw the blade.

But the wolf seemed to predict each attempt. Giovanni could either avoid the snapping jaws or help Turco. And the wolf knew it. He could read the monster's intelligence in its demon eyes, which were neither animal nor human.

Turco grunted when the wolf clawed his face, but his grunt turned to a tortured scream – his cheek had been torn open and his jaw dislocated. Still barely managing to deflect the beast's fangs, Giovanni realized with horror that the monster's swipe had ripped Turco's left eye from its socket and it hung from its optic nerve leaving behind a black hole in which he swore he could glimpse hell itself.

"Shoot him!" he shouted at Manfredo, who was frozen in place with his pistol extended, trying to draw a bead on the monster without striking either human. "Damn you, shoot him!"

Turco opened his mouth and screamed incoherently as the wolf suddenly gained the advantage and its snapping jaws tore the partisan's clothing to shreds and dug savagely into his belly.

Giovanni felt the gush of hot blood and intestines wash over his chest and pried himself out from under the dying partisan and the savage monster. As he rolled out from under the two, it was clear Turco was dead.

"Bastard, shoot him now!"

Manfredo snapped out of his trance and placed the pistol mere centimeters from the back of the wolf's head. The crash of the gunshot deafened Giovanni. Manfredo fired again and again, hot brass splattering from the breech. The slugs tore through the wolf's skull and exploded through Turco's head.

The wolf snarled and turned its blood-spattered muzzle toward Manfredo. It lunged and clamped its jaws on his gun-hand. Manfredo screamed as the wolf shook its head and tossed the severed hand and the pistol into the darkness.

Manfredo scrambled away, trying uselessly to stem the bleeding from the jagged stump. But before he could get clear, the wolf leaped off Turco's body and its jaws closed on the giant's unprotected groin. The demonic monster began shaking the shrieking partisan violently, blood gushing into its mouth and scattering like scarlet raindrops.

Operating now on instinct tinged with fear and rage, Giovanni scooped the dagger from the ground near Turco's body and slid it out of its wooden sheath.

In the darkness, the blade seemed to glow with a moonlit sheen.

He drew the wolf's attention from Manfredo, but before pulling away, the beast ripped into the wounded giant's groin once more. Giovanni knew enough anatomy to figure the jetting blood meant an artery has been torn.

Manfredo would bleed out if Giovanni didn't kill the wolf.

6

The monstrous wolf's eyes burned with supernatural intelligence.

What did Giovanni have?

A damned dagger from the Vatican and a drunken Jesuit's crazy story...

And a mission: he had a son to find.

The wolf advanced, snarling. Its bloody muzzle seemed to smile as Giovanni backed up slowly. Before he could refine his plan the monster was in the air.

Giovanni had feinted left and sold it well enough that the wolf went for him. While the wolf was committed to its attack, Giovanni sidestepped to the right. At the last second, while their bodies were in brushing contact, he brought the silver blade up and jabbed it deep into the monster's side before sawing with heart-clenching fury.

The wolf shrieked in pain; an unholy sound that hurt Giovanni's ears.

The blade furrowed the beast's fur and skin with ease, parting its flesh as if he were made of dough.

The stench of burning flesh and fur rose in a plume of disgusting smoke.

The wolf fell in a heap and flipped, attempting to lick his blackening wound closed, but its side was split and its organs and intestines were spilling out in a bloody jumble. The smoke continued to pour from the widening gash as if its innards had caught fire.

Holy fire?

Could it be true?

Pressing his advantage, Giovanni plunged the blade through the beast's right eye, into its brain. It died as soon as he slid the blade out, collapsing in a heap that now appeared to be burning from the inside out.

Body quivering, the wolf seemed to blur and Giovanni fell back and watched in wonder as it changed from animal to human and back again until it finally took the form of a naked man.

Gasping and wheezing, Giovanni stumbled as he tried to get farther away from the horror.

He checked Manfredo, but the partisan had died in a pool of his own blood. He stood for a moment, crying dry tears for the two heroic partisans who had given their lives to help him find his son, then he did as they had done with others' bodies.

Giovanni found the scabbard he had dropped and bent to retrieve it.

He gasped. Suddenly his right upper chest felt as if it had been split open and he straightened and bent over again so quickly he almost fainted. Slowly, he patted his destroyed blood-drenched clothing and realized that some of the blood had to be his own. He scrabbled through the ruined shirt and hissed in pain as he found the source, a series of deep gashes and a ragged wound.

Gesu' e Maria, he mumbled, *I'm wounded.*

Fangs or claws?

Did it matter?

His skin was bruised and rippled around the wounds, the flesh beneath blackening into a series of plum-colored circles. The bleeding appeared to have stopped – a blackened crust of blood was already hardening around each laceration.

He hastily rearranged the torn clothing to cover the hideous wound, hissing at the excruciating pain he felt as the fabric dragged across his flayed skin.

Gently he bent again, wincing, and retrieved the scabbard. Then he sheathed the dagger.

Did it hum in his grip?

He gathered his wits, found his bearings, and realized he was only a couple buildings away from his own. He retrieved the Beretta submachine gun and slung it painfully over his shoulder. One of his comrades' pistols went into a pocket. The dagger remained in his hand, comforting.

Hunched over in pain, and fearful of being spotted by another German patrol, he hugged the shadows and found his way home.

The building seemed unfamiliar and he had to check the address plate twice to make sure he had indeed reached his own home. His family's airy apartment was one of four located on the fifth floor. The lights in the lobby were out, but there was moonlight filtering through the skylight above him.

He shuffled up the stairs, the preternatural quiet frightening. Soon he was on his own floor. In the near-darkness, he saw that his apartment door was ajar.

Inside, the foyer was dark. His heart beat rapidly and his wound throbbed. He resisted the urge to touch it.

"Franco?" he whispered hoarsely. "Franco, are you here? It's your father."

After checking the small bedroom off the foyer, he advanced down the corridor. Franco's room was empty. The next room was the bedroom Giovanni shared with his wife, but it, too, was empty.

The last two rooms were a long narrow bath – empty – and the kitchen. Standing in the kitchen, he swore he could hear a small heart beating.

"Franco?" he called out in a whisper that threatened to become weeping. His heart throbbed in time with his wound.

A tiny whisper came from a cabinet below the sink.

"Papá?"

"Franco! Dio mio, is it you?" He ignored the pain in his chest and sank to his knees, crawling toward the sink.

A boy's face peeked from behind Maria's frilly curtain, Franco's face. But his eyes had aged since Giovanni had last looked into them. It was still the same day, but a lifetime had passed. Apparently for Franco, too.

"Are you all right, my son?" He didn't let him answer, but instead gathered the boy in his arms and they rocked together, tears flowing for a long time.

"I'm all right," Franco said. "And Mamma?" His voice trembled.

"She's fine, she's fine! We're in a shelter."

"I thought you were dead! Killed by those… *things*." Franco sighed, laying his head on his father's shoulder. "I've seen– Hey, there's a lot of blood! Papá, are you–"

"I'm fine! It's the blood of some brave men who helped me, God rest their souls." He slowly shifted Franco's face so he could see him better. "What about your friend Pietro?"

The boy suddenly started to weep. "We were great, we took them on, we saw them turn to wolves, we saw them kill, and then we ran and ran, but – oh, it was terrible! It caught us by surprise and it took Pietro, then it did terrible things to him. I ran away, Papá. When I could have helped him, I ran away, I ran all the way home and I hid like a baby."

"No, Franco," he soothed, "you couldn't have helped him. If you saw the wolves, you know you couldn't have fought them."

"But you did, didn't you?"

"I had help," he said. "I had lots of help." He touched the dagger in his pocket.

His son's eyes were wide with fear from the memory.

"Let's go," said Giovanni, and they stood. "We can be with your mother in a short while, if we're careful."

He retrieved his submachine gun from the floor, checked to make sure it was cocked, and then took Franco's hand.

As they walked out of the building and into the dangerous night, Giovanni wondered why his wound hadn't bothered him in a while.

After a tense but eventless trek back to the shelter, the family reunion was joyful, though tempered by the loss of two good men who had given their lives to bring it about.

The partisan brigade leader, Corrado, had flown into a rage when informed the mission had cost two of his best, most experienced men, but a sober look at the condition of Giovanni's blood-splattered clothes caused him to pause. Plus, the fact that he had not lost the Vatican dagger redeemed the situation in a small way.

"I have seen the dagger's power," he told Corrado, as he held hands with his son and wife. "And I'd like to be its guardian."

He didn't tell anyone he had been wounded in his life and

death struggle with the wolf. He didn't have to. The wound had disappeared by the time he'd changed into a borrowed shirt and jacket.

He was afraid of what that meant.

7

Giovanni awoke and sat bolt upright. It was dark in their sanctuary, though in some distant corner he could see the flickering glow of burning lamps or candles. And he could hear the disembodied voices of partisans talking quietly.

He felt strange. Dizzy and hot and itchy, like he was lost in a fever dream.

Maybe the past few days *had* been a dream, or more precisely an *incubo*, a nightmare. All of it. That certainly seemed more likely than the existence of savage German wolf-men. But he'd seen the truth of it with his own eyes, hadn't he?

Giovanni wondered what day it was. How long had he slept? He remembered finding Franco hiding in their apartment and bringing him to their new home. They had returned just before dawn, and now – though it was nearly always dark where the partisans hid underground, a tiny bit of daylight trickled down through their many secret routes to the streets – it was clearly after nightfall. Had he slept all day, or even longer? Two days? Three?

Giovanni's skin tingled where the wolf had wounded him. He reached up and touched it. The injury had somehow miraculously healed before he and his son had returned to the Sanctuary. He wondered if he had been mistaken, and what he had at first thought a wound was in fact Turco and Manfredo's blood. Or if he had seen anything at all.

He wiped a sheen of sweat from his forehead with his shirt sleeve. More flowed from his pores.

Behind him, on a mattress tossed on the ground that had become their new bed, Maria and Franco lay sleeping peacefully.

Giovanni rose and swayed unsteadily. His head swam, from nausea or hunger, he couldn't tell. *More like starvation.* And he was so damned hot. Without thinking of anything but relief from the sudden oppressive heat and itchiness of his clothes Giovanni stripped down, leaving every stitch in a pile beside the mattress.

Then he moved quietly, shambling to the nearest exit – a set of uneven stone stairs that led to a hidden exit that opened onto the ruins of the city above. He needed some fresh air.

The stairs felt cool and damp under his bare feet, and the chilly night air felt good on his burning skin. In fact, it felt invigorating. It was the air and something else... the moonlight.

He could see it shining in through the cracks at the top of the stairwell, cool white light. It seemed to be calling to him much as it pulled the ocean tides. It drew him in, tugging at the small hairs on his naked arms and legs. It felt like it was causing his hairs to grow, pulling them as it summoned him to bask beneath its mesmerizing glow. As it did, he thought he saw a forest whipping past his vision as if he were running, running, ducking the shadows of trees in order to playfully catch the silvery moonbeams. These images playing across his mind's eye suddenly seemed frightening, but he couldn't deny them.

When he reached the top step he looked out over the decimated neighborhood's crumbling walls. The piles of debris from the bombed out building looked oddly beautiful bathed in the full moon's light. Nearby, a young partisan sat guarding the hidden stairway entrance. Giovanni recognized him. His name was Vincent. Rags that were once his Sunday clothes served as his uniform. He had a Beretta submachine gun resting on his knee and a hand-rolled cigarette hanging from the corner of his mouth. He looked out at the street's ruined structures, unaware of Giovanni approaching him from behind.

Giovanni opened his mouth to whisper a greeting, but what emanated from his throat startled him and young Vincent both.

Instead of whispering or even speaking, Giovanni *growled*.

The young guard whirled, abject horror engulfing his features. The cigarette dropped from his mouth as he leveled his submachine gun at a confused Giovanni.

Suddenly having no control of his own actions, Giovanni leaped forward – *an incredibly far, impossible distance* – and pounced on the terrified guard. And to his panic and amazement what he thought were his hands had somehow become a massive set of *lupine paws*.

Horrified at what he was doing, he sank his teeth – *but they were fangs, weren't they?* – into poor Vincent's neck and tore away a huge chuck of warm flesh. He swallowed and went back for more.

Vincent fell backwards. All that was left of his throat was the vertebrae of his neck surrounded by a few thin strips of grisly meat. His life jetted from the ruined artery in a fountain-like gush.

The beast that Giovanni had become stood in the growing pool of hot blood, which he lapped up greedily.

He fought to control himself, to stop the horror of what he tasted, but despite every bit of his will he couldn't even bring himself to step back from the slaughter. It was as if he were a passive observer – watching through a window, or a mirror, as a monster fed on the still-jerking remains of a human being – but it was obvious *he* was the monster, even though he wasn't controlling the muscles or the claws, or the jaws.

Something else had taken control.

The Devil.

It had to be the Devil, taking him for the evil he had done.

And as punishment, he couldn't even look away or close his eyes to the horror before him. He had to live through every moment of it, watching through the window that was a mirror to his actions.

Showing its incredible intelligence, the beast Giovanni had become dragged the partisan's warm corpse away from his sentry position and – once hidden in the shelter of a crumbling building – tore into Vincent's belly and feasted on the soft, bloody innards. Within the body of the wolf-monster, what was left of Giovanni-the-human prayed to wake from this terrible nightmare as he tasted the flesh, chewing and swallowing like a machine. The fresh meat invigorated his body even as his mind screamed in revulsion and disgust.

But the beast wasn't sated.

No, there was a deep-belly hunger the likes of which Giovanni had never experienced, and he knew the monster in front of his eyes wasn't finished, not yet.

After finishing the choicest parts of the sentry (his name had been Vincent, and hadn't he offered Giovanni's family his mattress?), the beast he'd become began to prowl, looking for more food.

The creature moved effortlessly and without a sound through the rubble, the new and expanded palette of scents and sounds suddenly exploding in Giovanni's brain. Even though he couldn't make sense of the jumble of olfactory and auditory sensations, the beast took it all in and used it to hunt new prey while avoiding potential adversaries.

Ahead there was movement and the beast closed in as stealthy as a shadow in the dark.

Within the skull of the wolf-monster, Giovanni screamed when the creature spotted its newest quarry – a woman escorting two young children through the ghost of the city.

Straining with everything he had, Giovanni fought to stop the beast, or at least distract it. But it was futile. He knew now he was inside the monster – part of him at least was completely aware of it – but it didn't seem as though he could influence its behavior.

The beast trailed behind the woman and her children, stalking them through the desolate, detritus-strewn streets.

Was it toying with them?

The woman glanced over her shoulder repeatedly while herding her babies, seeming to intuitively sense the presence of danger. And through the creature's senses, Giovanni smelled the woman's fear, her nervous sweat, and heard the heart pounding in her chest, her quickened breaths.

And despite his horror, Giovanni felt *excited*.

Sexually excited.

When the woman spotted the monster, her eyes grew wide with fear. She turned on her heel and pushed her young ones ahead of her. "Correte!" she said with a hiss. *Run!*

But the wolf was in no hurry. The prey couldn't outrun it. He loped behind them, gathering speed, easily avoiding the scattered bricks and broken glass that littered the street, which the humans had no choice but to navigate carefully.

They were too frightened by now.

The woman stumbled over a mound of broken bricks and Giovanni could only look on in horror through the wolf's eyes as it decided to end the game.

"Presto! Correte piu' presto!" the woman yelled. *Faster, run faster!* She shoved her children even as the wolf pounced on her back, knocking her violently to the ground.

What was left of Giovanni cried out in torment as the wolf's jaws – *his jaws* – sank into the back of the woman's neck, snapping the bone as if it were a pencil.

The younger of the two boys stopped and turned back, his eyes and mouth gaping as he watched his mother's terrifying fate. The child's older brother grabbed his hand and jerked him away. *"Vieni! Corri!"*

The monster didn't care. They would be easy enough to track. He gave a powerful twist of his neck and tore the woman's head from her shoulders, enjoying the crimson gout that poured out of her and puddled on the paving stones. He licked at it, enjoying the freshness and the unknown element that made the blood of a frightened human so much tastier.

He then rose to pursue the two smaller male humans.

He could smell them – the sweat oozing from their pores, the urine staining their undergarments... *and their sweet, salty blood.*

He could hear them, too, softly weeping in heightened fear and grief.

He found them a few ruined buildings away from their mother's cooling, headless corpse. They were huddled together in the space between two collapsed walls. The smaller of the two clutched some kind of plush figurine that smelled of sawdust.

As the wolf approached them, growling, strings of drool escaping from its jaws, Giovanni's conscious mind could no longer accept the bottomless well of suffering he was causing. Mercifully, he blacked out, and the wolf went on without him.

8

At dawn, he awoke shivering from a nightmare, bathed in cold sweat. Faint echoes of the dream lingered like the previous night's moonlight, and he shrank at the images of blood and fury. God knew he had experienced enough of both recently. Where was he? Why was he shivering?

He was curled in a tight ball, trying to keep skin on skin so he could stay warmer. Had Maria opened the window again? She tended to feel too hot, whereas he craved warmth in the night.

He shivered more intensely now. His head ached, throbbing with a hammer-like cadence that threatened to overwhelm him. Slowly he became aware of the cold wetness covering every part of his skin. The tiny, hard points prickling his side puzzled him. The scratchy wool blankets piled on his side of the bed didn't usually feel like pine needles.

Pine needles?

Suddenly his throat screamed for water, as if he had swallowed a bucketful of desert sand.

He remembered then that the shelter they had been forced to inhabit was below ground. He wasn't in his own comfortable bedroom, where the creamy stucco walls bore only a crucifix and a portrait of Mary. He almost smiled at the memory, but his head hurt too much. And he remembered the shelter was windowless.

He opened his eyes and leaped up, shocked to see that he had slept on a gently sloping hillside – in a clearing, trees cluttering his view all around. Over him the drooping branches of a weeping willow seemed to cascade like tears. The long, narrow leaves dotted his naked arms and chest. Where was his nightshirt? Giovanni always wore a thick layer of clothing to bed, but now he was naked and the leaves tickled his skin.

He hugged himself, trembling uncontrollably. Cold, wet dew numbed his toes. His penis had shrunk and sought shelter between his thighs, and small twigs made sticky knots in his pubic hair.

"Ma che cosa—?" *What was going on?*

He tore his right hand from under his left armpit, where he felt a semblance of warmth, and cupped his genitals to preserve some body heat.

It was dawn, the sky dappled with patches of light. A cool wind swept across the overgrown grass of the clearing. The slope meant he was back in the hills, but where? How far? And how had he gotten here? And why had he shed all his clothing? His feet squished in the wet grass as he started in one direction, stopped, then tried another.

It all looked the same. Every side of the clearing faced him with a thick stand of trees. Under the canopy of their leaves it was still dark. He didn't know what had happened to him.

And yet...

He stooped to swipe off some leaves and twigs and recoiled to see that his feet weren't only wet with dew – there were splashes of dark red. Was it...?

Giovanni's breath caught in his throat.

Blood?

He checked his calves, thighs, and ankles thoroughly, but no, he saw or felt no new wounds.

He scraped at the blood stains. Dry, mostly dry. He looked at his fingers. Flecks of dark matter was crusted under his nails.

"Gesu' e Santa Maria," he said softly and crossed himself, forgetting his nakedness for a moment.

He sniffed his fingertips.

It *was* blood. He had smelled enough of it.

He sidled toward the clearing's edge. The approaching sunrise might well cause him to be seen by people who awakened for field work or farm chores, or to attend mass or one of the meager markets. He had to find his way home.

Home?

Not home, but the partisans' secret shelter that had become his home.

With a deep breath he abandoned any modesty that might have crippled him and sprinted through the dew toward the thinnest face of the forest.

Giovanni was still shivering, now with fear as well as cold. The blood, the naked romp outside, and the lack of memory. There was no accounting for this, none at all.

Unless…

Giovanni looked at his arm, which itched unbearably as if he had a rash or had dragged it through a patch of poison ivy. Below his right shoulder, where that monstrous creature he had fought had torn and ripped the skin with grotesque fangs or claws was throbbing painfully and itching madly.

Both arms tingled, and he thought he felt the tingle reach his shoulder and spread across his back. He scratched at the edges of where the wound had been, but it wasn't enough to slake his need. In fact, the itch seemed to be spreading to the other arm now. He would have given anything for some immediate relief.

He licked at the tingling arm absent-mindedly, his nakedness momentarily forgotten.

Then Giovanni stopped in mid-lap. What the hell was he doing, lapping at his arm like a dog?

Porca Madonna!

He shook his head and scraped the area around his mouth with one hand. Dried bits of red flesh flaked off his skin, leaving bloody smears on his palm. Some of the bits were sharp, bone-like. He sniffed at the debris. Smelled like… like slaughtered meat. He'd seen enough farm slaughters in his youth. The smell overtook his senses and the sudden urge to vomit rose. When he forced himself to swallow and breathe deeply, the taste of raw meat and bone and rancid blood came alive inside his mouth.

His throat gurgled and hitched and a stream of bloody vomit spewed onto the ground, splashing his feet before he could side-step.

It looks like pieces of my lungs, Giovanni thought as he wiped his mouth. The bloody taste still on his tongue.

What is wrong with me? A strangled sob escaped from his lips.

He gagged again, but this time it overwhelmed him and more pieces of bloody flesh and bone came gurgling up his throat and through his lips in a disgusting stream.

After the spasm passed, he opened his eyes and beheld the grotesque contents of his stomach, now splattered onto the grass. He turned away, dizzy, trying to keep his gorge from rising again.

The shivers he felt had nothing to do with the chill in the air, and the madness was just beginning.

Because not far from the clearing away from which he stumbled, Giovanni found a child's shoe, tattered and bloodstained. And memories of the previous night, horrible memories that he had buried to protect his sanity, flooded back in one irreversible rush.

He screamed, and he was certain he would never stop screaming.

He was able to loot someone's abandoned clothes from the debris of a ruined building. Then he stumbled back to the shelter.

9

In the coming days, Corrado's men met German patrols made up of humans less frequently, while their encounters with the supernatural members of the Werwolf Division increased. The Werwolf members had been left as a rear-guard, and while Hitler's regular ground forces retreated through Northern Italy and met up with those retreating from Normandy, the monstrous soldiers took over the last-ditch duty of harassing the partisans who paved the way for the Allied forces that advanced from the south.

And during those days, Giovanni Lupo became Corrado's best werewolf fighter. In his hand, the Vatican blade became a scythe that mowed down every wolf who dared attack him.

Father Tranelli noted that Giovanni seemed to have become feverish and reckless in his encounters with the monsters. "He is on a mission," the old priest said to Corrado. "A holy mission, perhaps. But he may not see the end of this accursed war if he doesn't watch himself. What of his wife and son?"

Franco grieved for his friend Pietro, but worry about his father seeped into his grief. And Maria Lupo wondered at her husband's newfound obsession with killing werewolves. Although the few wives who remained with their men told her how heroic her Giovanni was, she wondered what had made him so dedicated to killing at the constant risk of his own life.

For his part, Giovanni grew silent and, despite his great love for his family, distant to the point of being morose.

Corrado often looked at him with some vague suspicion on the tip of his tongue.

The fighting intensified, and Giovanni found himself celebrated as the unit's best and most skillful wolf-killer.

It was cold at night, so no one questioned why he wore gloves on patrol. Only one person noticed that he wore them in daytime, too.

Franco.

10

Corrado's partisan brigade was pinned down by rifle fire from a crow's nest of granite boulders above the sloping mountain path.

They'd been climbing, their guard lowered because the territory had been recently cleared of Germans. But the first rifle rounds brought down two good men and Corrado shouted at the rest of his column to seek cover as best they could. One side of the path dropped off, forming a deadly steep cliff. The other side afforded little cover.

While the partisans were kept down by the accurate gunfire, a pair of Nazi werewolves pounced on those in the rear.

The snarling of werewolves and the screams of men being slaughtered behind them were punctuated by rifle fire that kept the rest of the partisans pinned and helpless.

Giovanni started snaking back down the path, retrieving one of the daggers from under his coat. The other dagger was with a second patrol.

"Get down!" Corrado hissed. "You can't take them on yourself!"

Giovanni ignored him. The brigade had run out of silver bullets days before, so the wolves would be able to work their way back up the path and butcher each partisan one by one, unless someone counterattacked. And the holy weapon was the only way to win a clash with the shapeshifters.

He scrambled down the rocky incline, past the huddled partisans, avoiding their eyes. In a minute he had reached the slight turn in the path they had recently traversed. The snarling continued, but the screaming was silenced – the men were surely dead.

The first of two werewolves materialized as if magically on the path just below him, its eyes widening with glee and gluttony at the sight of prey, but he was ready, the dagger held close to his body until he could smell the beast's breath.

When the wolf's muscular legs propelled it into an uphill lunge for his throat, Giovanni judged the timing perfectly, unsheathing the dagger just as the animal reached him, side-stepping it and throwing it off-balance long enough to drive the dagger's point through its neck.

The wolf's scream of tortured pain effectively hid Giovanni's. His hand smoked where the silver scorched his skin and flesh, turning it black. The pain was excruciating, but he still managed to stab the wolf once in the heart as it collapsed at his feet, its wounds flaming and its blood boiling in the veins.

Giovanni whirled to face the second wolf, but this time he'd misjudged the angle of attack and the red-eyed demon knocked him painfully to his knees. He tried to bring the dagger around, but it was still buried in the dead wolf, which was flickering like a candle back and forth from monster to human.

By the time he ripped the dagger out of the corpse, the second frenzied wolf snatched his hand with its jaws and he dropped the dagger with a scream of pain and frustration.

Holding his burned and wounded hand, Giovanni backed up against the rocky slope, knowing the nearest partisans watched helplessly a few meters away, their guns useless and their heads still pinned down by the sniper fire from above. The wolf's jaws trailed bloody drool as it approached, its eyes staring intensely at this new enemy. Its scrabbling paws avoided the toxic dagger, but its body prevented Giovanni from retrieving it.

Before he knew what he was doing, Giovanni felt the rage take him.

He had secretly learned a little about his new condition in recent days, but he barely understood how the beast inside his bloodstream could take over.

He tried desperately to reverse the feeling, but he felt the changes inside his body and the terrible itch of his fur suddenly sprouting along his arms and back, and then—

—then he was *Over-over-Over*, lost inside the instincts and defensive rage of the Beast he barely understood.

The last his human ears heard was the shouting of his partisan companions, horrified by what they saw: one of their own now taking the form of the wolf – the dreaded enemy.

His ruined clothes dropped beneath him as his wolf's body took the enemy wolf by surprise.

Jaws snapping at each other, the two werewolves closed and fought, biting and retreating, their claws slashing.

Growling, shrieking, they attacked and feinted, bit and retreated, rolling over and over, the advantage constantly switching.

Lead bullets struck them both, but did no damage. Their fangs drew blood from wounds that hurt excruciatingly, but which began healing and closing up almost immediately.

Suddenly the beast that had been Giovanni was backed up against the hillside, his paws losing their purchase on the rocky path, and the other wolf seemed about to go in for the kill.

But instead the German regained his human form and, while Giovanni tried to make sense of it, reached down and snatched up the dagger and its scabbard. Naked, he sheathed the dagger and inserted it into his mouth, then – before Giovanni could act – returned to his wolf form and bounded away down the hill and around the curve.

The wolf that had been Giovanni regained its footing and scrambled down the hill, human screams following him until he was gone.

The other wolf had too much an advantage, and even though Giovanni had the other's scent in his nostrils, he couldn't see and was forced to run blindly. In his brain, where Giovanni and a terrible monster both jostled for control, all he could think was that he had lost one of the special daggers.

And that he could never go home, for now he was unmasked as one of the enemy. A monster.

I am banished.

11

They'd long since told him his father had died, but he knew they still whispered about him and his mother when they thought he was asleep.

His father was a *hero*. He was a *monster*.

He could never return.

Franco understood then that his father was still alive, but that he was *dead to them*. Because he had become a monster. He had become one of *them*.

There was no consolation in anyone's eyes, and Franco felt the hate that begun to bloom against his mother and himself. As if they had helped his father fool the partisan brigade! As if Giovanni Lupo had intentionally put one over on them.

"We should have never allowed someone named *Lupo* to join us!" one shouted in a drunken rage. "Never again!"

There was muttered agreement.

Then they turned and stared at his mother. And at Franco.

Their days with the partisan brigade were numbered.

And early one morning, after the new year had come, he and his mother took their few belongings and stepped into the hidden staircase exit, the staring eyes of Corrado and the Jesuit Tranelli and the few remaining men and women of the brigade boring into their backs, refusing to stop them or send them off with a wish of luck or farewell.

And they had headed for his uncle's farm in the hills, neither of them knowing whether the older man still lived. Their trek took two weeks of arduous climbing along narrow paths, always on the lookout for desperate German soldiers left behind to die.

At the end of 1944, the partisan resistance had risen up against the weakened German occupiers and formed provisional governments which sought and received foreign recognition as sovereign states, but the Germans and the remainder of the Italian forces still loyal to Mussolini were successful in quelling the rebellion and executing its leaders.

Now, all the disparate partisan units could do was await the Allies, whose painstaking advance had been mired by the vicious rear-guard action of suicide patrols who would fight to the last man, and elements of the Nazis' Werwolf Division.

They didn't know it wasn't merely a code name.

When the Allies finally arrived, their field guns audible in the distance, the withdrawal of the few surviving Wehrmacht and ragged Werwolf units left an almost tangible vacuum.

Franco and his mother had been safe on the desolate farm, but the boy could not forget what they'd said happened to his father. The nightmares kept him awake, and his mother worried for his health and sanity. In his sleep, he saw the wolves come for him and his family, but instead of being a German werewolf who battered in their door it was his father, jaws slavering and red eyes glaring with hate. *And hunger.*

One morning, when Maria went to wake the boy, he was gone.

Franco had grown rapidly, and in a few weeks he already appeared years older than his actual age. What he had witnessed, suffered, and lived through had toughened him, but those things had also changed him in ways he could only suspect. Frequently he found himself awash in a rage, yet unable to understand or explain why. Until one day, when he realized that he needed to face his father – the partisan who had become a monster and shattered their small family.

But where could he find Giovanni Lupo? Where would his father have sought refuge?

Instinct and keen insight into his father's mind brought him back to their old neighborhood. Franco sensed his father would have hidden in their old apartment if he could, perhaps to await their return. Not knowing what he would find, the boy – now just barely a teenager – made his way along the street on which he had grown up. Several buildings had been demolished since the last night he had spent here, and others had been damaged, some walls sheared away to expose their insides like grotesque layer cakes. Mountains of rubble lay at the bases of their surviving structures.

Franco looked at all the places he had played during more innocent times. Everything that had happened since then was a nightmare from which he could not wake.

He pushed open the door of their old apartment and was overwhelmed by the stench of rotted meat and dried blood. Franco stood in the doorway, breathing through his mouth to avoid being sick.

"Papá?" His voice was soft and tentative and echoed in the high-ceilinged space. "Sono io, Franco."

He heard a shuffling from the kitchen, and stepped into the long corridor that led there. He was reminded of that night, when his father had found *him* hiding here. A strange reversal. He pushed the memory aside.

"Papá, I've come to bring you back home with me. Our new home."

He held his nostrils. He remembered this same smell in butcher shops down the street. He entered the kitchen. The lights didn't work, but there was enough light from the balcony door to see the form in the shadows at the far end of the massive room.

It was his father, his clothes ragged and his hair growing wild.

"Papá!" he said, startled by his father's appearance.

"Hello, my son," Giovanni said and then his voice broke and he was sobbing. "I knew you would come back to me. I felt it. And your mother...?"

"She's safe on Uncle Vittorio's farm, but she sends her love."

"Dio mio, what a terrible time it has been."

"Yes, Papá, it has been."

Giovanni stepped farther out of the shadows. Franco gasped when he saw the bloody smears around his father's mouth, crusted in the stubble. Giovanni blinked rapidly, as if this was too much light for him.

"I've been hiding here for weeks, hoping you would return. I– I've changed, Franco, I'm not the way I was. I get these urges; I become hungry as you've never known hunger. I become another person altogether, a creature. I try to control this *hunger*, this cursed hunger, but the moon brings it out in me. Sometimes I think I can control it, but then I cannot, and I do terrible things." He put his head down and wept.

"Papá," Franco whispered. "It's all right."

"I prayed, you know. I prayed that it would go away and leave me alone. I prayed that I could go back to that day when you were playing with your friend and I was trying to earn some money for food, and if we had both just... just come home. If we hadn't... But it's the past now and we can't change it, can we?"

"No, Papá." Tears squeezed from Franco's eyes.

Giovanni came closer to his son. He reached out and touched Franco's face.

"Don't cry," he said. "Things will be better now."

"Yes," Franco whispered.

"I hear the Germans are finally on their way out of the city. The Allies are only a few days' march away. The war is almost over for us." He spread his arms. "We can be together again, a family. We'll go and fetch your mother."

Franco stepped into his father's embrace. It felt good for a few moments, like it always had. He laid his head on his father's chest. Felt his father's heartbeat.

Giovanni kissed his son's cheek and caressed his face with rough hands.

"My son–" Giovanni's body stiffened and he began to pull away. "What...? Franco, I feel... *Franco?*" His voice rose as the fear took him. "My son, what have you done?"

The heat must have become suddenly obvious. Franco held his father close, his strength surprising the older man, while his hand had reached behind his back where he'd tucked the dagger stolen from the priest. As soon as the blade was free of the wooden scabbard, Giovanni had sensed the heat of the silver dagger.

Franco brought it around quickly, before his father could free himself of the embrace and flee.

But Giovanni didn't attempt to flee.

Franco buried the dagger in his father's chest, hitting the heart on the first try.

Giovanni screamed and the wound caught fire, as did his clothing around it, and the boy plunged the blade in and out several times, the reek of scorched flesh and blood enveloping them as they embraced one last time.

The creature within Giovanni began to manifest, the hair lengthening and his face beginning to change, his mouth becoming a snout, and Franco thought his father would take him along to hell. He twisted the knife cruelly within each new wound, each twist and each stab piercing vital organs and liquefying them in a flash of silvery heat.

Franco watched as his father's form flickered from human to wolf and back again, his eyes bulging and finally exploding in a shower of blood and gore, and his hands – which were now claws and could still have raked Franco's face and head – spreading in helpless surrender.

The boy stepped back and his father collapsed in a burning, smoking heap onto the marble floor.

"My son," he cried in a sickly whisper through charred lips. "Grazie…" *Thank you.*

And then Giovanni Lupo's body once again resembled that of a human, no breath left in him.

Franco left him in the ruins of their old home. He walked out with a new need in the pit of his stomach, his hand gripping the dagger with a renewed sense of purpose.

He had wolves to hunt.

JESTER

Jennifer R. Povey

It was a pretty ordinary sortie right up until Caveman bought it. Things went downhill from there, and the diminished squadron fled back towards the White Cliffs at full speed, pursued by a couple of Germans. Half-heartedly, because the Germans had no wish to tangle with British air defences during daylight hours.

Jester's engine stuttered, its sound rough as it began to fail. It struggled back into life then faded out. He tugged the ejection handle, the canopy breaking away in a rush of wind, the chute threatening to pull his shoulders from their sockets as it tore him free. He knew he was going to come down closer to France than England, and hoping to come down very close - better to risk capture by the Germans than to drown. Prisoners of war could escape. Yes, that was his thought as he fluttered down into the shallow water. He cut the parachute free, leaving it to float in the still ocean, and scrambled ashore, making sure his sidearm was in his pocket.

His best chance was to find somebody connected to the resistance, some fisherman who could maybe smuggle him across the Channel. It had happened to others. A long shot. Especially once he looked around.

Jester had got lucky in terms of almost hitting on land, but not lucky in terms of the bit of land. No general would choose this place to land troops for the rumoured invasion. The beach was a thin strip of beautiful golden sand... but that was all before the vertical cliffs started. Or nearly vertical. After a moment, his eyes found a narrow trail leading upwards. He wasn't sure if it was man-made. Looked more likely to have been created by sheep. Or maybe mountain goats. Staying on the beach, though...

151

well, perhaps somebody would sail past. He contemplated the matter at some length; the tide was close to high, so the beach wasn't going anywhere. At the same time, there wasn't any food.

More critically, there was no fresh water. He checked himself for injuries, found nothing but bruises, and headed towards that horribly narrow upward trail where golden wild flowers dotted the slope above.

He could almost imagine there wasn't a war on. Almost. He heard a buzzing overhead that was probably... yes... those German fighters returning to base. He tracked them, knowing they might see him and report his position. Or not. Either way, he probably didn't want to be in this position much longer. With a sigh, he hiked the rest of the way to the top of the cliffs.

At the top, no fence blocked his way, but he saw a field full of cows to one side and a German pill box to the other. He didn't voice the swear word, but ducked and ran for the cows, hoping to use them as cover if whoever was on watch spotted him. He was almost certainly going to be caught, but why make it easy for them?

He refused to sit out the war in a POW camp with a bunch of idiots who couldn't come up with a good way to escape, and frankly, Jester's luck lately pointed to that being right where he would end up: in the worst camp with the worst fellow inmates.

Shaking his head, he darted towards a copse of trees, but no gunfire came from the pill box. Perhaps they didn't want to hit the cows. Perhaps the occupiers had some understanding, here, with the occupied.

That understanding scared him. Rumours of what might or might not be happening somewhere in Germany or eastern Europe scared him. He wouldn't be telling any jokes until he was back at base, back where he belonged. If that happened, this would be a bad dream, but he wasn't able to wake up just yet.

On the far side of the woods sat a farmhouse. Jester crouched at the treeline, watching. Soon, a little girl in a floral dress came wandering out. She looked healthier than the British kids... at least the city kids. A farm. No rationing to thin her lines. He'd rather have the rationing than the Nazis, though. Had they already measured her Aryanness?

The girl suddenly yelped then ran back into the house. Once more, he didn't voice the swear word. She had certainly seen him. He didn't want to run, though.

The scent of fish stew drifted into his nostrils, causing his stomach to rumble. He never ate much before sorties. Hunger held him in place longer than good sense should have.

He wanted that stew so badly it was all he could do to keep actual control over himself. Did he want it badly enough to risk being captured? As he had that thought, a burly farmer emerged from the door.

"I know you're out there," the man called in French, a language Jester struggled with fluency. "Come and get some stew."

He hesitated then sighed. Living off the land, oh, he could, but sooner or later he would be caught, and sooner or later worse might happen. Slowly, he stood, hands where the farmer could see them, and walked towards the farmhouse.

"Quickly!" the farmer urged.

He sped up, and ducked into the building.

"Got shot down, did you?" the farmer added, sympathetically, once Jester was inside.

Jester nodded. "Yeah. Look, don't want to get you in trouble with the Huns. Or anyone else."

"Eh. Wouldn't mind trouble with the Huns, if it wasn't for Francine."

That had to be the little girl. "For her sake, don't court it."

"They'll never know you were here. Have some stew."

Hesitating, looking around, he followed the man into the kitchen, hunger overcoming fear for now. There was no sign of a wife. Perhaps she was dead. Perhaps she had left him. Neither option being pleasant, Jester didn't ask, but he did think of a certain young woman. And this was why they couldn't be together right now. He didn't want to have her worry about him getting shot down, killed, caught. He didn't want to be caught, but he knew his luck.

"I'll take the stew," he finally said, his stomach growling.

The man nodded, filling three bowls. Francine came bouncing in to claim hers, youthful energy radiating from her. "Truth is, I don't like the Germans much either, and if I could get Francine out of here…"

The girl, no doubt a pitcher with big ears, just watched them then started to eat. Jester tucked in himself.

It was good stew – the kind of fisherman's stew that was made with whatever came out of the sea fresh that morning and the garden that afternoon. Jester didn't ask or care what was in it. It filled his stomach; didn't seem to be drugged or poisoned. There was nothing more he could ask for. Well, except for a way back across the Channel before he was caught.

They insisted, nonetheless, that he stay the night. He refused a bed. Instead, he made up a bedroll on the floor. He'd slept rough before; he'd practiced doing so at some level for exactly this situation. The floor of a farmhouse was nothing compared to a tent in the woods, but in the morning, he would go.

He was woken before dawn by hushed yet urgent voices in French, a woman's voice among them. He thought he might have heard a door opening or closing.

Hope rose within him. The absent wife, perhaps; not a ghost or a hole in their life, but a spy working for the resistance, working with the allies.

If it wasn't for Francine… Perhaps the pretence was that she had left, and perhaps he had a hidden radio, had called her back.

"He's just some British airman. We'll toss him on a boat tomorrow."

The woman's response. "And if he saw something he shouldn't?"

"He's British. You really think he'll care as long as it hurts the Germans?"

It would have been rude to keep listening at that point. He rolled to his feet and stepped outside. "I don't care as long as it helps us win the war.

"See?" the farmer said.

The woman? Her stance was that of a predator, her head held high with a pride he'd never seen in a woman before. He wanted to run from her. Or run towards her. Something about her drew and repelled all at the same time; yet was oddly familiar.

"Airman," she said, turning to face him. For a moment, her eyes flickered yellow.

Quiet, but knowing that if anyone else could hear they were likely already in real trouble. "Spy."

"Indeed." Her lips curled. "So. We put you on a boat back to England. Unless, of course, you can be... useful. Or, perhaps..." Her head tilted to one side. "Oh, yes, I could make use of you."

His hackles rose. "I'm not a very good spy." A pause. "I'd be more useful back with my squadron, trust me."

"I don't know about that, Airman."

"He's not yours!" the farmer snapped. "He's not yours any more than Francine is."

"Maybe we can just make you even more useful to your squadron. Come with me."

He tried not to follow, but that gold came into her eyes again. It drew him, and he found himself walking out into the dawn. "What do you want with me?"

"I want you to help us kill Germans. That's all."

"I can do it better from my fighter." He kept his eyes on her, and kept them up. Her arse was worth looking at, but he knew if he started thinking like that he'd lose what remained of his self-control. Or he could run. He wanted to run.

"But I can make it so you can do it better yet. Besides, I don't plan on giving you the choice. Come."

She led him into the woods, and he was pretty sure she was walking to show off her mesmerising attributes, just for extra persuasion. *Do it better yet?* She was sure as heck no flight trainer.

Can't have Francine.

Was this Francine's mother? This beautiful, terrible being who... Yes, he knew what she reminded him of – the Regents Park wolf pack, before the war. They'd taken them somewhere out of the city now, safe from the blitz. He wasn't sure where. It didn't matter. But this woman. "You're a wolf."

She turned, smiled, fangs glinting in the dawn light. "Of course I am."

He wanted to run. Then he didn't. "*Loup-garou.*" He knew the word. *The werewolf resistance?* It was a ridiculous idea. "Brakes on, lady. There's no such thing as a werewolf, and if there was, well... I don't want to turn into a wolf every time the moon is full, even for somebody as hot as you."

"And you don't want to be stronger? Faster? Better reflexes? Better night vision? That's what I offer, even in human form. And besides, I hate the Germans."

"Let me guess. They're experimenting on werewolves."

Her lips twisted into something half smile, half grimace. "That and keeping us as pets."

There was a rumour Hitler was obsessed with wolves. "Only German werewolves, no doubt."

She laughed, a sharp, harsh sound with little humour in it, then turned to face him. "You will do what it takes to hurt them. So will I. I will show you... and then you can decide."

"And if I say no?"

"Then we'll send you back to your squadron." This time it was a smile, almost a nice one. "As much as I want to keep you, we won't remove an asset."

"Then send me back now. I don't need to see what you want to show me, I don't need your recruiting..."

Gunfire. Ahead of him.

The woman swore in what he thought was actually Italian. Then... she became a wolf. It was a melting, a blurring. It wasn't something he enjoyed watching or something he ever wanted to see again. But she became a wolf. And set off towards the sound of the shots, not waiting for him, not looking to see if he followed.

He thrust a hand into his pocket, where it rested on his gun then set off after her, or more accurately after the sound. No way he could keep up with a wolf, *were* or otherwise, or even a dog that size. He knew that, but still he ran. Her alarm... was the rest of her pack in trouble?

The rest of her pack… He sped up, pulling the gun from his pocket but not clicking the safety off just yet. Just six shots in the Enfield; he had to make them count. The revolver had never been issued for pitched battles.

Which this was, by the sounds, and he slowed his approach, ducking behind a tree. He saw the fight now… the darting forms of the wolves and a half-dozen German soldiers. Make that five – one man went down, his throat ripped out. Jester took aim and fired, feeling the kick of the gun in his hand. He had never fired a sidearm in anger, only on the range. It was an odd feeling as his target staggered, a kill somehow more intimate than anything in the air. If, that was, he had actually killed him. He wasn't sure, but at least the man was out of the fight.

He readied another shot. No matter what the woman might have intended for him, he definitely hated the Germans more. They weren't trying to kill the wolves… no, definitely not, two of them had now thrown a net over one member of the pack, who snarled and then subsided, as if some enchantment on it had stilled it.

Jester fired again. Missed. The bullet slammed into an innocent tree, sending chips of wood flying. One of the Germans turned, sending a round flying past Jester who fired again. *Nailed him this time.*

Three bullets left. *Have to make them count.* He ducked behind the tree; there were more Germans than bullets, but they were trying to retreat with their catch rather than take out the rest of the pack. More Germans than bullets, yes, but there were also the wolves, with their teeth and claws – their natural weapons. They had to get close, though. One of them was hit. Yelping, it fell to the ground. A frown formed on his lips - *didn't you need to use silver bullets?*

He shot the Germans holding the netted wolf. First one, then the other. One went down. The other didn't, but he dropped the net, turned, made himself vulnerable.

Then a burning pain struck Jester in the chest. It was suddenly no longer possible to merely stay on his feet. The last bullet flew, but he wasn't sure if it hit anything, and then the world tunnelled down to a narrow place, and then to darkness.

He woke up flat on his back on the forest floor, looking up at a canopy of trees. Feeling fine. Not feeling as if he had been shot. No, no feeling of that. "What...?"

"You were dying. We had no choice."

He actually did snarl. That was how it came out. They had had a choice. They could have let him die as a man, not live with all of this energy flowing through his veins. He could smell them. He could smell, too, the dead. He hoped only German dead. "Your..."

"She lived. They sought to take her alive." It was the woman, kneeling next to him. "You should stay."

"My squadron still needs me." He found it in himself to move, to roll to a kneeling position, to face her. "It's my duty."

Could he, though? Or would he turn into a wolf in the cockpit. Would he lose control... Would he? But he felt more in control than he ever had; felt the beating of his own heart. Smelled her, wanted her, desired her and knew it was returned. "Tomorrow."

She smiled. "Tomorrow."

THE WILD HUNT

James A. Moore

The snow was coming down in frenzy; not drifting lazily to the ground, but hammering the earth and everything it touched. Cars were merely shapes under the thick blanket of frozen white and while the houses hadn't disappeared yet, it seemed a real possibility.

Mark Loman was just fine with that. He hadn't wanted to go into work today anyway, and now all he had to do with his time was watch a few movies and put up with his wife and kids. Lou and Ellen were good kids; they were easy to deal with. Donna, his wife, was another story entirely. Ever since she'd gone back to work, she'd become a shrew of epic scale.

He looked to where she sat with her little laptop, chain-smoking her damned cigarettes and managed not to sneer. When they'd married she would have been best described as 'handsome'. With a thin build and her auburn hair, her easy going smile and her sense of humor, she was always fun to be around, but she'd never quite made it to beautiful. Now, after almost twenty years of tanning herself whenever she got a chance and eating enough food to keep a sparrow underweight, she was all bones and leathery skin. She looked more like one of the stuffed hunting trophies in his den than like the woman he'd fallen in love with.

She looked up at him and smiled, and her face was closer to what he liked to see than to the pinched, hard expression he had grown used to of late. She was back to handsome, at least and that was a step in the right direction.

Did he love her anymore? He really didn't know, but he was certainly comfortable with her and just too damned lazy to change. He looked away after throwing her a quick smile of his own in return and looked at the two kids on the floor, watching the Wizard of Oz. Lou and Ellen were good, sweet kids. He was proud of them despite their occasional shortcomings — Lou liked to go out and party too much and Ellen was happiest when she was being a drama queen like her mother — and he loved them with all of his heart.

If he didn't, he'd probably have left Donna instead of just finding some action on the side.

The wind picked up outside just as flying monkeys were attacking the scarecrow in the movie, and both of the kids jumped a little as the hard breeze slammed into the house with enough force to shake the windows. Mark smiled and stood. "Gonna make some popcorn, guys. Who wants some?"

Lou and Ellen were both crying "I do!" around the same time the front door exploded inward.

The house was built to withstand the sort of weather going on outside and Mark stared hard at the fractured wood sliding across the hardwood floor and running down the short foyer leading into the living room without any real idea of what the hell had just happened. His kids didn't know either but they let out ear shattering screams just the same. Donna let out a squeal of her own and judging by the ache in his throat that hadn't been there a second ago, he must have let out a good one, too. He didn't remember screaming but that didn't mean it didn't happen.

The cold from outside moved into the room with all the subtly of a sledgehammer and brought with it a feral stench. Not foul, exactly, but musky and wild. Mark turned and headed down the hallway toward his den, where he kept his firearms. He saw something in the open threshold, a dark, furry shape, and decided the best thing he could do was be armed when whatever was out there came inside.

Donna screamed, "Where the hell are you going?" and ran toward the two children, ready to grab them off the carpet and hide them away, which was exactly what he'd hoped she'd do.

Mark didn't answer. He was far too busy opening the locked door to his private sanctuary and grabbing for his shotgun. Most of his weapons were locked away — he had kids, after all and he didn't want them ending up on the news for accidentally blowing each other away because he got stupid — but he kept the one firearm socked behind the door and hidden behind an American flag for any possible emergencies. The weapon was loaded and the box of shells was at the base of the flag. He had both in his hands and was heading back down the hallway before he could really give any conscious thought to the action. He'd done his time in the service and he'd remembered the lessons he learned.

He moved back into the hallway as he checked the chambers and made sure the .12 gauge was loaded. By the time he was back in the living room, the TV had moved on to another singing number and his wife and kids were backed up in the corner by what looked at first like a bear.

Mark's heart skipped three beats while he reassessed the situation. It wasn't a bear, and it wasn't alone. Black fur covered a hard, muscular form that was designed as much for speed as for power. *Not a bear*, he thought, trying to decide exactly what it was. It was closer to a wolf, but the body shape was still wrong. The thing paced in front of his family staring with oddly glowing eyes. It kept a bared muzzle full of teeth close to the legs of his loved ones.

There were three more of the things in the living room, all of them staring hard at the hallway where Mark stood.

"Mark! Do something!" Donna's voice cracked and strained as she looked at the thing in front of her. Lou and Ellen were held close to her, partially behind her as she shielded them with her own body. In that moment she looked more beautiful than he'd ever seen her.

Mark lifted the shotgun to his shoulder and sighted it at the monster closest to his family. "Donna, don't you move a muscle, honey."

A chorus of growls answered his gesture and the one nearest Donna snapped its teeth inches away from her left knee and sent the children into tears.

Mark's hand trembled a bit. He wasn't sure if he could kill the thing without at least injuring his wife. The cold from outside was spilling in a thick layer of snow and chilled his body, adding to his doubts about making a clean kill.

"Now, I wouldn't go and do anything too hasty there, fella." The voice came from the doorway and Mark spun hard, his eyes focusing on the man standing there. He'd seen him somewhere before but couldn't for the life of him remember exactly where.

"What the fuck is going on here?" He looked at the stranger, doing his best to sound like he was in control of the situation. He was good at bluffing that sort of thing; it was how he'd managed to turn his single bay garage into the biggest chain of automotive repair stores in the Midwest.

The stranger stepped closer, into the light of the living room, and revealed more of his face. He stepped forward with the confidence of a general facing off against a battalion of fresh recruits.

"What's going on here depends on you, Mr Loman." The voice was deep, and the man was just a little intimidating. He was tall, easily a few inches over six feet, and he was dressed in a hooded parka that was still covered with melting snow. Denim pants layered with a crust of ice and thick, black leather boots that dropped crushed slush to the hardwood floor finished off the outfit.

"What do you mean?"

"I mean I want some answers from you. If you answer me truthfully, we might just go away and leave your family alone. If you lie, we'll kill you, but make you watch them die first."

Donna started crying, and the kids increased the volume of their own wails of misery. Mark kept the business end of the shotgun aimed at the stranger's chest.

"What the hell are you talking about?" He asked the question, but even as the words left his mouth, he thought he knew.

The broad, weathered face looking at him wore a small, knowing smile. "Do I have to say it in front of your family, Loman? Do you really want me to do that?" His voice was soft, barely even carried to him past the wind from outside, but Mark saw the look on Donna's face switch for a second from panic to curiosity.

"I-No. Just ask your questions."

"Who else was there?"

He looked into the man's eyes, puzzled by their color. Hadn't they been blue a moment before? He couldn't be certain, maybe it had just been the lighting, but now they were brown, dark and deep and focused on him to the exclusion of everything else.

"I don't know. I wasn't there when that happened."

Those dark eyes stayed on his, and he swallowed softly. He was also a very good liar. He had been for a long time.

Finally the man nodded. "Kill his bitch."

"What? NO!" Mark started pulling the trigger on his shotgun and felt the impact move up his arms as the stranger grabbed the long barrel and pointed it toward the wall. The hammer rose and fell and set off an explosion that blasted through the wood paneling along the wall and shattered the plaster behind it.

Mark looked past the stranger's brutal face just as the thing on the ground stood, rising in height until it could barely stand in the room. When he'd been young Mark had a St Bernard that used to stand on its back legs and place its paws on his shoulders when it came to greet him. That old dog had stood close to six feet tall when it was in that position and it had weighed in at 185 pounds. The thing that reached out with one paw and grabbed Donna by the throat and yanked her forward was much bigger.

Donna let out a cry of fear and desperate pain as the claws on the thing sank slightly into her neck and drew blood. She was lifted completely off her feet and hauled toward the bared teeth in front of her. Ellen and Lou tried to hold on, to anchor their mother, but were shaken off easily by the monster.

Mark tried to keep his grip on the shotgun, but the man he'd just tried to kill ripped it out of his hands and cast it aside. The parka covered arm wrapped around his neck and spun him forward into the living room proper as the other dark shapes moved easily out of the way.

Mark struggled, he did, but it didn't seem to do him the least bit of good. He fought and kicked and cursed, his mind focused solely on getting to Donna and saving her.

"Watch this, Loman. You did this. Remember that." There was no humor in the voice, only regret tinged with anger.

"Oh, God! Please! I'll tell you whatever you want to know, just leave her alone!" His voice trembled and broke as he pleaded.

The man behind him grabbed his hair in one hand and held his skull with enough force to make the bones creak. "Keep watching! You keep watching, Loman or I swear I'll make your children suffer for hours."

Donna had tears running down her face and her teeth bared as she hyperventilated. She'd been trying to get away all along but the grip on her neck was simply too powerful and despite trying to rake her nails over the furry arm that held her, she hadn't managed to get through the thick pelt of hair to catch any flesh.

For the first time, Mark finally, really focused on the face of the thing that carried his wife closer. He was a hunter; he knew damned near every animal on the planet well enough to identify it. This grinning thing was nothing that should have existed. There were marks in the black fur, patterns within the shadow of the rich, dark pelt. The face bore every indication of belonging to a predator, from the forward facing eyes to the wrinkled muzzle above a set of teeth designed to cut flesh and break bones. It was standing on two hind legs, but the way they bent made it obvious the thing was more comfortable running on all fours. The torso was wide and, being a man who prided himself on staying in shape, Mark knew that some of the clusters of muscle that stretched over the ribcage had never been designed to accommodate a four-legged creature.

The eyes looked back at him and took his measure and found him lacking.

"Mark! Please! Don't let them do this!" Donna was panicked, and he couldn't find any fault in that. He was terrified himself; imagining the damage the teeth would cause and already knowing the reasons for the attack.

"Oh, Donna. I'm so sorry, honey."

The stranger spoke again, his voice a deadly rumble. "Are you now? You certainly weren't crying then, were you?"

164

"She has nothing to do with this!" He tried one last time to break free, and felt the fingers holding his head push forward, driving thick nails into his scalp. The pain was enough to make him stop, to make him scream out again.

"I know. She's innocent in this. That's what makes it such a shame."

The beast holding Donna looked at the man behind Mark and turned its head quizzically.

Two words and every hope that Mark had of coming out of this alive fell to pieces. Two words and his entire world exploded into ruin.

The man said, "Do it."

Without any hesitation, the beast opened its mouth and lunged forward, pulling Donna closer in at the same time. Her flailing arms beat up and down on the creature's head, her fists striking as hard as they could, even as those teeth ripped through her shirt and carved trenches into her breasts, her sternum. Donna bucked hard, her hands unclenching and grabbing at the thick fur around the thing's head, pulling, trying to wrench the pain away.

A shower of bright red blood came out of the wounds even as Mark heard the bones in Donna's chest break. The teeth let go for an instant and then sank in deeper as the nightmare in front of him broke her chest cavity open. When it finished ripping a wound wide enough, the foul thing began shredding the organs underneath. Donna let out one more powerful screech and her body stiffened with agony. The monster reared back and pulled a mass of raw, bloodied flesh from inside Donna. Viscera painted her body, her face, the floor, and her dark-furred assailant in a dozen shades of crimson.

As Donna's body relaxed the creature let her drop to the ground, a lifeless wreck, a ruined parody of the woman Mark had married.

Mark stared, too stunned to even move, barely even breathing as his wife hit the floor. The kids were on the ground, gasping out jagged sobs, their faces tear-stained and red.

Mark was shoved forward and stumbled, his foot catching on the leg of one of the damned beasts surrounding him. He fell, his hands outstretched to catch himself, and landed across Donna's still form. Warm blood covered his hands and face, his left palm slipped into the hole in her chest cavity, bending his fingers almost to the breaking point, and his elbow slammed into her face, breaking her nose.

Mark backed away in a raw panic, screaming hoarsely as he realized what was covering him. He wanted to act, wanted to grab his shotgun and kill the bastard that had just murdered Donna, but his body wasn't listening. He wanted to protect his children, too, but that was beyond his abilities.

The four beasts leaped across the living room, knocking aside the coffee table and scattering a week's worth of magazines and unread mail in the process.

Dorothy cried on the TV screen and the children, who meant more to Mark than anything else in the world, cried with her as they were surrounded.

"Wait." The voice came from the man again, the stranger who looked so damned familiar.

Mark turned his head slowly, barely able to manage the feat, and blinked Donna's blood from his eyes.

"Take them. Don't kill them." The man was looking at him, his eyes blue again. "Don't harm a hair on their heads."

He moved over to Mark again and squatted on his haunches, his right foot crushing Donna's hand in the process. Donna made no noise of protest. She couldn't, she was dead. Dead, dead, dead, dead, dea—

"Pay attention, Loman." The man slapped him across the face hard enough to leave a heavy red mark and bring Mark out of his daze.

"Why...? Why did you?" The tears came then, tinged with a dark pink color, washing the last of her blood from his eyes.

"Shut up. Pay attention. I've decided to give you a fighting chance; more than you and yours ever gave, I suspect. You're going to answer my questions, or I swear to you I'll mail you back a piece of your children every day for a month. Do you understand me?"

He didn't trust himself to speak. Mark nodded instead.

"Good. I want their names. The names of everyone who was with you. I want their addresses and phone numbers. You do this, and your children get to live."

Even as he spoke Ellen was screaming, her cries muffled by the furry hand cupped over her face. Lou was silent and staring into space. Both of them were held close to bestial bodies, dwarfed by the things that carried them.

Mark knew all the information he needed and got it out of his Rolodex under the supervision of the stranger with the hellhounds for pets. He handed over the five business cards. He could almost think again, could almost reason, and the grief he felt was gradually becoming something else.

"I know you want me dead, Loman. I understand your anger." The man put the cards away in his parka and sealed the zipper over the pocket as if he were carefully securing a vital treasure.

"I'll see you dead, too, you bastard."

"Maybe you will." The stranger nodded his head. "You'll get your chance. Hide the body of your wife or call the police. It won't matter in the long run." He looked at Mark with a fury of his own, a dark rage that wanted to come to the surface. "By now your children are gone. If you're smart, you won't warn your friends. You might need them. Like I said, I'm going to give you a chance. If you behave, you and your friends will get your children back. If not, I'll kill them all and then I'll come back for you. Do you understand me?"

What could he do? Mark nodded.

"I already have your name and number. I'll call you sometime soon. Once we're ready for you. Don't be stupid. Don't try to find us before it's time. I crossed over five hundred miles of this country to get to you, to track you down. Don't think I won't do it again."

The stranger turned and moved toward the open front door with the grace of a gymnast, and headed back into the storm.

Moments later the house was silent except for the movie that was playing in the living room and the sound of the wind howling out its cold dismay.

For a time, Mark Loman joined in its song.

* * *

Scott Lassiter was in a good mood for the first time in weeks, right before the phone rang. The business deal he'd been trying to work out finally went through, his commission on the sale of all the equipment needed for a national chain of discount warehouse stores was now a reality instead of a pipe dream, and his commission was enough to add two zeroes to his yearly income.

So he was just as happy as he could be when he reached over, grabbed his cell from its holder and answered the phone.

His joy lasted exactly seven seconds.

"Hello?"

"Scott!?!" He recognized Allison's voice instantly. His wife of two years and the girl he'd dreamed of being with for as long as he could remember. Her voice was ripe with fear and his heart almost froze inside his chest.

The road around him was spilling over with cars all heading away from Atlanta's busy traffic flow and toward the suburbs to the north. He turned on his flashers and pulled to the side of the road, moving on autopilot. He'd always been a very cautious man.

"Allison? What's wrong, honey? Is it the baby?"

Her pregnancy had been touch and go from the very beginning, and much as they both wanted children, the little one growing inside of her seemed almost determined not to survive.

"Scott! Scott!"

He gripped the phone so hard he thought for sure he was going to shatter it, but he couldn't make himself stop. "Allison! Listen to me, honey, calm down and tell me what's going on."

The voice on the other end of the phone was sedate and cold. "Hello, Scott. This is a kidnapping call. Listen very carefully if you ever want to see your wife again."

"What?" His pulse slammed into overdrive and he looked around as if he might, somehow, see the man speaking to him past the traffic and the fourteen miles he still had to travel in order to get back to his house.

"You don't have time for questions. You don't have time for anything. Pay careful attention. Your wife is in my custody. If you attempt to call the police or interfere, I'll kill her. Wait for a phone call. I'll use your cell phone number. Oh, and make absolutely sure you act like everything is just fine. You have a little boy on the way and the only way he's going to make it is if you do as I say."

The click of the phone on the other end terminating the call was loud and made him flinch.

Scott stared off into the distance, seeing nothing as the heavy traffic moved past him.

"Allison?" He spoke only to himself, knowing full well she couldn't possibly answer him.

* * *

George Heatherly walked into his house at the usual time, his car keys bouncing in his hand. Coming home meant a lot more to him these days than it had in the past. These days he had company waiting for him when he stepped through the door and dinner either waiting, or almost prepared. Cheryl was good to him like that.

He'd never expected to find anyone who could fill the void left in his world when Amy passed away, but after years of being alone, Cheryl was there to make him feel complete again.

If it wasn't actually love, it was a damned fine substitute.

He ran across Cheryl when he was waiting at the doctor's office for his yearly check up. The red head was waiting too, and despite the fact the place looked deserted except for the two of them, there didn't seem to be anyone who was in a hurry to see them.

She was the one who started the conversation, displaying a razor sharp wit and damned fine looks to boot. Somehow, six months later, she moved into his house and sort of took over. Most of the time he was too dazed to question it, and even when he did decide to sit down and assess the situation, he fully acknowledged that he was better with her in his world than without her. Also, the sex was amazing and her cooking beat all hell out of another take-out pizza.

All of that and more flashed through his mind as he moved inside and carefully took off his coat, placing it in the small closet just inside. That was one of the rules he'd gladly accepted when she took over: coats were to be put away immediately and shoes were to follow them into the closet.

He put away the coat and slid his shoes where they belonged and then moved into his house.

And stopped dead in his tracks when he saw the devastation. The black leather couch had been thrown across the room and shattered the TV set. The long sheet of glass from the coffee table was now scattered across the plush carpet, a sea of shimmering reflections.

George stared at the scene with a blank expression on his face as he tried to absorb the damage. "Cheryl? Hon, are you here?"

No one answered him at first. But he heard a floorboard creak in the direction of the kitchen and felt his mouth go dry and his bladder threaten a revolt.

Some of his friends liked to keep a dozen or so firearms in the house, liked to go on talking for hours about how good they were with their weapons and how much fun it was to blow away a hundred or so Osama Bin Laden faces on the targets at the local range.

George didn't give a good damn about weapons. He went hunting with the guys because it was fun to get together with his old high school chums once in a while.

Oh, Lord in Heaven, how he wished he had their obsession on his side tonight. He didn't even own a gun. He borrowed one of Mark's every year when they got together.

George looked around for anything that would make a suitable weapon and found nothing.

In the hallway, he heard a footstep hit another of the loose floorboards, this one several feet closer to where he was standing.

"Cheryl?" He could barely manage a whisper. The chill from outside was still sticking to his body, but a sheen of sweat seeped from his pores just the same.

"She's not here." The voice was deep and bordered on a growl. The man who walked into view was a complete stranger as best he knew, but looked like he should have been locked away on general principles. He stood six feet, four inches in height. His broad shoulders threatened to split the seams of the dark blue flannel shirt he wore along with dark jeans, dark boots and a black leather belt that was cracking from age. The man had a mane of golden brown hair with a blend of silvery and reddish highlights and the clearest blue eyes George had ever seen. His face was wind burned, a little weathered, and broad.

"Who are you?"

Blue Eyes looked at him for a moment and shook his head. "You really don't remember me?"

"No." George was unsettled, but doing his best to keep a level head. It didn't pay to jump to conclusions. The man might be an ex-lover of Cheryl's, he might be an old high school buddy who hadn't aged well, or he could even be a cop. Not every person he encountered had to be somebody sinister, even if the man in question had no reason at all to be in his house.

"Well, that's a peach, isn't it?" The man stepped closer and his eyes narrowed. "I remember you, George. I remember you very well. You were the one who told them to stop."

He looked at the stranger and shook his head. "I'm sorry, but I have no idea in hell what you're talking about. Why are you in my house and where is Cheryl?"

"Cheryl has taken a vacation, George. She didn't want to go without leaving you a message, but I convinced her that I would explain everything to you."

George felt his calm exterior starting to crack. "What have you done to her?"

"Not a blessed thing." The man crossed his thick arms and looked down at George. "And I won't do anything to her, either, as long as you follow a few simple rules."

He'd tried so hard, been so good about not losing his temper, and he wanted to keep that inner peace, but the man standing in front of him was making it very difficult. "Listen to me. Whatever game you're playing, I don't want any part of it. Bring Cheryl back here, now, and this doesn't have to get ugly."

The man smiled — smiled, like they were having a smoke break together — and shook his head. "That's not the way this works, George. You have to play by the rules, *my* rules, or the only way you'll ever see Cheryl again is in a morgue."

"You miserable fuck." His vision went red and the muscles in his body tensed. Adrenaline kicked into George's body like an old familiar friend, and before he knew what he was doing, he'd grabbed the bigger man by the front of his shirt and lifted him off the ground. George slammed the man into the wall, his teeth bared, his breaths coming in hard fast gasps, and he snarled as he spoke. "You don't want to fuck with me! Where is Cheryl?"

The knee that hit him in the solar plexus hurt, but George was almost beyond feeling anything. He grunted but didn't let go of the man he held against the wall.

"You're about to get me angry, George. Don't do that." The broad, almost brutal face looked different, but he barely noticed the transformation. George was too busy losing his ability to stay calm.

"Where is she!?!"

The man sighed and slammed his knee into George a second time with far more effect. George let go of him and staggered back, his body bent over on itself and he fell against the far wall, gasping for air.

The stranger jumped as he landed on his feet and in the space of a heartbeat, he had his hands on George's lapels and was returning the favor. George was not a small man, he was taller than average and a little heavier than was healthy, but the man shook him like a temperamental toddler and slammed him into the wall with enough force to crack the plaster.

"You're not listening to me, George! I said if you don't behave yourself you'll never see Cheryl alive again! Pay attention!" The voice was deeper than before and rumbled; the blue eyes had gone so dark they looked almost black, and when the man spoke his lips peeled away from teeth that barely seemed to fit inside his mouth.

"You don't get to hit me, George. You don't get to threaten me. The only reason you're even alive is because I'm nicer than most of my kind and I decided to let you have a fighting chance."

"What the fuck is wrong with you?" George struggled, even with the wind knocked out of his body and the giant of a man — six foot four? Hardly, closer to six foot eight! —holding him off the ground it was hard for him to listen to the words and make himself calm down.

"You told them to stop, George. I'm giving you points for that. But you didn't even try to *make* them stop. You just watched."

The Incredible Growing Man spun George in a half-circle and threw him toward the distant kitchen. George was reunited with the floor in a painful collision that left his arms tangled with a chair from the dining room set and eyes that refused to focus.

Before he could get to his feet, or even to his knees, the man was back again and this time he took the offensive, pushing one foot against George's neck and pinning him in place. "Keep it up, George, and I'll tear Cheryl's heart from her body. Do you understand me?"

George stopped struggling and took several deep breaths, focusing himself, pulling back from the anger that still threatened to erupt. Finally he nodded, knowing that all the rage in the world wouldn't help him right now.

The man nodded and stepped back, his face still locked into a snarl. "Good. Listen to me and listen carefully. Go about your life like nothing is out of the ordinary. I'll be in contact with you in a few days." He moved toward the front door. "Don't get stupid, George. You do anything you shouldn't, and Cheryl will be the one who pays for it. Oh, and keep that temper of yours at the ready." He paused and looked back at George, still on the ground. "You're going to need it."

* * *

Cullie Landers didn't have a family. He was alone in the world and that suited him just fine. He tended to think of himself as a man without a care in the world, and most of the time he was right. His parents had left him a fortune when they died, and he'd been wise in how he spent it. The house was bought and paid for, the cars in the driveway all belonged to him and he was cautious about going crazy with the spending. He didn't live beyond his means and with a little careful financial maneuvering he'd managed to set most of his assets aside and still give himself a spending allowance of almost three thousand dollars a month. When it came to living on Easy Street, Cullie was an old pro.

When it came to having a good time, he was even more of a seasoned veteran. So it wouldn't have surprised anyone who knew him to hear that he staggered into his house at just after two in the morning, wise enough at least to have taken a cab home. He could always pick up his Bronco in the morning.

Cullie opened the door and stumbled through the threshold as the room did a small spin to the left. He reached back to close the door and encountered a very warm fur coat instead.

He turned back with unfocused eyes and looked at the thickly muscled torso he was touching, felt the flesh move as the thing standing in his doorway breathed, and then looked up at the face.

He meant to scream "bear!" but never had the chance. The fist that clocked him was as big as his face, and drove him to his knees. He was unconscious when he was lifted from the ground and carried out into the cold night air.

* * *

Captain Eric Fulford was not happy. He was, in fact, absolutely miserable. The diner in front of him looked perfectly comfortable, but he sat in his car anyway, smoking a Pall Mall and trying to keep calm.

Four days earlier his wife Sarah's car had been found abandoned on the side of the road. Foul play was suspected. Two days later, he was home on emergency leave, trying to figure out exactly what had happened to Sarah and the boys. Lance and Tyler were good kids, but too young to do much if something had happened. He took out the last picture taken of the whole family together and stared at each of his loved ones' faces, memorizing them.

The phone call had come just after two in the morning, and he'd answered it quickly, praying it was Sarah. No, instead it was a stranger's voice.

"Captain, we have Sarah and your twins. Lovely boys they are, too. They're all fine and they miss you horribly."

"Who is this?"

"Don't concern yourself with that. Right now what you need to worry about is getting your family back. So here's the deal. I want you to go to the Wilmont Diner on White Horse Pike, do you remember the place?"

How could he ever forget? "Yes, yes I do."

"Excellent. I want you to meet me in there at seven pm on Friday night. The place will be crowded, but I've arranged for a very large table. You'll find several of your hunting buddies waiting for you there. Like you, they have family members to consider. Do you understand?"

"Yes." His heart felt like it was going to explode, but he made himself as calm as he could manage.

"Do I have to explain what happens if you're late? Or if you bring reinforcements with you? I know what you do for a living. I know you've been out of country, dealing with a few problems in the Middle East, and I have to be honest here, I'm sorry it's had to come to this."

"I won't be bringing anyone with me."

"Excellent." The voice was pleasant enough, but there was a sarcastic tone that grated on his nerves. "We all want this resolved, Captain. One serviceman to another, I hope we can bring about a painless resolution to the problem at hand."

"What is this all about?"

"Murder, Captain. It's about the people you and your friends murdered."

The phone cut off before he could respond.

He'd had to drive most of the last day to get here, but he'd managed it, juiced on more coffee than he ever thought it possible for one man to drink and enough roadside burgers to feed his full battalion.

Now the only problem was getting motivated enough to leave the relative safety of his car. The diner was a brick affair, with chrome around the widows and doors and enough neon to light up a city block in Las Vegas. He could see through the windows, and he knew several of the men sitting at three tables that had been put together. Of course he knew them; they were his buds from all the way back in high school and, in a couple of cases, even earlier.

He saw Mark and Scott and Cullie and George. The only person who wasn't there yet besides himself was Tony, and Tony hadn't been with them when everything went down.

So maybe they were just waiting for him. Maybe Tony wasn't a part of it.

"Let's just get this done. I can't sit here all night." Eric climbed out of his Ford and locked the doors before heading into the diner. He walked slowly, despite his own admonitions. Fear can do that to a person.

* * *

The three tables were joined in a larger block, a chunk of the room that dwarfed everything else. When Eric sat down the total number of people became an even dozen. He didn't nod or do anything but sit. Cullie was next to him, his eyes blackened and his nose swollen to the point where he barely looked like himself.

The strangers at the table were, as a whole, quiet, giving off a calm that was unsettling under the circumstances.

One of the strangers, a large man who had his longish hair pulled back into an efficient ponytail, tossed a menu toward Eric. Eric took it.

"Order something to eat. You'll need your strength." Eric recognized the voice from the phone.

"Do you want to tell me what the hell is going in here?" He'd been as calm as he could, but the time for patiently waiting was done with.

The man nodded and gestured for the waitress. The woman wore her nametag and blouse over jeans that looked almost painted on, but she wasn't even remotely attractive to Eric. She could have been dancing around naked and she wouldn't have even caught his eye for more than a second.

"He'll have a steak dinner, make it rare, and a large coffee." The woman nodded and turned away. "You looked awfully cold out there, Captain."

The man cleared his throat. "Now then, you're all here for a reason. You're here to deal with a matter of bloodshed and how it will be paid for."

"What the hell are you talking about?" It was Scott that spoke up, confused. He was, as always, the most naïve among them.

The leader of the group around them shook his head and stared at Scott. Scott, the go-getter salesman, dressed in his jeans and his thick preppy sweater and his perfect hair, facing off against a man who looked like he would probably be at home leading a Viking raid on another village. Oh to be sure the clothes were modern, but the man still looked like a savage trying to hide among civilized people.

There was something about all of the strangers that felt the same way. It wasn't the style of clothing they wore — which spoke more of rural common sense than fashion — it wasn't that they were unclean or bore a thousand tattoos, but there was something about them, about the way that they carried themselves that drew the soldier's eye in Eric. They were, for lack of a better way to put it, seasoned warriors. He had no doubt in his mind they had fought together before and maybe even killed together.

"Not this last November, gentlemen, but the year before that, you were out hunting together, do you remember that?"

Eric and the others nodded their assent to the question.

"While you were hunting, you did what almost everyone does. You camped out, you had a good time, and you maybe drank a few too many beers. Nothing out of the ordinary there." The man took his time and fixed each and every one of them with his stare.

"Except on your last night." Eric saw it, and felt his stomach drop. Scott didn't flinch when the Viking talked about the last night, but Cullie, George and Mark all did. Eric flinched too, but for different reasons. He hadn't been with them. He didn't know all of the details, but he knew that something had happened that night, after they'd packed up and headed their separate ways.

Scott shook his head, puzzled, and proved again that in his way he was the most naïve, or just maybe the most innocent of them. "I still don't know what you're—"

The Viking lifted his hand. "I'm getting to that." He shot a look to his friends around the table, and without a word between them they communicated something vital. Eric didn't know what they'd said but they were definitely talking.

"On the last night, after you broke camp, you left in three cars. One of those cars took off with Anthony Ridgemont behind the wheel and went south. The other two vehicles moved to the north and east, heading in this direction. Do you remember that, gentlemen?"

Once again they all nodded their heads. "Excellent. Mr Ridgemont is no longer a part of the story. The closest he came to doing something wrong was failing to put out the fire as well as he should have, and that was fixed easily enough."

"But the rest of you? Well, now, that's where things get interesting. I'm an excellent tracker, and I had a little help along the way, but it was rough weather, there was rain, and there was even a little sleet. It's understandable that one of the gentlemen driving lost his way a bit and managed to slide into a ditch."

Of course they all remembered. Eric and Scott had turned around after getting a call from Cullie's cell phone almost an hour and a half after they'd left. The car had gone off the road and run into a tree. Because Scott was smart enough to rent a well-equipped Jeep Wrangler, they'd managed to pull it back up to the road. No big deal, just a few hours of lost time before they all got home.

At least, that was what Eric had thought at first. It was later, when he asked why the others had taken so long to call that he suspected something else might have been up.

"Which three of you were in that vehicle?" The Viking looked at each of the men, and none of them was willing to raise a hand. "Let's try this again. Which of you were in that vehicle, gentlemen? The other two are free to go."

"What about our families?" That was Mark. His voice cracked when he spoke, dried and dusty, his eyes shining feverishly.

"The men who weren't in the car can collect their families and leave, but only after this is all resolved."

Eric spoke softly, his voice as controlled as he could manage. "What happened in that car?"

The Viking looked at him. "I was hoping you weren't involved, Captain. I meant what I said. I respect what you're doing for this country."

Eric ignored him and looked at Mark. His old friend couldn't look him in the face.

"What happened in that car, Mark?"

Mark shook his head.

It was George who finally spoke up. "I was in the car. So was Mark. So was Cullie. Eric and Scott didn't have anything to do with it."

The Viking nodded and stood. "That was about the way I remembered it, but I couldn't be sure."

He was about to speak again when the waitress came back and set down Eric's meal. Eric nodded his thanks and she went on her way.

"Eat up, Captain."

"I'm not hungry."

"Take it to go; you and Mr Lassiter are free to leave. Your families are being taken care of and you'll have them back when this is done." The man's eyes barely even looked in his direction. Now that his part had been played, Eric ceased to be important.

Hell with that. "What happened in the fucking car?" His voice was rising and a few of the diners at nearby tables looked in their direction, but quickly looked away when they saw the strangers surrounding the table. All of the men with the Viking had stood.

"That doesn't concern you any more, Captain. Leave it like that. I'll call you when everything is finished."

Scott shook his head. "No way. I want to see my wife. Now.

"Mr Lancaster, I know you're missing your wife. I appreciate that. But it just isn't going to work out that way for a while. I have business to take care of with your friends. That's all you need to know."

Scott opened his mouth to speak. "That's not going to work for me! My wife's condition is delicate!"

Eric shook his head and responded at the same time: "This is nonsense. Whatever happened, you can take care of it in a court of law."

George stood at the same time, shaking his head, red faced. "I didn't have any part in it, I tried to stop them. I didn't kill anyone."

And all of the voices together stopped as George's words rang out through the cacophony.

Scott spoke first, his eyes wider than usual and his voice shaken by the words he'd just heard from a long-time friend. "Wait a minute. Wait a goddamned minute! Who got killed?"

* * *

Just a few words at the wrong time can put an awkward spin on a situation. The Viking looked at everyone at the surrounding tables and shook his head: *Can you believe the lack of tact from some people?*

The people around their joined tables suddenly decided they had better places to be. Four couples and at least two families got up and headed to the cash register to pay for their meals, several of which were barely even touched.

The six men who had called Scott and his friends to the diner stood looking pointedly at the people who'd had their meals interrupted until they left the building.

There was a long few seconds of silence until the last of

the diners left and then the guy with the ponytail spoke again. "Would one of you like to tell Mr Lassiter what happened? Or would you prefer I do it for you?"

None of the three men looked at Scott. The big guy finally shrugged his shoulders.

"I guess it's me then. While you were driving on your way and these three were doing their own thing, they hit something on the side of the road. They ran over a wolf."

"We didn't see it." That was Cullie, who was whining.

"You had your chance. Shut up." The man skewered Cullie with a glance and then went back to his tale. "Now, accidents happen, I'm the first to acknowledge that. They're unfortunate, but they really can't be avoided." Scott was fascinated by the man's face. The features were all where they belonged, but the way his eyes moved, the way his lips worked as they formed words, seemed just slightly off-kilter somehow.

"What would you have done in their situation Mr Lassiter?"

"I would have stopped to see what I could do to help and I would have called emergency services." That was, to Scott's way of thinking, the only thing to do in that sort of situation.

"You see? That's where you and I are on the same page. You render aid. If aid is not possible, you might even get a guilty conscience and just scamper on your way. It happens from time to time. I spent twenty-five years with the Highway Patrol. I saw more accidents than I ever want to think about."

The strangers around the table were all looking at Cullie, staring hard, their silence filling the air with tension.

"What your friends here did, however, was first check to see if the wounded animal was alive, and then torture it to death."

Eric looked at his three hunting buddies, his normally stoic face showing disgust. Scott looked at them and shook his head. "That's not possible. They wouldn't do that."

"Didn't go so well for all of you guys on that hunting trip, did it? I believe you and your friend Anthony were the only ones who managed to bag a deer."

"Yeah, so?"

"So all I can figure was that they didn't want to go home empty handed. They backed their car off of the wounded wolf." And here he paused and looked at each of them men who were in the hunting party before he continued. His face when he stared at Eric and Scott was calm and conversational. His expression changed substantially when he stared at the other three, as if the only thing stopping him from killing them right then and there was the lack of a handgun.

"When they saw what they'd hit, George actually wanted to call 9-1-1. He reached for his phone and he started dialing." Those deep blue eyes stared hard at George, who looked down and shook his head, blinking his eyes against tears. "Before he could finish, Cullie Landers said he had a better idea." And again the eyes moved, staring hard at Cullie, who stared back defiantly. The two men locked gazes and while it took several seconds, Cullie finally looked away. "Cullie thought it would be fun to play with the poor thing, to make it suffer a bit more and then to take the pelt home with him."

The man turned and looked at Scott again, his features once more softening from what looked like homicidal rage. "There are laws against it, of course, but what the hell, maybe he could get it treated." A shrug of broad shoulders. "It might have worked out that George won the argument. Your friend George seems like a decent enough man. But then Mark Loman decided he wouldn't mind having a prize himself."

The man moved across the side of the table until he was inches away from Mark. Mark was hyperventilating. He was sweating enough to look greasy, his dark hair was plastered to his skull, and he trembled.

"What was it you took, again, Loman? The head, I believe?"

Cullie roared when he opened his mouth again. "It was a fucking dog! Who cares?"

All six of the men around them did something completely unexpected. They growled. Not a little low noise like clearing the throat, but a deep rumble that came from their chests as their lips peel back from the teeth.

The leader spoke again. "Show them, John. Show them why we would care about a 'dog'."

One of the men with him stepped forward and quickly unbuttoned his shirt, setting it aside. Scott and his friends all watched while the man disrobed completely, down to nothing but his underwear.

The man was lean and hard, athletic enough but definitely not a body builder. Scott, who tended to work out regularly, was about the same height and had him by easily thirty pounds of muscle.

John stared directly at Cullie, his face still set in a sneer, and started breathing fast. His breaths were almost silent at first, but then there was a light whimper followed by a full-out groan.

Scott watched it happen, every last second of it, his mind frozen, his eyes bulging.

The man threw his head back and gasped and as he did so, his skin split, tearing like thick paper and revealing a different shape beneath its surface. There was no long drawn out process as he'd seen in several movies, there was simply a sudden growth spurt as the average sized man became something entirely different.

What shook off the shredded remains of a human being was a werewolf, one that stood easily seven-and-a-half-feet tall, and had to weigh at least a hundred pounds more than the man it had replaced.

The guy with the ponytail kept speaking, while every one of the hunters who'd been called to pay a debt scrambled away from the beast looming over Cullie.

"Wolfmen, werewolves, lycanthropes, whatever you want to call us, gentlemen, we're very real." He moved forward and looked the beast in the eyes. Scott could only stare in awe, but his friend Eric had a different look on his face. Eric looked like a man who'd just had an epiphany.

"Sweet Jesus," Mark spoke softly, his voice shaking.

"Keep your gods to yourself, thank you." The man staring at the monster in front of him stepped back and the werewolf fell forward, onto its hands and knees, even as it once again became the man named John. John very calmly put his clothes back on, leaving behind the shredded underwear.

"Hate when I forget the briefs," John muttered almost apologetically as he got himself back into his jeans.

"Would you like me to tell you the rest of the story now, gentlemen?" The obvious leader of the group settled down against one of the tables and crossed his arms. "This is the part where things get grisly, and since you wanted the truth, you'll get it."

He looked over at George when he spoke. "George wanted them to stop, but I guess he didn't feel too strongly about the situation. Instead of making them leave the wolf alone, he lit a cigarette, grabbed himself a beer and went into the woods.

"So he didn't get to see everything that Cullie and Mark did. He didn't watch while they took turns cutting at the crippled animal on the ground." The rumble was back in the man's voice, a sound unsettlingly like a dog growling as it ate. "He was busy leaning against a tree and then puking his guts out when he heard the animal's cries change."

He pinned Cullie with his glare and continued again. "What gets me, what really amazes me above all else, is that your friends didn't stop with the cutting when the wolf started to change shape."

Mark was hyperventilating, his hands were clenched and his eyes were locked on the ground at his feet. Cullie was looking at the ground too, but more like he'd been caught in the act of doing something he wouldn't have minded doing as long as no one knew about it. He looked more like a man accused of public masturbation than a murderer.

"When the change happens, there's no mistaking that what you are dealing with is human. You saw that yourself a moment ago, gentlemen. But Mark and Cullie here? That didn't stop them."

He moved away from the edge of the table and looked at the two men. Turning his head from one to the other, his own breaths coming like a bellows stoking a furnace, he made sure to look them both over.

"In the very farthest stretches of polite society, it's possible that someone could have overlooked their killing a wolf, even if they felt the need to torture it to death. But I ask you gentlemen, what do you think about your friends murdering a twenty-year-old woman?"

Eric shook his head; his face pale and sickly.

Scott felt his gag reflex try to force his recently consumed dinner into reverse and dry swallowed until the impulse vanished.

"Now, how about we add one more factor into the equation, one I'm sure neither of these fine, upstanding citizens decided to mention, even to George over here. The girl, my daughter and John's wife, was pregnant when they hit her."

"Oh for fuck's sake you've got to be kidding." The words were out of Scott's mouth before he realized that he had spoken. The giant of a man turned on him and nailed him in place with a stare.

"I wish I were. I'm not. They murdered my daughter and my grandchildren, Mr Lassiter." He walked closer until he was physically looking down at Scott. "They murdered her and then, to make sure no one would ever know, they dug her a shallow grave and buried her. On the bright side, at least your friend Loman was good enough to bury her head with the rest of her body."

"How do you know all of this?" Eric spoke, as calmly as he could. He looked a little green around the gills, but still composed.

"I guess I edited the story a little. You see, they didn't hit one wolf. They hit two. They just didn't notice me when I crawled away to tend to my own wounds." He looked over at Eric as he spoke. "We're a hearty breed. We have to be. We can heal from almost any trauma, but it takes time. They'd shattered my hips and broken my back when the car hit me. Two days later I was fine, but until then, it took time to mend. Much as I wanted to stop them, to explain what they were doing, I couldn't do anything but listen to the sounds they made."

He moved again and this time he faced George, who was trembling. "That's right. I had to listen while they murdered my little girl, same as you chose to listen. The difference is, you could have stopped them."

George looked at the man and trembled, not from fear if Scott had to guess, but from shame. That was all it took to convince Scott that the werewolves were right.

Their leader turned around and walked away from George, effectively dismissing him.

"And there you have the story. It took me two days to get better. By then all of you were long gone, of course, but I took the time to memorize your scents, and then I started tracking. It took a long time. Longer than I want to think about, but it was worth it."

"Look, this is all crazy!" Mark was pacing, upset and nervous. Even Scott could smell his fear. "You already killed Donna! You've had your fucking revenge. Just, just call this done and let us go!"

"We already discussed that, Loman. You killed your wife. Not me and not any of my friends. You did that by lying to me."

"You fucking animal!" Mark had his fists clenched, his face set in a scowl, but Scott could see the tears threatening to fall from his eyes.

The man smiled at him. "Yes, actually, I am an animal. But because I don't act like a rabid one, I've decided to give you a chance to survive the sadistic murder of my only daughter." He moved from Mark to George and finally to Cullie as he spoke. "So here's the deal, gentlemen; we're going to blindfold you and take you out into the woods. Once we're where we want you, we're going to take off your blindfolds and give you a map. That map will show you a ten-mile long course. Once you are on your way, you'll have one hour to get a head start, and then we are going to start hunting you." His lips pressed into a thin, angry smile. "And if we catch you, we kill you. It's that simple."

"Wait a minute." Eric spoke up, and shocked damned near everyone. "Wait one minute. That's hardly what I'd call a fair fight, even with the head start."

"True enough." The big man looked Eric over and shrugged. "But it's better than just ripping their throats out."

"Give them a fighting chance at least."

"Why? Have you ever given a deer a fighting chance?"

"Hell yeah. Normally I'm too drunk to shoot and smart enough to know it."

The leader looked at him for a moment and then laughed. "I like you. Fine. They can each have one knife."

"Still not very fair, you'll all have teeth and claws."

"They'll have teeth, Captain. They may not be as sharp as ours, but they'll have teeth. And as for claws, that's why I'm allowing them each a hunting knife."

"What about my kids?" Mark was sweating, but his eyes looked less panicked.

"What about them? You fulfilled your part of the agreement. They're safe and they'll remain that way, regardless of what happens in the woods."

"How can I be sure?"

"You can't. I'm not going to call and let you hear their voices. You'll just have to accept that. In the meantime, I hope you brought good coats. It's supposed to snow tonight."

Eric looked like he wanted to say something; he was even opening and closing his mouth.

"Was there something else you wanted to ask, Captain?"

"I want to go with them."

"Excuse me?" The man stared at Eric for several heartbeats. "Why would you want to go with them?"

"Because they're my friends and the odds are stacked against them."

"The odds were stacked against my daughter, too."

"I know the risks…"

"Then think about your wife and your children! Don't be a fool! If you go out with them, you'll be as hunted as your friends. There will be no quarter given. Do you understand me?"

That shut Eric up, which was good, because if the man who'd set everything up didn't stop him, Scott would have.

"Say goodbye to your friends, gentlemen, and wait here. Order something to eat if you'd like. My treat. One way or another, we'll be back here in a few hours." Having said those words, the leader turned to his men and all six of the strangers pressed in closer to George and Cullie and Mark.

A moment later, they were out the door and heading into the night. Eric and Scott sat down. The same woman who'd served them earlier came back and gave them menus while two older men bussed the tables all around them.

Scott resisted the urge to laugh. It was a little too surreal.

"They're gonna die, you know that, right?" It was Eric speaking, but he sounded completely wrong. His voice sounded... hollow.

Scott sat still for a moment and thought about what they had done, how they had gotten into their present situation, and nodded. Much as he wanted to, he couldn't bring himself to care. He was too busy worrying about Allison.

* * *

The three of them were shoved into the back of a police van, with benches built into the sides of the interior. Before they could do much by way of protesting, they were on their way, moving first down smooth asphalt and then after a series of turns that had them feeling rather seasick, they could feel the bounce and jostle that marked their change over from paved road to dirt trail.

None of them wanted to talk about it, so they sat in silence for most of the trip.

It was George who broke the silence. "I'm sorry about Donna."

Mark nodded and then looked at the steel plates of the floorboards.

Cullie started crying. George thought about trying to comfort him, but couldn't bring himself to do it. As much as he loved the men with him like they were brothers, he wouldn't have been in the current situation if they'd listened to him.

He closed his eyes and remembered the damned night that he'd tried so hard to forget.

They'd all been wearing their street clothes, having traded out of their hunting gear when they left the campsite. It'd been a good time, even if only two of them had caught anything. Besides, Scott promised to send him a leg from the deer, and that was more than enough venison to keep him happy for a while.

He was thinking about the meat and how he'd roast it, what he'd use to marinate it, when they hit the wolf. She'd come out of nowhere, and he could remember the way the wheels lifted and dropped, lifted and dropped on the right hand side of the car even now.

He didn't want to remember the rest. He didn't want to think about the creature shuddering in the middle of the road in a thick smear of blood, or the way it snapped and whined as it lay dying. George wasn't really much of a hunter. In all the years they'd been doing their annual trips, he'd never bagged a deer. He just couldn't bring himself to pull the trigger at the right moment.

And had Cullie gotten pissed when he tried to call the authorities? Oh, hell yes! Cullie'd thrown an absolute fit, because he was the one driving and the smell of beer was still strong enough to be an issue.

With his eyes closed against the flood of memories, George shook his head and grimaced, angry with himself now. Yes, he had told them to stop, had tried to speak reasonably, but in the long run, the asshole who'd taken Cheryl and beaten him down was absolutely right. He'd let Cullie and Mark do their thing, even knowing that it was wrong, because he always let them win the arguments. It was easier than trying to keep his cool.

And deep inside, down where he tried to hide the worst memories, he could remember the sounds that came from behind him as he chain-smoked a dozen cigarettes. If forced to admit the truth, yes, he heard the sounds of a woman screaming. No animal he'd ever encountered could have imitated that sound, and sure as shit, none of them could have begged for mercy.

So yes, he knew inside that he was at least partly to blame for the situation. He'd been afraid of cutting loose, of letting his temper get the best of him. He'd spent years in therapy for his anger management issues and it was hard to break that sort of training.

Still, he wouldn't have given Cullie comfort in a million years.

* * *

The van finally came to a halt, and all of them leaned forward to counter the sudden change in speed. For a few moments longer, there was silence, but before any of them could grow bored with it, the doors were opened. Four men stood outside and waited for them to climb out.

Eventually, they did, but none of them were in much of a hurry.

The largest of the men, the one who was the obvious leader, stepped toward them and handed them each a hunting knife. The sheaths were well worn and tended to, obviously not new.

"It's a last minute thing, gentlemen. Take them, use them."

Cullie had managed to stop crying, but his nose still felt damp and his eyes were hot with irritation.

He looked at the big man and swallowed hard as he took the blade.

"Why don't you let them go? Just take me. I'm the one that started it." He said the words before he could lose his courage.

The man looked at him and shook his head. "You might have started it, but you didn't finish it alone."

The words hurt, but Cullie shook his head. "Then let George go. He didn't do any of the cuttings. He tried to talk us out of it."

"I've already made my decision, Landers. George had his part to play in all of this."

Cullie nodded. The answers were exactly what he'd expected, but he at least had to try.

It was Mark that asked the next question. "What are the rules of this little game?"

"As I said before, there's a spot ten miles down through the woods. If you reach that spot before we can kill you, you're free. If we get to you first, you're dead." He made a point of looking at each of them, but Cullie felt the eyes on him for the longest span.

"John has a map. It's accurate." He nodded and the freak they'd watched change earlier handed the map to George. "There are five possible trails you can take, gentlemen, each has its own risks and advantages." He shrugged. "You can decide amongst yourselves how you want to handle all of this." The man looked at his thick left wrist and tapped his watch. "You have one hour, starting…now."

Without another word, the strangers all climbed back into the van and drove away.

Cullie watched the taillights as they faded.

"Get over here, Cullie. We need to get to work." George didn't even look at him as he spoke. He just unfolded the map and started looking it over. When Cullie got a look at it, he groaned: it was a topographer's map, clearly showing the elevation for the surrounding area. There was a small red arrow marked on one of the roads, and another red mark, shaped like a cross, almost a foot away.

They each looked at the map and studied it as carefully as they could, painfully aware of the time that was passing.

While the other two were looking at distances and topography, Cullie made up his mind. "Okay. I'm going this way. You guys do your own thing."

Mark looked at him sharply. George shook his head and got an I-knew-it look on his face.

"What the hell are you talking about, Cullie?" Mark stared hard at him.

"I mean it's better if we split up. At least one of us might make it that way. Good luck."

Before either of them could try to talk him out of it, he started moving. Cullie had been hunting with his father since he was a child, and he knew how to move through the woods. Part of his reason for separating from them was exactly the reason he claimed. The other part was simply that he knew he could move faster without them.

Neither of them tried to stop him as he left. Part of him wished they would have.

* * *

The rain started about five minutes after Cullie left. By then George and Mark were both on their way. Much as they hated to agree with Cullie, it seemed best to break up. Mark said it best. "Either they're going to kill us or they aren't. Not really a lot we can do to defend ourselves with or without each other as back up. If we split up, maybe they will too."

He wished George the best of luck and then ran, sliding down into the lower woods on the side of the road and heading for the most direct path through the forest. He knew there were risks. The path showed the least obstacles and the most direct route, but he had to hope that meant he could get more of the ten miles covered faster. He was athletic enough that he thought he could make the full distance if he concentrated and kept a steady pace.

The path that was marked on the map was fairly easy to see, right up until the time the rain started coming down. It wasn't exactly a torrential downpour, but it was fast and heavy enough to run into his eyes and blur everything ahead of him.

The chill seeped into his clothing, ran through the layers of fabric in no time and then into his skin. Mark did his best to ignore the sensations as he started to run, breathing in through his nose and out through his mouth, just like Coach Walker had taught him back when he was a runner.

In a very short time he'd developed a good rhythm and a better pace. All he had to do now was make sure he didn't fall and break his fool neck as he moved through the woods. Even with a path, there were a lot of obstacles.

Off behind him and to the right, he heard the sound of George jogging along. Like Mark, he'd apparently decided the best way to live was to cover some serious distance. Unlike Mark, he was wearing a thinner coat that was waterproof. "Lucky bastard."

It happened sooner than he expected. In what seemed like only minutes, he heard the howl of the things in hot pursuit. When Mark looked back he realized the road was long gone from his view, hidden by the trees and the shape of the land, but he knew where the howls came from.

They were long and low and mournful, the sounds he'd heard far more often in movies than he ever had in real life, and they froze him in his tracks.

It was beginning now and he had no point of reference, no idea how far he'd run. He could only pray it was far enough.

* * *

His name was Roland Weilland, and he was a werewolf. Roland had led the local pack for a long time, both in light of his command abilities and because he was still the fastest and meanest of them.

He folded his clothes neatly, placing them inside the police wagon. When he was completely stripped, he placed his books on the clothes to weigh them down. The air was just above freezing and getting colder by the second as the storm moved deeper into the area, but he barely noticed it as he stood and looked down at the woods below.

John was looking at him, his face set in lines of anger. John still wasn't thrilled with the decision to make this a hunt instead of merely killing the humans that had done in his wife. He didn't understand the reasons for it, and in all fairness, Roland hadn't shared them.

He wanted a hunt because he could feel his younger charges growing restless. They had everything they needed, including secrecy, and several of the men folk had started taking up new hobbies to stop themselves from going mad with boredom.

Settling down had seemed like a good idea at the time, but now he wasn't so sure. Maybe they weren't meant to sit still and get jobs; it was the human way, not the way of werewolves. But damn it, it had made sense. It was harder to hide yourself when the world around you kept changing.

He let the beast free and reveled in the sudden pain of transformation. His form didn't grow slowly, but in a sudden explosion of cellular activity. Bones shifted and muscles stretched to accommodate a new position; his teeth swelled inside a growing mouth and his nails thickened even as his hands took on a new shape.

When he yelled to release the pain, his voice had changed and the sound quickly became a roar. Dead skin fell away from his body as he shrugged and his fur pushed out from beneath. In a matter of seconds, Roland and his charges were all in their truest form, breathing in the cold night air and shaking away the freezing precipitation that pelted their hides.

They did not need words to understand him. Their eyes could see the expressions he made, the simply gestures he used were easily recognized. "We hunt," he said. "Pick your prey."

John did exactly as he expected, and chased after the lingering scent of the human called Cullie Landers. He chose the trail that Mark Loman had taken. John wanted the man who had started the desecration of his wife. Roland wanted the man who had ensured her complete death by hacking through his daughter's neck until her head fell away.

The rest left to go after George Heatherly.

As he moved, he called out for the hunt to begin. The others responded, their voices mingling with his and echoing off the trees around them.

He followed the scent of fear Mark Loman had left behind, taking his time. The man was running, and would probably get careless. More importantly, the man was scared.

He had every reason to be afraid. Roland intended to kill him, and to date no one had ever escaped from the leader of the group when he went on a hunt.

* * *

Eric Fulford stood up and walked toward the restrooms, his eyes shifting constantly to see who was near him and whether or not he could make a break for the door.

He was not being hunted, true enough, but he also didn't know if he trusted the man who'd said they would be safe. Want to know what will make a soldier paranoid? When every single person left in the diner looks at him as if he were potentially a meal.

He wasn't sure, but he thought it was very possible that every single person left in the place was a werewolf.

Instead of going for the bathroom doors, Eric made a sharp right turn and pushed through the front exit of the building. No one came after him, despite his fear.

The air had grown a lot colder and the road outside was starting to turn white under a layer of ice. For a moment he thought about running for his car and driving off to find his family, but one look around stopped him. The biggest problem was simply that he had no idea where his family was being kept.

The door opened a moment later and Scott coughed into his hand rather than trying to touch him.

"You all right, Eric?"

"No." He shrugged. "How can I be all right? I want my family back." He looked back at Scott and saw the same desire in his friend's eyes.

"Listen, I figure if that guy wanted us dead, we'd be in the middle of the woods right now." He paused a moment and they both heard the sound of distant howls carried by the wind. They couldn't have proved a damned thing, but Eric knew they were both thinking the hunt might have just begun. "I want to help them too, Eric. But you have Sarah and the kids to think about and I have Allison."

"I've been thinking a lot about that." Eric nodded and looked back at his friend. "I'll accept his reasons for all of this, but if he did anything at all to Sarah or the kids, I swear I'll kill every last one of them."

Scott shook his head. "I don't think they did anything to them except maybe settle them down somewhere and keep them locked up."

"Why do you think that?"

"Because he seems like a fair enough guy. I think maybe he doesn't even like what he's done so far, but you know what? I think if I was in his shoes, I might have just gone and killed everyone instead of checking first."

Eric looked hard at Scott, surprised by the comment. "Really?"

"Seriously. What would you do if someone had killed Sarah like that?"

He nodded.

"I hope you're right."

"All I know for sure is he sounded sincere. And I think if he wanted everyone dead, he could have saved himself a lot of trouble. He gave them an out. Maybe not much of one, but he gave them something."

"What I don't get is he said his daughter went back to her human form when she... when they killed her. So why not report it to the police?"

Scott shivered a bit and coughed a plume of steam into the air before he answered. "Too many questions."

"Like what?"

"I don't mean official questions. No matter what shape she took, it would have been easy enough for him to find the evidence. He could have said he was an eyewitness and I bet most of the people in this county would take one look at his record on the highway patrol and side with him in a court. But if they're trying to hide what they are, and George and the others said they hit a wolf and we're so sorry and all of that crap, it would have made somebody look twice, maybe a reporter from a piece of crap like the Enquirer or maybe someone from the local news. Whatever the case, it might have started rumors."

"No one would believe them."

"Maybe not, but I don't think I'd take chances like that if I was a werewolf, or whatever."

"Given this a lot of thought, have you?" He looked at Scott and gave a small grin.

"Not really a lot else to do right now."

"You think they have a chance in hell, Scott?"

"Yeah, well, I've been giving that a lot of thought too, and I don't really know if I care anymore."

"You can't be serious."

"Dead serious, dude." Scott looked at him hard, and the innocent expression he was used to seeing was completely erased, covered over with anger. "I don't care if they started on a wolf or not, they killed a pregnant woman and then they hid that fact away. That makes them about as low as anyone can get in my book, Eric."

"What about George?"

"What about him? He should have stopped it from happening and he didn't. I don't care if they were both bigger and meaner than him, Eric, and you know he could have at least taken out Cullie. He should have stopped them and instead he went where he didn't have to watch."

Eric nodded. Much as he felt like he was betraying his friends, he also understood exactly how Scott was feeling.

"Okay, so even with the risk of being marked as a werewolf, he could have reported the murder."

"Let's forget the fact he was stuck for two days in the woods while he healed himself. Let's forget all about that and pretend he was just a witness. Have you noticed what happens to a lot of the murderers out there, Eric?"

"A lot of them get the chair, especially for murdering and torturing a pregnant girl."

"A lot of them get to sit on death row for fifteen or twenty years and their families get to reflect on why the asshole who murdered their loved one isn't dead yet."

"But they get killed eventually."

"And a lot of them paint pictures, and write books and get released from death row because the laws were changed." Scott shrugged.

"I thought you were opposed to the death penalty anyway."

"I am. Mostly. If someone's innocent, they shouldn't fry. If a society convicts and then kills an innocent man, then the society is no better than the person who committed the crime in the first place. But this is different."

"How is it different?"

"They all confessed. They tortured a pregnant woman to death."

"You sure you aren't letting Allison's pregnancy color your views?"

"I don't really care if I am. All I have to do is think of her in the same boat and I know I'd want all three of them dead myself. Especially if I watched them do it."

"So you think he just doesn't like the chances of all three of them going to death row?"

"He's not after justice, Eric. He's after revenge. I can't blame him. I wish I could, but I can't."

Eric sighed and headed for the door. "Neither can I, damn it."

Not a person inside had left their seats, but the tension he'd felt earlier seemed to have gone away. If the people were waiting for him to make a break for it, he guessed they felt a little more comfortable about his staying where he belonged now.

Part of him still wanted to find his wife and kids, but he decided he could wait it out for now. In the long run, he didn't really have much choice in the matter anyway.

All he could do was wait, and wonder whether or not he should pray for the safety of his friends.

* * *

Cullie was panting like a dog when the howls started up. He was taking a much-needed breather and trying not to freeze his balls off when the sound hit him and sent feverish chills running down his back.

"I get out of this alive, I swear I'll kill George." It was a hollow threat, but it made him feel better. George was always trying to do what he thought was right, like narcing them all out at the diner, which had led Cullie to his current predicament.

Well, okay, and killing the wolf when it turned into a pregnant girl.

He started moving again, and as he did, he replayed the most powerful memory of his life. It had been cold that night and the wolf had steamed as the blood flowed from multiple lacerations. The animal was beyond being helped, but she had a beautiful pelt, at least the parts that weren't soaked in blood. For the first time ever, he couldn't resist the temptation.

As soon as they were out of the car and assessing the damage — the good news was that the dent on the front end was minor — George had pulled out his cell phone and started looking to see if he had good enough reception. Cullie'd snatched the phone out of his hands before he could do more than blink, and started on the browbeating.

The good thing about George was he was wishy-washy. Five minutes was all it took in most cases to convince him to change his tune, and with Mark helping it hadn't even taken that long.

But he'd still wussed out and refused to take part in the fun.

There was a part of Cullie that had always wanted to be in a situation that allowed him to try torture. He was just drunk enough that night and as an added bonus, so was Mark. Okay, so he had to give Mark the head, but it didn't matter.

Cullie took his time making the right cuts, not because he wasn't in a hurry, but because the sensations he got as he started skinning the wolf alive were downright erotic. He'd never had a problem with getting laid, but this? Cutting the wolf made sex seem like a pale imitation.

Was it sick? Yes, but he didn't care. He liked it.

He kept liking it, too, up until the moment the wounded animal became a woman. He was watching when it happened, amazed by the sudden transformation. One second he was peeling the fur from the broken right forepaw of a bloodied, oversized dog and the next his hands were gripping the soft, almost velvety flesh of a girl in her prime.

Mark had staggered back, shocked by the change. Cullie would have probably backed off, too, but at that moment he experienced the most shattering orgasm of his entire life. While his friend was screaming in shock it covered Cullie's own yelp of pleasure.

Either the girl was beyond the ability to speak, or he didn't want to remember her words. Either way, he sped up the cutting, not giving himself a chance to change his mind. There was no way the girl would live through what they had done and no way he wanted to stop now that he'd started. Without a second thought, he ran the skinning knife down her belly all the way to the edge of her sex and before Mark had even begun recovering from the shock, he gave a savage pull. Flesh peeled away just as easily on a human as it did on a deer. The difference was the deer would have been dead already and he would have missed the sounds of the girl screaming in pain.

The best part, the thing he would never admit to anyone, was how pleasantly surprised he was to realize she was still alive, even after he'd finished skinning her. Even thinking back on it, even in his current situation, he felt himself get aroused.

The thoughts were pushed out of his head when he heard the sound of a branch snapping in the distance. It wasn't close by, but it was definitely closer than he wanted to think about.

Cullie cursed under his breath and started moving faster, his eyes keeping careful track of the land in front of him.

After the incident was finished, Cullie thought long and hard about whether or not he'd ever be able to kill another person and enjoy it the same way. He thought he would, and he'd been preparing for that possibility. Medical books can show you the most amazing things, like which clusters of nerves are most vulnerable to blunt force, and which tendons would cause crippling. He didn't know if he'd ever get a chance to use his new skills, but he surely did hope so.

He also didn't know if the same spots would be vulnerable on the monster he thought was tracking him, but he prayed so with all of his heart.

The rain started coming down even harder, the cold drops hitting like pebbles now instead of just splashing against his skin. It didn't take much to let him see that the centers of the drops were turning into ice.

If he was lucky, really, lucky, the rain would wash away his scent and make it harder for the things in the woods to find him. He wasn't counting on it, but he could hope.

His left foot slipped in the slush that was falling and Cullie took a spill into the ravine to his right. He tried to catch his balance and failed, rolling down in an uneven bounce that seemed exactly rough enough to keep him from grabbing hold of anything to slow his descent. Despite the thick layer of dead plants that coated the ground, rocks and branches still beat into him to the point where he finally gave up and pulled himself into a rough fetal position with his hands covering his face to avoid any more grievous injury.

He came to a halt in cold, running water and sputtered as he felt the runoff cover his face. He rose as quickly as he could, shivering and spitting the water from his mouth along the way.

"Fuck me! What the hell kind of shit is this?" All of his thoughts of surviving the night evaporated in an instant, replaced by the sudden realization that he was in the middle of nowhere and would be lucky if anyone even realized he was missing.

Up above, where he'd been standing a moment ago, he saw movement through the surrounding trees. Cullie did his best impersonation of a statue, forcing his muscles to stay still despite the chill.

His eyes had long since adjusted to the darkness as best they could and he saw the beast as it moved into view. In the center of the diner he'd been too stunned to really see much of anything, but watching as it moved from a distance he could see the play of muscles moving under fur, the impossibility of its shape and the unsettling grace with which it moved.

He could also see with perfect clarity when it suddenly turned its head and looked down the hill for him.

"Oh, God, no."

The teeth of the black furred beast stood out remarkably well as it grinned and looked him in the eyes.

Cullie turned and ran, his feet lifting and splashing down into the cold stream of run off, as he did his best to escape. What in God's name had he been thinking when he was toying with actually trying to hurt that thing?

"Ohgodohgodohgodohpleasegod."

The monster dropped to all fours and bounded toward the stream, its forepaws almost looked like hands, but its hind paws were designed for pushing and clawing.

The thing leaped and cleared the last twenty feet, splashing down five yards in front of him.

"I swear I didn't know! I thought it was just a dog! I know I was wrong, but I didn't know any better!"

Hot tears spilled from his eyes, washed across his face in thin lines of warmth as the creature came closer. When it was in front of him, it rose on its hind legs and studied him with deep green eyes that showed no sign of mercy.

Cullie was still crying when he pulled the knife from its sheath. "Fine. Come on then, you fucking *pussy!*"

The werewolf lunged, growling deep in its chest, and he swung the hunting knife hard and low, trying to cut through its defenses. The blade glazed the long torso of the creature: its claws ripped into his jacket, tearing through the heavy padding and taking close to a yard of material with them.

Barely believing his luck, Cullie swung again and this time felt the blade push through the thick fur and slice deep into the monster's muscles. The beast grunted and twisted, taking the knife from his grip as it fell back. Blood drooled from the wound, and the black furred nightmare carefully gripped the handle in a hand never designed to carry a weapon of that size. It looked like something from a kid's play set in that massive paw.

Barely even letting himself think, Cullie charged and slammed his shoulder into the creature's side, staggering it. The werewolf rolled onto its back and snarled as it hauled the hunting knife's eight-inch blade from its ribcage.

He didn't know if the wound was fatal or not, he just knew he couldn't take any chances. Cullie swung his fist hard and slammed it into the creature's armpit, pounding at the spot where a nerve cluster would be on a human body. The creature let out another yowl as it dropped the hunting knife, and Cullie dove for the blade.

The weapon fell into the cold waters and he reached for it, his hand scrabbling, touching first the sharpened blade — that sliced into his ring finger and his middle finger — and then grasping the hilt again.

At exactly the same time he wrapped his hand around the weapon's grip, the teeth of the monster sank into his foot and his calf, pushing through clothing like it was air and then driving together, cutting past flesh and meat and shoe with remarkable speed. Cullie was dropping the blade and screaming around the same time the werewolf ripped his Achilles tendon away from his body.

Frigid water mingled with hot blood as Cullie flopped into the stream, clutching at his ruined leg with both hands.

The werewolf shook off his hide, reversing the transformation until the man he knew as John was looking at him, panting, bleeding from his chest, and grinning around a mouthful of Cullie's leg. He spat the piece of meat away and swayed, naked in the cold night air.

"I thought a big hunter like you would be a challenge, Landers." His form was human again, but the words were still a growl. "I thought you'd do more than scratch me."

Cullie shivered, his hands the only part of him that felt warm as blood flowed from his leg. "Just go ahead and kill me! Get it done!"

"No. Not yet. I'm going to watch you die slowly for a while, and then when I'm sick of looking at you, I'll finish the job."

Cullie reached into the waters a second time, wincing at the pain in his entire leg, and grabbed the hunting knife. The naked man stepped closer, smiling.

"You gonna' try to kill me, Landers? I'm right here."

"F-fuck you!"

He squatted, not five feet out of Cullie's reach and shook his head. "I'm right here, big boy." His voice was a calculated taunt, and Cullie knew it, but he still wanted to live and he wanted the man dead almost as much. "Prove to me that you're really a man. Prove to me that you can do something other than torture a woman to death." John shrugged. "Do that, and maybe I'll let you live."

Cullie thought hard about that, and even as he thought, he repositioned himself in the cold water. He didn't stand, but he put most of his weight on his good leg, trying to decide if he could reach the man in front of him and hit him with the blade before John could change again.

"That's right, Landers... What have you got to lose? You might be able to get me, might cut my throat before I can do anything about it. You know you want to. You know if you wait too long, the blood loss will do you in, so come on…Come and get me."

Cullie pushed off with his good leg, and much as it hurt, he used his wounded limb to add a touch of support before he was airborne. John started moving at almost the exact same second. The distance between them grew smaller until, at last, Cullie brought the knife down, his aim was flawless and the blade plunged toward his enemy's throat. John was faster than he looked. The weathered hands caught Cullie's wrist and twisted hard before the knife could finish its descent. Cullie let out a yelp of frustration and then he let out a squeal of pain as his body was thrown down and he hit the rough stones John had been crouching over.

The impact was much greater than Cullie'd expected. His front tooth splintered as it hit the rock and he let out a grunt of pain as his nose and lips were dragged across the stone. He coughed hard and tried to roll over, but before he could, John was on him. The man pulled hard at his good foot and yanked his shoe away. A second later the maniac pulled what was left of his other shoe from his other foot and Cullie almost blacked out from the exquisite pain. While he was still trying to recover from that, John reached out and pulled at his belt until it came loose. Then his pants and his underwear were next.

Cullie bucked and panicked, convinced that the man was going to rape him. He imagined the pain and humiliation and screamed, pushing with good leg and bad alike to get away from the mad man standing naked above him in the cold waters. John's bare foot slammed into the small of his back and knocked him back down, half drowning him before the man moved away from him.

"You stink, Landers. You smell as bad as you look."

"You get away from me you sick fuck!" Cullie's voice broke and he started pushing up from the water again, desperate to get away from the madman he knew was going to sodomize him.

"Not a chance." John reached out and grabbed the back of his jacket, pulling hard. Cullie was lifted half out of the water before the ruined material let out a rude noise and fell away from him, dropping him once more into the rapidly swelling run off.

"Oh God! Please!" He was crying again, as John came closer, the knife that Cullie'd been ready to use on him now held casually in his left hand.

Cullie looked over his shoulder in stark terror, ready to do anything this man wanted him to in order to avoid what he knew was coming.

The smile had left John's face, and the rain that fell was beginning to stick in his hair, to freeze there. He dropped down on his knees behind Cullie and grabbed his good leg, clenching his fingers and digging deep into flesh. Cullie tried to kick with his other leg, but it lacked the strength to stop his attacker.

Without another word, John brought the knife around and in two deft strokes had cut a circle around Cullie's ankle. Cullie shrieked again and tried to pull away with the strength of his arms, but the blade had done to his good leg what the monster's teeth had already accomplished on the other side. He lacked the power to escape.

John leaned back for a second; his face a little pale, and shook his head. "I know what you're thinking. You think I want to fuck you. You're wrong."

Despite his situation, the panic level lowered itself a bit, and Cullie crawled forward a few paces, solely because John let him.

"If you were the only woman left on the planet and looked like a Playboy Bunny, I still wouldn't want you that way." John stood again and came closer, his flesh shivering in the cold.

"You just relax yourself, Cullie Landers. This is gonna' hurt." He moved forward again and this time when he grabbed for a limb, it was Cullie's left arm. Cullie fought, he swung with his free arm and kicked as best he could with both of his legs. John pinned his left hand in the water and ignored the blows, barely even flinching when he was struck in the side of his face.

Then he started cutting, tearing through the tendons in Cullie's wrist with ease. "Figured you deserve what you did to my girl, Landers."

He slapped Cullie with a savage backhand that knocked the wind right the hell out of his sails and moved to grab his one unmarred limb before he could recover.

Cullie screamed all the louder as the blade cut skin and tendon again.

John sat back, panting from his efforts, and stared hard at him for a moment.

"Make you one last deal, you sick fuck. If you can get up and walk away when I'm done skinning you alive, I'll let you alone."

Cullie kept screaming until he blacked out.

* * *

George heard every sound, every scream that echoed through the woods, and he did his best to ignore them.

He knew that somewhere downstream, Cullie was dying, and he ground his teeth together, wishing he could shut out the sounds.

Cullie had fallen across the waters in the gulley by accident; George found them deliberately, hoping that the frigid stream would mask his scent. He'd seen at least a dozen movies where it worked for prisoners, but never had a reason to test whether or not it really had any affect, at least not until now.

At a guess, he'd made it around half way to where he needed to be. The rain was coming down too hard for him to even consider looking at the map. All he knew was that they'd used a cross to mark whatever the final destination was supposed to be.

He didn't allow himself to think or strategize; he refused himself the luxury of panic. He simply ran, doing his best to forget everything that had happened back in the woods when he'd let them do what they did to the girl.

Instead he focused his attention on the simple task of moving one foot in front of the other as the cold sapped his energy and the freezing rain fell on his balding head and clothes. It was all he could do if he wanted to survive, and he wanted that desperately.

What had started as rain and moved into freezing rain continued to change, falling slower now, as a mix of hard ice pellets and snowflakes. He kept sloshing through the water, breathing hard and doing his best not to fall on his face in the growing current.

Cheryl would hate him, of course. Even if he lived through all of this, he knew he couldn't keep her in his life. There was no doubt in his mind that one or more of the monsters would have told her why this was all happening. The one in charge struck him as exactly the sort that would enjoy the theatrics of telling her the gory details.

"No one to blame but yourself, George. Just you remember that." He spoke to himself, a habit he'd picked up a long time ago, when he decided it was time to get help for his anger issues.

At age fourteen, he started letting himself go, and got into a lot of trouble at school. It was seldom a week went by without him getting into it with someone. By sixteen, he wasn't just over-reacting to situations anymore; he was starting a lot of the fights. By his second semester in college, he decided it was time to do something about his rage. He hadn't just hurt a kid he decided to fight with – he'd hospitalized him.

When the fight was done he turned himself in to the authorities and faced the consequences of his actions, not because he felt he was in the wrong exactly but because he was afraid of what he might do the next time he lost his temper.

George caught his foot on a loose stone and fell into the water, landing on his ass. Any hope he'd had of keeping his privates warm was immediately destroyed, and the cold that had been gnawing at his flesh sank teeth deep into his bones as he rose from his fallen position.

He thought about heading for the shore, but still liked his chances better down in the water. That decision didn't make moving in sodden clothes any easier and neither did the chill that refused to leave him.

He'd gone another hundred or so yards when he was first aware of the lights up ahead. Red and blue strobes started splashing the trees and the ravine alike and George stopped for a second, completely shocked by the sudden light.

After a moment he realized there was a bridge up ahead, nothing fancy, but still an unexpected surprise. It didn't take him long to realize there was a road running through the area, but he couldn't remember seeing it on the map of the area and he wasn't about to check at the moment.

The bridge looked like an old concrete piece from the depression era, complete with rusted guardrails, one of which had been ruined. A black shape that strongly resembled the silhouette of a small car's front end could be seen dangling over the side, along with the mangled railing. It was from behind that particular obstacle that the lights originated.

He was tempted, so damned tempted, to go up and see if he could ask the cop for help, but he knew there was no way in hell the police in the area would believe there were monsters after him and there was Cheryl to consider.

When he stumbled and fell into the water the second time, he decided he'd ask for help anyway. Shivering violently, he scrabbled up the side of the ravine's incline, clutching at whatever he could to keep from sliding back down. By the time he'd reached the side of the road he'd managed to drive several thorns into his hands and knees, but he didn't dare stop.

The road was covered in a thickening layer of ice and George understood immediately what had happened. There had been a one-car accident and either by use of cell phone or by blind luck, the police had shown up.

His eyes ached with every pulse of the police car's lights, and he squinted against the glare as he moved toward the vehicles and the three people standing outside of them. One was a woman dressed in a thin coat and a formal dress. She was shivering in the cold as one of the police officers took down her information. She might have been in the car, but judging by how much of her vehicle had left the road and was now dangling over the side of the bridge, it was probably wisest to freeze instead of risking a seventy-foot drop to the bottom of the ravine.

There were two cops, both far better dressed for the weather, and both busy with the task at hand. George could have wept at the sight of them.

"Hey… " His voice sounded too weak for them to hear so he yelled. "Hey! Can I get some help?" He called out as he moved closer and saw all three people turn to face him. The lights kept their faces hidden in shadows, but he imagined they were surprised to see him.

"Where the hell did you come from?" That came from the larger of the two policemen, a six-foot-tall man with a build like an armchair quarterback.

"I was down there." He pointed down to the ravine.

"What were you doing down there?" the younger officer asked. He looked like he was in better shape.

"I'm being chased, and I need to get away from here."

"Well, we're in the middle of an accident investigation, but if you want to wait a few minutes we'll see what we can do." The older cop stepped forward enough to let George catch a glimpse of a round face and a thin mustache as he spoke. "We're a little thin on help right now, there's been a lot of fender-benders tonight, but if you can be patient, we'll find out what's going on." He sounded friendly enough, but George could tell he was less worried about what might be after him than he was about making sure George wasn't actually just a mental case traipsing through the woods. George really couldn't blame him for that, but his sense of urgency hadn't changed.

Still, he had to try to explain without sounding like he was, in fact, a mental patient and that was going to be tricky. He couldn't just say a pack of werewolves wanted him dead, after all. Even thinking about the beast he'd seen in the diner was enough to make him want to wet himself. Maybe bears would work as an explanation.

"I'm pretty sure there were bears down there, and they seemed sort of ticked off."

"Bears? This time of year?" That was the younger cop again. He shook his head and frowned. "They should all be hibernating. What? Did you go looking in a cave and find them?"

"All I know is whatever they are, they're big and hairy and growl."

He could see the look of disbelief on the man's face and he also got to witness that same expression change as he looked behind George and looked up.

George turned just in time to see the monsters coming. All the time he'd thought he was safe had been a mistake. The werewolves came over the side of the bridge one after the other, easily leaping over the railing and landing in the shadows of the road.

There were four of the things all told, massive shadows one second and equally large nightmares the next. Every time the lights from the cruiser hit them their eyes flared with the reflected glow and their bared teeth gleamed in red or blue.

"Mister, those aren't bears." The young cop was staring and had reached for his weapon.

The older cop already had his drawn. "Move out of the way!"

He didn't have to tell George twice. He bolted for the squad car and prayed he'd have no trouble getting there.

The werewolves moved forward, two of them on their hind legs, and two on all fours. They didn't move fast, but crept at a casual pace, as if deciding what, exactly, they wanted to do about the policemen.

The younger officer finally got his weapon clear of the holster and pointed it at the closest bestial face. The werewolf looked at the business end of the service revolver and bared his teeth even wider as he let out a warning growl.

"You be a good boy and we won't have to kill you." The kid was nervous, but his hands were steady.

The werewolf stood still for a moment and then rose up to its full height. The cop kept his grip on the revolver and kept it sited on the powerful chest of the thing now standing fully a foot taller than him.

As for the woman next to her ruined car, she was staring at the animals with wide eyes and a fearful tremble running through her entire body.

The werewolf closest to the younger cop reached out its paw and placed it gently over both of the hands holding the firearm. And then it spoke in a voice that was garbled, but understandable. "I know you, Sam Farber. We want the stranger. Leave this place and we will leave you in peace."

The younger officer, Sam Farber apparently, stared hard at

the monstrous face and shook his head, refusing to believe what he had just heard. While he was doing the unreality shuffle, the werewolf plucked the weapon from his hand and moved past him.

The other cop, older and more experienced, was just as stunned. "Hey, give him back his gun." He might have been trying to speak with authority, but what came out of his mouth was a nervous whisper.

The woman was staring at the beasts as they walked, and one of them looked at her, returning the gaze. She was dwarfed by the thing, which did nothing but look at her.

It might have all gone differently if the older cop hadn't finally snapped out of his shock and taken aim at the closest monster. The furry head turned sharply and vulpine lips that had been slowly calming down peeled back from the wicked looking teeth as it snarled.

The cop pulled the trigger on his revolver again and again and George looked on as dark red blossoms of meat and viscera flew from the back of the werewolf.

The monster staggered back, pushed by the force of the bullets ripping through its chest and shoulder, crying out with a sound like locked tires sliding on rough asphalt.

Even as it fell, all of its partners started moving. The one that had been staring at the woman next to her car leaned down almost as if it planned to kiss her and then bit into her face with an audible crunching noise. If she screamed, it was hidden inside the sounds of bones breaking.

One of the beasts that had stayed on all fours, bolted forward, bounding over its fallen brethren, and hit the older cop in the chest with both front claws. The palms of the beast's hands pushed hard and the talons at the end of each finger sank in deeply, past the coat and the uniform below and into skin and meat. Even as the officer fell back, the thick nails of the creature pulled away and took a few pounds of flesh.

The werewolf that had taken away the younger cop's revolver turned fast and sank its teeth into the young man's shoulder and neck, savagely shaking back and forth as it worried the new wound. The rookie screamed, a lot.

George took one quick look at the squad car and opened the driver's side door. The engine was running, the keys were in place and the werewolves were busy. Three seconds later, he was inside and revving the engine.

The wounded werewolf stood back up and let loose a growl that shook its entire body. The one on the older policeman stepped forward and dropped down on top of the bloodied man and began tearing into him, shredding clothing and flesh with powerful hands before sinking teeth deep into the wound and ripping away at what looked like part of a heart and a lung. The officer's chest had bloomed like a bizarre flower that steamed in the cold night air.

The young cop was still screaming, bucking and trying to get away from the snarling giant that tore the wound in his shoulder into a lethal hole.

The woman was dead; her body sliding down as the werewolf pulled away from her, chewing at whatever prize it had pulled from her face.

George shifted into drive then hit the gas. The squad car jumped forward, slamming into the furry shape that loomed over the older cop and then driving over the dead man and the snarling nightmare alike. The tires spun against the cold, icy road and caught extra traction as they ran over both forms.

He wasn't thinking at all, really, just doing his best to get away from the madness. The gun-wounded werewolf didn't seem to see it that way. It lifted its good arm and brought it down with a hammer blow that caved in the front of the squad car's hood and rocked the vehicle on its shock absorbers. The car decided at that moment that stalling would be a good idea.

George couldn't have agreed less.

The beast roared again and rather than climbing on top of the car, stepped around to the side to get at George. It reached for the window and plowed through the glass with surprisingly little effort. Fragments of the broken window exploded into the interior and showered George, who was doing his very best to get out through the passenger's side door at the same time.

He had just managed to open the door when the thing's claws hooked into his foot and ankle. George yelped and kicked, trying to get free, trying to stop the pain that went running from his lower leg, when the door near his head was ripped completely away from the hinges.

There were snarling faces above him and below and George decided enough was enough. He cocked back his mauled foot and then drove the heel of his boot into the snout that was snapping at him. Something in the monster's nose crunched and the beast pulled back, shaking its head violently from side to side.

The one near his head was reaching in to grab him and George returned the favor; even as the long, deadly fingers of the werewolf were grabbing at his clothes, the beast got close enough for him to drive his thumb into the left eye of the thing.

It tried to pull back, but George used his other hand to grab into the thick ruff of fur near its neck and forced his thumb deeper into the soft tissue, snarling himself.

He was as good as dead, so he decided to at least leave them knowing they'd been in a fight.

As the werewolf jumped back, George followed; his face in that moment was almost as feral as the ones on the wild things near him. The werewolf snarled and came for him, one eye closed against the furious tearing and, yes, the blood that was flowing from it. George drove his fist into its throat as hard as he could and was delighted to hear it let out a choking cough. He liked the effect so much, he did it again while the giant thing was hacking and trying to catch a decent breath.

The werewolf backed off, clutching at its throat and half growling, half whining. George moved forward again, determined to push his advantage over the unnatural monstrosity.

The weight that hit him from behind slammed him into the road with enough force to knock the wind out of him and to crack a couple of ribs. George grunted and tried to breathe again as the pressure increased.

"Get the fuck offa me!"

The one he'd struck in the throat fell to all fours in front of him and vomited a stream of blood. It looked at him with both eyes, one still red and swollen looking, and then loped forward until it was staring him in the face.

All the anger left his body even as he managed to draw in a decent breath. Out with the bad air, in with the fear. He'd hurt it, but the snarling thing staring into his eyes was far from out of the fight and another one was sitting on top of him, pinning him in place as it huffed warm breaths on the back of his neck.

As he lay there, waiting for the creature to kill him, the others came closer. Apparently they had finished their murderous appetizers and were now ready for the main course.

* * *

Mark Loman panted heavily in the deepening cold. The run wasn't that long, only ten miles, but still he was exhausted and the arctic air was scouring his lungs with every gulp of oxygen he took in.

Not surprisingly he reflected back on the night he helped murder an innocent woman as he kept moving.

He'd thought Cullie was joking at first, and had said he'd take the head. It seemed like a good joke right up until the time Cullie started cutting.

He should have been disgusted. He should have knocked his friend on his ass and been done with it, but once the animal's cries started, he found himself fascinated.

Mark had been a hunter since he was very young and he'd never once felt any regrets for his actions or pity for the creatures he killed. He'd been raised to believe that man was the ruler of the world by God's decree; everything else was here for man's use. His family had owned only a few pets, and in all cases they were servants as well. Hunting dogs. He'd never gotten close to any of the animals because his father had always believed that the dogs were tools, not toys.

So, no, there had never been any guilt, but he'd also always made it a point to make sure he had a clean kill. The animals were here for man to use, but not for man to misuse. None of God's creatures were meant to suffer if it could be helped.

Until that night. Watching Cullie cut and abuse the animal hadn't been as exciting as it had been fascinating. Okay, he was a little freaked out when he realized his friend was, well, getting into the torture a bit much, but Cullie had always been weird. That didn't really mean much as long as he kept it to himself. He'd even decided to talk to Cullie about it later.

When George started puking his sad guts out, Mark turned to make sure he was all right. He only saw the transformation out of the corner of his eye, but seeing the mangled, wretched animal turn into a wounded woman threw him for a loop. Okay, to be honest, he'd freaked out. It was one thing to torture a dying animal, but something else entirely to hurt another human being. He screamed, and he staggered back, horrified by what he saw. He was just as horrified when he saw Cullie grab the — and here his mind tried to make the memory a lie and show him a wolf being maimed beyond all repair: he did not allow himself that luxury — woman's bleeding arms and rip back with all of his strength. For one brief second it looked like Cullie was peeling away a shirt, and then the blood came, spilling from the bared muscles and tendons, the lacerated underlying layer of tissue that separated skin and the body beneath.

The woman (*wolf*, his mind insisted) had let loose a scream that still haunted him on nights when he went to bed sober. She'd sat up, for the love of God, and the sounds she made sent fever chills through Mark's entire body. Her face was unmarred, and her wide blue eyes stood as far open as they could get as her mouth strained against the sounds escaping her.

For one heartbeat his entire world became terrifyingly clear. He heard the poor girl screaming, and under that he heard the sounds of Cullie grunting and whining in pleasure. In the distance, almost sublimated by those overwhelming noises, he heard George crying, sobbing into his own hands and then getting ill again.

He saw Cullie's hands holding that flesh shirt, saw his friend keep pulling, separating the skin garment from the body

215

it belonged to, and saw the way his friend trembled. He looked into the girl's eyes, and all but felt the pain coming from her in waves.

Worst of all, he knew that Cullie meant to keep cutting and skinning until the girl died. He knew the kid he'd all but grown up with meant to make her suffer for as long as he could.

He moved forward and knocked Cullie aside even as he was reaching for his own hunting knife. He drove the blade in with all of his weight behind the strike and felt muscles part, hot blood wash his hands and finally, the sickening crunch of bones breaking from the force of the attack. Mark held his breath as he kept sawing at the open wound he'd made, using more strength than he actually knew he had to stop the scream still echoing through his mind. She kept screaming long after he'd removed her head. The sound slowly faded, but still seemed deafening even after they'd buried her body.

As for the burial itself, he barely remembered a damned thing except panicking. All he clearly recalled was digging and then George trying to get the rental car back on the road and running into a tree and finally, Cullie calling the other guys back to haul them out of the ditch.

Mark pushed the rest of it away. He was close to where he needed to be, and he wanted to concentrate.

He was pretty sure the landmark he was looking for was almost his. All he knew for sure was that it had a cross as a symbol. Maybe it was a church or maybe it was a tree, he had no idea for sure.

As he finished scrabbling up a steep slope of jagged stone he saw what he'd been questing for. It was a church; or rather it had been a church once. Now there was little to see save the burnt remains that sat under a sheath of ice from the growing storm. The wood was old and water-soaked, but even in the darkness he could make out the shape of fallen pews through the holes in the front of the building and the slightly bent cross that still perched on the roof. A narrow dirt trail stood in front of the place but it was overgrown now and obviously no longer in use.

He almost sobbed as he staggered forward, his body shaking with cold and exhaustion.

He did sob when he saw the golden mane of the werewolf. It stepped around the side of the building, looking directly at him and grinning. The thing towered over him, close to eight feet in height on its back legs, and moved closer with slow, predatory steps.

He almost pissed himself when it spoke. "She'd have lived if you hadn't cut off her head." The words were clear enough to understand, but only barely.

He looked at it for several seconds and it, in turn, waited for a response. "I have no excuse for you. I was wrong."

Instead of speaking, it merely nodded.

"Will... Are my kids going to be okay?"

It nodded again.

"Then I guess let's get this over with."

The werewolf didn't tear him apart. Instead it moved forward and struck him with a backhand that sent him sailing five feet backward.

"You've got a knife, Loman. Use it."

Mark crawled back to his hands and knees and looked at it for a moment, surprised.

The thing came closer, dropping to all fours. "I said use it."

He nodded and reached for the sheathed weapon. It waited patiently until he was up and standing, ready to defend himself, and then it charged, roaring a challenge.

Mark stepped to the side and swung the blade in a low, fast arc, hacking through fur and muscle across the creature's back. It let out an almost human yelp and spun around, glaring hatred in his direction.

Before he could even think about how lucky he'd just gotten, the creature lashed with one forepaw and cut four trenches down his face. Mark fell to his knees from the pain and the force of the blow, the knife forgotten and all the fight taken from him.

"Pick up your knife and try again." The voice was infuriating. "I wouldn't want you thinking you didn't get a fair shake out of this."

He spoke as carefully as he could through the heavy lacerations on his mouth. "You're going to kill me either way, right?"

"Oh, yes." The monstrous face nodded, the blue eyes burned with the desire to rip him apart.

Mark reached down and grabbed the knife. He didn't want to die; it was as simple as that. If he could at least incapacitate the thing, he might have a chance.

His face felt like it was on fire and the rain and snow that struck it only made matters worse, but his adrenaline levels were climbing now and the cold seemed to have left him. Mark shook the blood that threatened to spill into his eyes away and lowered himself closer to the ground, covering his most vulnerable areas as best he could.

He was a hunter, too, and he knew what the werewolf would try for. The same places he knew he would be trying for.

The werewolf moved, stalking closer. Mark faced it, his hands and knees shaking with adrenaline and exhaustion.

It was time now.

Man and wolf-man both charged, both growled as they met, and Mark ducked under the monster's body and slammed the knife he carried into the heavily muscled stomach of the creature, not trying to hack in and pull out, but instead sinking the blade in deeply and then forcing the edge to run up from just above the creature's navel all the way to the hard sternum. Thick hot fluids ran from the gaping wound and the werewolf let out a shriek of pain. The claws of the beast raked across his back, tearing through waterlogged clothes and grazing his ribs on both sides.

Mark let out a scream of his own and pulled the weapon free, stabbing again, this time into the heaving tender spot under the thing's arm, slamming the blade through muscles and blood vessels and once again dragging the weapon as far as the bones would permit to open another long gash. The werewolf clubbed him with its elbow, trying to break free, but Mark knew better than to let it. He pulled the knife away and lowered his aim, cutting into the meat and organs just above the werewolf's pelvis, trying to saw through as many vital organs as possible, to inflict as much pain as possible, anything he could do to stop the animal in its tracks.

The hind claw of the thing left the ground and caught his leg just below the knee, ripping flesh and clothing away in a downward stroke that took most of the meat from Mark's shin in the process.

Mark screamed and kept stabbing, hoping he could stop this insanity, praying he would live through it.

The werewolf pushed away from him, thick trails of blood falling from every open wound he'd made.

Mark groaned, feeling the hot run of blood coursing over his face and over his leg. Aside from that unexpected heat, he felt almost nothing. Shock was surely setting in.

The beast stood still, panting heavily and looked at him. Its unsettlingly human eyes stared a little glassily. There was a part of Mark Loman that had always been a hunter and always would be. That primal aspect of his soul wanted to roar in victory. He kept staring back, and that predatory piece of him suddenly shivered.

The werewolf was standing back, not attacking, because it wanted him to understand what he faced. Its fingers parted the fur around the worst of the wounds he'd given it, displaying the massive gash that ran from chest down nearly to the groin. Mark stared, stunned as the flesh there began to heal.

He watched, too shocked to consider running or fighting, as the flesh and organs exposed by the deep cut pulled back together. Blood stopped flowing, and then the heart he'd nicked mended itself, the muscles bunched and twisted until they were once again whole and the skin practically zipped itself shut.

The other wounds mended as well, and the beast stared at him, the glazed look gone from the cold blue eyes.

"That was to let you know, to make you understand." The voice seemed more human now, or maybe he was just adjusting. "She would have healed even from the skinning your friend gave her, Loman. She would have recovered given time."

The thing stepped forward again, lowering its head until they were almost at the same height. Mark's eyes looked at the same spot where he'd seen the wounds vanish. There wasn't even a serious scar left to show that he'd almost killed the thing.

"Landers did the maiming, you son of a bitch. But you killed my baby girl."

The werewolf hit him hard with a closed fist and Mark heard something inside of his chest break under the impact. After that he felt nothing at all.

* * *

Roland Weilland looked down at the unconscious wreck of a man and stared. The pain from his wounds was little more than a memory now, and he lifted his head to the sky and called out to his brethren. His voice clear and pure, echoed off the trees and hills and carried longer than most would have thought possible.

He looked at the still breathing man on the ground and shook his head. He knew this was the part where it would get tricky. Now it would not be his decision alone, but John's as well.

The snow fell heavier now than it had before, and Roland sat, saving body heat while he waited.

Eventually they came to him. The rest of his pack moved with the sort of grace that all of their kind had, and all of them carried their burdens.

Two dead police officers — both of whom Roland knew, and a faceless woman were included in the bodies brought along. John came forward carrying Cullie Lander's skinned body and wearing the flesh he'd peeled away as if it were a cloak.

All three of the men they'd hunted were still alive, though none of them would be for much longer and the odds were good that if they'd been conscious they would have been begging for death's release.

"It is the time of judgment. What say you about the offenders?" His voice was calm and solemn.

John would decide their fates as his wife was the one they had killed.

John called to hear how each had fought and listened to the stories told.

He listened well, and as the storm raged around them he thought over the options and made his decisions.

* * *

The diner had attracted a new crowd of customers and Scott watched them all as they came past, wondering if any of them might be shape changers, or how they would react if their entire world were thrown into chaos.

"If I don't get to see Allison soon, I swear I'll go crazy."

Eric simply nodded, his back ramrod straight and his eyebrows drawn together. Scott remembered the same expression from when his friend was still in high school, but that was before he'd gone into the military and become a walking brick wall. Of all the people he kept in touch with from back then, Eric was the most changed and, ironically the most the same. He was different in appearance and in the way he carried himself, but he was still, deep inside, a decent human being. That was really what bothered him the most about the situation they were in. The others had pulled the wool over his eyes and he'd let them. He hadn't wanted to know that they had changed and so he'd let himself be blinded.

But looking back over the last decade, he could see where the signs were all there. George had been the original Angry Young Man, and somehow he'd gotten past that and become a wimp. Cullie had gone from being a loud and obnoxious creep to being just a creep. Only, really, he'd probably just learned to keep his opinions to himself instead of advertising. He couldn't for the life of him remember why they hung around with Cullie back then or why they'd continued doing so after high school. And Mark? Well, Mark didn't seem to have changed, not on the surface, but he could still remember a few times when Cullie and Mark had cornered one kid or another for a little fun and games. They'd never beaten the crap out of the underclassmen; they'd just tormented them enough to make the younger students leery of getting too close.

Eric looked at him and shook his head. "I think if I get out of this with Sarah and the boys, that'll be enough to make me happy."

Scott nodded.

"And if anything has happened to them, I'll be coming back around here and taking care of business." Scott didn't need to ask for clarification, he knew exactly what Eric meant and he felt the same way.

Scott's stomach twisted and roiled inside his body at the thought of what Allison was going through and what condition the baby was in.

"I'm trying hard to understand all of this, Scott. You know what I mean?"

Scott nodded. "Oh yeah. You better believe it." He took a sip of his coffee and leaned back in his seat. "I never would have thought in a million years that we'd ever be sitting here and having a discussion like this one, you know?"

Before Eric could answer him the door leading into the diner opened and the six men who had sat with them earlier re-entered the place. All of the men looked solemn, as well they should.

Neither Eric nor Scott stood, but at least in Scott's case it took effort to remain relatively calm. The men walked over to the booth where they were sitting and stood looking down at them.

Eric was the one who spoke first. "Have you finished your vendetta?"

"We're done." It was the big man who spoke. "The weather's a bitch out there, but I'm guessing you gentlemen would like to be with your families."

Eric nodded and stood and Scott followed his lead.

A few moments later they were all outside and the truth of the Viking's words was made painfully clear. Scott had barely bothered to look out the window; he'd been too busy worrying about Allison. While they'd been waiting, a full inch or more of new snow had accumulated and the temperature had dropped by what felt like at least ten degrees.

The leader looked at the two of them for a moment and then spoke calmly. "We're going to blindfold you gentlemen, and then we're going to take you to see your wives and children. The house where they're staying isn't far away and this won't take long."

Neither of them resisted as they had their eyes covered and were led into an oversized van. The men who handled them were gentle, and spoke only as much as was required to let them know what they had to do.

Scott closed his eyes behind the blindfold and prayed as hard as he ever had. His fears about Allison and the baby grew worse instead of better.

Eric was quiet beside him, but the tension coming off of him was palpable. Neither of them spoke until the vehicle finally stopped.

When they were led from the car and their blindfolds were removed, they looked around in the blustering veil of snow and saw only one house, a large affair with three stories and a fireplace that was burning. They also saw the for sale sign in the front yard, though it was half buried under snow.

The men led them to the door, and knocked softly. A moment later the door was opened by another stranger, who looked around and then nodded his head and let them pass.

Eric smiled for the first time since he'd shown up, just as soon as he saw Sarah and his twin sons. Lance and Tyler looked up from the Disney movie they were watching in the model home, and let out squeals of joy even as they rose from in front of the 32-inch television. Twin bullets of flesh launched themselves at their father and he caught them silently, pulling them up to the level of his face, one on each arm, and hugging them. It was practically a miracle he didn't crush his sons from enthusiasm alone.

Sarah stood and looked at him for several seconds, shocked to see him. Sarah was not what Scott had ever expected when it came to his high school chum. She had short brown hair and a body that hadn't quite sprung back from giving birth to the twins. Scott would have expected his friend to marry a cheerleader type, because they were all he ever fell for when they were both younger. Instead Eric had married a woman who was moderately attractive and almost as tall as he was. She also had a brain and was at least as opinionated on every subject as her husband.

If her sons were energetic in their reunion with their father, she was more reserved, but no less happy to see him. She walked calmly to where he was and stared into his eyes like he was the most important thing in the world. Aside from the children they shared, Scott had to guess that was the absolute truth of the matter.

He was happy for Eric. He was happy for his friend's family. He wished every joy and good moment for his friend that the world could provide. He also wanted to see his wife.

While Eric was hugging his family and listening to the three most wonderful voices that could exist in his world, Scott looked around to see if Allison was in the room and saw only the Spartan furnishings and a total of ten strangers standing around.

"Where's Allison?" He spoke, but the words didn't travel far. He couldn't seem to catch enough breath for that.

The Viking came over and placed a hand on his shoulder. "Allison is fine, Mr Lassiter." His voice was soft, pleasant now that the growl had left it. "But there were complications."

* * *

Roland walked slightly ahead of the younger man, his grief almost enough to overwhelm him.

Scott Lassiter was an innocent in all of this, and his wife, Allison was even more of an innocent. He didn't know them and didn't need to know them to feel bad for their involvement in his personal war.

They moved to the back of the house, with Lassiter almost whining in the back of his throat. The man was worried, terrified of what might have gone wrong.

Three of the women who'd been left to watch over their guests were in the master bedroom with Allison, tending to her needs as they entered the room.

The woman lay on her back, sweating, and crying softly as the labor pains continued.

Scott Lassiter shoved past him and moved to his wife's side, dropping to his knees at the sight of her. The baby was coming now and there was nothing that could be done to stop what had been started. He hoped for the sake of the couple now reunited that the birth would bring a healthy child, but he had his doubts.

He was still well connected with the local people and he'd made a phone call already to get an ambulance to them, but the storm was growing worse and there were so many accidents on the road that he worried more than he would have expected.

Lassiter looked at him for a moment and then turned back to his wife.

Allison Lassiter bit her lip and moaned as she arched her back; another contraction and this one was apparently worse than most of the others.

"I've called for an ambulance, Mr Lassiter. I have to be honest, the chances aren't very good for one getting here any time soon."

Lassiter looked at him again, this time his anger showing clearly through the confusion and worry. The man stood and walked away from his wife, bristling with the need to do something about her situation and his own growing fury.

"She shouldn't be here, mister. She should be at home, or in a hospital."

"I agree." He shook his head. "I am truly sorry for this, Mr Lassiter. I can't apologize enough."

"No, you can't." He moved closer, looking up into Roland's eyes. "There's no way you can apologize enough. Especially if my wife or my child dies because of this."

That hurt. That hurt a lot. He wasn't much of one to feel guilt very often, but the situation was entirely his fault. If he'd gotten the facts from Loman instead of getting dramatic, he could have spared them all a great deal of trouble. Instead, he'd dragged the woman in the bed and the man in front of him into this nonsense.

Lassiter jammed a finger into his chest with enough force to actually sting. "What makes you any better than my friends if they die? Tell me that."

Roland leaned down, his teeth bared, his nostrils flaring and his blood pressure rising. "I'm trying to make amends for my actions, Lassiter. They never did."

"How can you make amends for this, you son of a bitch?" It wasn't often that anyone, man or wolf man, stood up to him.

Roland looked around the room and then walked over to the window. The snow was falling harder than ever and didn't look like it intended to stop in the next few hours.

He looked to Susan, his wife and one of the women attending to Lassiter's wife and she looked back, communicating that the chances for the baby were not good without a medical team.

Roland nodded his understanding and began taking off his clothes.

"What are you doing?" Lassiter was looking at him like he'd lost his mind somewhere along the way.

"I'm going to keep your wife and son safe, Mr Lassiter."

The transformation was as painful as ever, but he stifled the urge to howl. Lassiter, who'd only seen John earlier in the diner, had apparently forgotten exactly what he was dealing with. The change left him stunned for a moment.

Roland stepped past him and moved to the bed. Allison Lassiter stared at him in complete horror, and he leaned in closer. "I'm going to take you to the hospital," He spoke as clearly as he could, moving his lips in ways that felt completely wrong when he was in his hybrid state. "Do not panic and do not struggle. I will not hurt you."

She stared at him for several seconds. They'd met and spoken a few times and while she'd been upset with being taken, she had never been stupid about it. Finally she nodded her head and waited.

Lassiter moved to intercept and both Susan and her sister Laura blocked him.

Without another word — there were several coming from Scott Lassiter — Roland picked the woman up and carried her from the room. The hallway and living room were full of his brethren, and he made his intentions known. John came with him and called for another member of the pack to join them. John changed without bothering to strip down. This wasn't a time for decorum and it wasn't a time to worry about a pair of jeans. The other started disrobing and changed his mind when he saw John split out of his skin and then impatiently tear away the remains of his old flesh and his wardrobe.

The woman in his arms cried out in pain again and Roland left the building, starting to run the second he was outside.

The hospital was only a few miles away if they chose to take the roads. Roland cut through the back yard of the house and started through the woods, already knowing better ways to handle the obstacles nature put before them.

* * *

Eric set his sons down and hugged Sarah to him, incapable of speaking for several moments. Through all of his time in the Middle East, through every combat situation he'd gone into and survived, the main reason he longed to come back home was now in front of him. He wasn't stupid enough to think he was invincible. He never once went into a combat situation with delusions of being a hero and saving the world. He went in thinking about his wife, his sons and their lives together.

When he thought they might be dead, a part of his mind shut down like a child holding his breath to get what he wants.

For the first time in a week, he could feel his mind breathe.

"Did they hurt you?" He asked the question because he had to. Sarah looked fine and so did the children, but he had to know. Looks could be deceiving, after all.

"No. They just... took us. They haven't been anything but kind aside from keeping us here." She looked into his eyes and tried to read whatever he might have stored behind them. "Eric, what's going on here?"

"It's a mistake. They thought Scott and me were involved in something. They wanted to make sure we showed up, so they took you and the boys and they took his wife."

"Eric, I don't think she's doing well. She's back there trying to have a baby and I don't think she's ready. From what she told me, she's not due for another couple of months."

Before Eric could answer, one of the werewolves came through the door from the back room, carrying Allison. Eric knew her, of course, had known her since high school for Christ's sake and seeing her held in the arms of a monster was enough to jolt him.

"What the hell?" He started moving forward and two of the men in the room shook their heads at him. Another two stopped and did their non-verbal communication thing with the beast carrying Allison and then almost immediately began changing.

Sarah turned without a word and distracted both of the boys, hugging them and talking to them as she maneuvered them away from being able to see what was occurring.

The two that had spoken with their leader walked toward the front door and began changing as they moved. By the time they were out the door and moving into the storm they'd left piles of dead skin and clothing in their wakes.

Scott came out of the back of the house, his face tense with worry, ready to storm after them if he had to.

It was Eric who intercepted him and pulled him to the side. He asked what was up and Scott explained.

"Look, there's nothing you can do right now, Scott. If they wanted to hurt her they would have by now." He kept his voice as calm and level as he could, and low enough that the boys wouldn't hear what he was saying.

"I know that," Scott hissed. "But I mean it, Eric. If they let her die or our baby die, I'll come back for them."

Eric said nothing. He was already trying to figure out how they were going to really get out of all of this alive.

He wanted to believe the monsters around them would keep their word about setting them free, but he had his doubts. He hadn't seen Mark's kids or the woman George was now living with. That left him worried. Very worried.

He looked to Sarah and his sons and tried to remain calm. There was nothing he could do about their current situation except be grateful that his family was alive and unharmed.

His number-one priority was making sure they stayed that way.

* * *

What had started as freezing rain and moved into snow had now become a blizzard. The thick layer of white that dropped from the sky blanketed damned near everything.

George woke up in the middle of the woods, sheltered by the remains of what looked like a church. He hadn't really thought he'd wake up at all, so it was a night for surprises.

The cold sucked at his vitality, leeched away his will to do anything but sit and shiver. Outside of his shelter he heard the wind screaming through the trees. Not far away in the darkness of the abandoned building, he could hear someone moaning.

That was what got him to move. He recognized the sound of Cullie's voice.

He tried to stand and heard himself moan at the pain it caused. There wasn't a part of him that didn't feel like it had been beaten hard and kicked a few times for extra measure. Still, he had to see what was going on with Cullie.

He moved toward the dark lump on the ground a few feet away and tried to see clearly in the darkness brought on by the storm. The thing sounded like Cullie, made noises that should have come from his friend, but it wasn't Cullie. It couldn't be. Cullie had skin.

His hands and feet still wore flesh, as did his face. The rest of his body had been stripped raw, and even in the darkness he could see things that simply were not meant to be seen.

"Oh fuck, what did they do to you?" He blinked back the tears that wanted to fall, refusing to shed a tear for his old friend. He knew what had happened. He knew why it had happened.

Cullie looked at him with wild eyes, but he didn't think the man was really seeing him anymore. Despite the bitter chill in the air, the skinned man in front of him gave off heat. He was feverish.

He let out a small yelp of surprise when he heard Mark's voice. "I don't think he can talk. He's too far gone with whatever else they did to him."

George turned around and looked for Mark. It took him a moment to spot his friend. Mark was alive, his wrists and ankles bound in what was left of his own bootlaces. His face had been sliced into fifths, and the red wounds that separated the portions were starting to scab over.

"What the hell happened?"

"The big one, their leader, beat me in a fight. He could have killed me, but he didn't. I don't know why." Mark coughed. "Maybe he wants us to freeze to death so it looks like an accident."

"If anyone ever finds us out here, I don't think they'll make that mistake."

Cullie moaned again and fell into a coughing fit. George looked his way and then started untying Mark. There was no way in hell he could offer comfort to a man whose entire body was basically one raw nerve ending. He imagined that any place he touched would just add to his already considerable pain.

Mark waited patiently while he finished untying him and then started rubbing his wrists, trying to get blood back into hands that looked almost blue even in the darkness.

While Mark worked on untying his ankles, George dug into his waterproof coat and prayed that the zipper had kept his meager supplies dry. He found the map and, yes, his lighter.

The lighter worked just fine and even the meager light it offered was enough to let him see that something was written on the map. Mark watched him while he read the message. "'Justice is served. You are free to go.'"

"Free to go my ass! There's nowhere to go!" Mark was pissed off. George was still unsettlingly happy to be alive.

"We've got the map. We can find our way back." He was trying to be reasonable. It wasn't working as well as he would have liked.

"What about Cullie? What about Ellen and Lou? Hell, what about your fucking girlfriend, George?"

He clenched his jaw. "Her name is Cheryl. When we get out of here we'll figure it all out."

Mark was shaking with cold, his clothes half frozen to his body and his feet stripped of everything but a ratty looking pair of socks.

"I don't have the answers, Mark. I'm still trying to figure all of this out!" George felt his temper rising and decided not to stop it. He'd had all he could take of Mark and Cullie browbeating him. Jesus! He'd been in a fight with werewolves earlier in the night and now he just wanted to celebrate being alive for five minutes without Mark riding his ass.

He looked at his watch and was shocked to see it was only a little after eleven PM.

"Okay, if we're going to live through this shit, we need a fire." Mark looked his way and then gestured. "There's a dozen broken pews around here. Let's gather some up." He limped toward them and George saw the ugly wounds on his leg.

George killed the flame from the lighter and started gathering wood; mostly small pieces at first, kindling for the larger boards.

Ten minutes later they had a fire and light and warmth enough to give him a hope of not freezing to death. He also had a dead lighter. The Bic wasn't meant to last forever and it gave up the ghost by the time they'd managed to get the blaze going.

"We'll wait out the storm. When it's all over with, we'll try to find our way to somewhere. I saw a road earlier." He shut his mouth, remembering the cops and the lady he'd seen on that road and how his actions had lead to them being slaughtered. He sighed and told Mark what he could remember. "Maybe there will still be cars there. Maybe we'll get lucky and have a chance to get out of this."

"What about Cullie?" Mark looked over at their friend, who was still shivering violently, his face turned away from the heat.

"What about him?"

"We have to get him help. He's dying."

"I don't know if there's anything we can do for him, Mark. He's lost—" he bit back the nervous voice in his head that started screaming about lost flesh— "he's lost a lot of blood. Even if we get him out of here, he doesn't even have a coat. He'll freeze to death out there."

"This is insane."

George looked at him for a long time without speaking, as his body started warming up. "Yeah, it is. This is fucked up beyond all repair."

"Why didn't they just kill us?"

"I don't know." That was the end of their conversations for a while. They sat in uncomfortable silence that was broken only by Cullie's fevered moans and the winds that pushed through the openings and tried to steal what little heat they managed to capture.

* * *

The Hillside Township Emergency Center welcomed the men, despite their nudity. If a few people looked concerned or amused, they pushed those thoughts aside as Roland handed over Allison Lassiter.

He didn't wait around to talk to anyone, but turned around and headed back into the blizzard. There were still things that had to be taken care of, still dangers left for him and his to deal with.

They had only run a portion of the distance back to the house when John veered away from them and toward the woods where they had left the men.

Whatever he did, it was John's decision to make.

They'd discussed that earlier.

Roland had made his proclamation and John had given a great deal of thought to what to do. Both Loman and Heatherly had fought well and done all they could to survive. As Landers had handled the worst of the crimes, John decided to let them have another chance at living. In the end, he'd left them at the church.

"I told Landers if he lived through it, I would let him go." He said the words softly.

"What do you think his chances are?"

"I bit him and let him live."

"Will you keep your word to the man who killed your wife?" Dave had been the one to speak up. Dave, who was loyal to a fault and always willing to state his opinion; He also happened to be the police chief these days.

"I don't know," John had answered truthfully. "It might be dangerous to let one like that become one of our kind."

Roland laughed when he heard those words. "Might be? It is dangerous. Don't be foolish."

"You said it was my call, Roland!" He wasn't quite challenging, but he was getting closer to it.

"It is your choice." Roland had leaned in closer and snarled, and John had wisely backed down. "But your promise to let him live doesn't mean we let him into our community or stand by if he goes too far."

Now Roland was heading back to deal with Lassiter and Fulford. That was his place. John would have to handle whatever happened in the woods. That was his place.

Everything would work out. He promised himself that much. Everything would work out because it had to work out.

They moved through the storm, he and his two remaining companions, ready to deal with the issues that remained.

* * *

Eric wanted to leave, and had intentions of doing so as soon as it was possible, but first he had to deal with Scott, who was practically wearing a hole in the carpeting.

It was one of the women in the room who came up to them next. She was attractive, with dark hair shot through with gray, and could have been anywhere between her late twenties into her forties. She had a weathered look to her skin, but had not developed any of the physical signs that he associated with middle age.

There was nothing demure or shy about her attitude. She stepped forward and looked directly at Scott. "You want to go to your woman?"

Scott couldn't have said, "yes" faster if his life depended on it.

Without a single word beyond that, she did exactly as the men had done and began taking off the majority of her clothes. Unlike the men, however, she grabbed a bag and shoved her skirt and blouse into it.

One of the remaining strangers, a man, stepped toward her and whispered something softly into her ear. The expression on his face made it clear he wasn't trying to get romantic.

Her body was in nearly perfect shape. Her breasts were full, but gravity had taken its toll on them. Aside from this one admission to age, the rest of her figure belonged to an athlete. She nodded her head at the man's comment and handed him the bag to hold for a moment. Then she changed with the same violent abruptness as the males of her kind, literally ripping out of her skin to reveal a dark gray form covered in thick fur.

Eric looked her over, too shocked to speak for the moment. Her height was close to seven feet; her body was still hard muscle, her breasts were still there, though buried in the thick fur that trailed down her belly to join with growth of fur near her pubic region.

Without preamble she grabbed her sack of clothing and then draped it around her neck. "Come with me, Mr Lassiter. We'll find her."

Scott stared at her for a moment, just as shocked as Eric, and then headed for the door. She shook her head and dropped to all fours behind him, then brushed past him in the hallway. Three times she blocked his path and three times he tried to move around her before the man who had spoken to her explained.

"The storm is worse now than it was a while ago. The roads are impassable. If you want to see your wife, you'll have to ride her like a horse or you aren't going anywhere." He spoke calmly enough, but had an amused expression on his face.

Scott shook his head and after a moment of wondering how he was supposed to handle the change in plans, slung a leg over the monster's waist and then leaned forward until his arms were around her neck. If carrying a 180-pound man caused the creature any difficulty, she hid it well. A moment after that they were out the door and lost in the flurry of white that fell from the skies.

Eric shook his head, still trying to convince himself that every thing going on around him was real.

Sarah brought him back to reality when she came over to put her head on his shoulder. He looked back the way she had come and saw his boys had fallen asleep.

And exhaustion reared its head and reminded him that he'd been riding on caffeine for the last two days. All of his worries about his friends paled next to the siren call of sleep.

Eric and Sarah moved over to the couch near where the boys were sleeping, and his wife, already as close to a perfect person as he had ever met, slid the cushions aside to reveal a fold out bed.

The strangers in the house with them saw what was going on and moved away, leaving them in peace.

After they were both in the bed Eric looked at Sarah and smiled. "We're almost out of here, Sarah. We're going home soon."

"I hope you're right. I miss that stupid house."

In response he pulled her closer and rested his head so that their faces touched. He was asleep in minutes. His dreams were all nightmares, but he didn't remember a one of them when he woke the next morning.

* * *

They did their best to sleep, still shivering whenever a breeze pushed through the broken down walls of the church and slithered to their corner where the fire crackled and glowed.

Mark had more trouble with the idea than George, who was now curled up and snoring softly to himself. Cullie continued to hang on, whimpering occasionally and from time to time trying to turn over in his fevered rest. Mark couldn't understand how the man could do anything at all except scream in pain.

He drifted for a while, not quite asleep and not fully aware either. He might have actually been taken by dreams if it hadn't been for Cullie's sudden screams.

Mark sat up, blinking sleep from his eyes, and looked over at the pew where Cullie had been resting in relative peace. Cullie was still there, but hardly resting. The man's body was contorted, and his mouth was wide open as he gulped in air and started yelling again. With no idea what was going on, Mark stood and rushed to his friend's side.

And stopped dead in his tracks when he saw the bones in Cullie's body stretching. It wasn't one to two random bones, but damned near all of them at the same time. Cullie's hands and feet pounded at the pew, beating a furious tattoo. His eyes were rolled back into his head and showed only whites. His chest was expanding in a series of uneven twists that looked painful and had to feel even worse.

Mark had been unfortunate enough to suffer from several growth spurts in high school. He remembered them well because they hurt almost constantly. He'd been taken to three different doctors when he complained of pain in his legs before his parents accepted that the aches and pains he felt were nothing but the usual discomfort associated with growing bones. He was just sensitive enough to feel it more than a lot of others because his growth spurts were always extreme.

Whatever he'd felt couldn't hold a candle to what Cullie was going through. Mark could see the bones in his rib cage changing, growing and stretching in ways that must surely feel like the Holy Inquisition had chosen him for a year's worth of confessions.

"Cullie?"

Cullie groaned, the sound coming from deep inside his chest and accompanied by the sound of bones creaking, flesh stretching. It was when Cullie opened his mouth again that reality sank through the numb surprise. Cullie'd grown fangs, and it looked like his face was starting to change shape.

"Oh, fuck me, Freddie." Mark stumbled backward; shaking his head in denial of what he knew was happening. Cullie was his friend, true enough, but his mind looked past the ruined form in front of him and pushed images of what he'd done to the girl that had been a wolf on the that dreadful night. More importantly, his memories insisted on reminding him that his friend had orgasmed when he'd torn the flesh from the screaming wolf-woman. He'd moaned deep in his chest and messed his pants at the thought of what he'd done.

Mark kept thinking about that, too, as Cullie kept changing. This wasn't the seamless, sudden transformation of the other werewolf he'd seen change. No, this was a slow and almost random thing. Cullie's body was trying to recover from heavy trauma at the same time, and the changes seemed less organic than with the others. Maybe his body had to get used to the idea of becoming something inhuman before things went smoothly.

And all Mark could think about was the physical pleasure Cullie'd received when he tortured the pregnant woman. He kept going back to that no matter how much he didn't want to think about it. Because, really, he was starting to realize why he'd been left here with George and with what should have been their dead mutual friend but was instead their changing mutual friend.

"George. George?" Mark almost stepped into the fire as he kept backing up and finally tore his eyes away from Cullie's agonized transformation. *Sweet Jesus, he's growing skin again. He's healing and when he's done, what's to stop him from getting off that fucking pew and tearing us both apart?* He knew the answer of course. Not a damned thing would stop Cullie. If he got good at the whole shape changer thing, he'd be nearly unstoppable, and he'd start killing whenever the mood struck him. Cullie, who'd always been a little weird, always been the one to talk about what he'd like to do to this girl that made him hot or that guy that pissed him off, Cullie who'd blown a fucking wad while he had torn the skin from a pregnant woman, would heal faster than ever, be stronger than ever, and never leave a single bit of evidence that proved a human being had been involved in a murder.

Werewolf? Fuck that! Can you say serial killer with claws?

"George! Wake the fuck up!" His voice cracked as he screamed and George finally came out of his slumber, waking instantly.

Mark didn't try to explain, he just pointed a finger. He saw the same realizations going through George's mind that had gone through his and when he thought the troubles had cemented themselves, he asked, "What are we going to do here, George?"

George stared at Cullie for all of ten seconds, and then stepped toward the still growing beast on the pew and grabbed the closest limb, in this case the left foot, which had started sprouting fur.

George was not a small man. He was out of shape, but he was also big enough to make most people think twice about screwing with him. Mark stared with his mouth hanging open as George put his weight into it and practically hurled Cullie onto the fire.

Flames leaped and danced around Cullie as he hit the blazing collection of wood, and Cullie did more than scream now. He rose from the burning flames and roared, as the changes in his body accelerated.

Mark swallowed hard and shook his head, refusing to believe what his world had come to. The damned thing kept changing even as it burned, growing larger and more ferocious. The sounds coming from it were undiluted rage and pain and loud enough to leave him half deafened.

George didn't stand by and wait for Cullie to die. He grabbed a board from near the fire and swung it as hard as he could, landing a savage blow across the side of its still burning head. The board shattered, and so did the back of Cullie's misshapen skull. Cullie fell back into the flames, screeching as his hands were buried in the coals, and the flames licked across raw parts of his body that had not yet re-grown flesh.

George was screaming now, too, as he took the remaining length of wood and drove the edge into the monster's back, pushing as hard as he could, ignoring the flames that threatened to ignite his clothing. The edge of the broken board was jagged and disappeared at least a couple of inches into the raw meat on the Cullie-thing's back.

Cullie fell into the fire completely, his face buried in the ashes at the center of the blaze, and still George held him down, pushing with trembling arms. The sounds the half formed werewolf made would haunt Mark for the rest of his life; he knew they would.

Cullie pushed and fought back, but despite his changes, he was still too damaged to hold his own. One hand slid out of the pyre, scattering coals across the ground, and trying to reach George, but he was quick enough to step aside. Mark watched the fingers lengthening, watched the nails grow thicker, even as the heat started cooking the meat away from the bones.

George's boots were smoldering, the laces on one of them already burning before he stepped back and left the board behind, sticking out of the spot where it had pushed through the muscles and possibly even through a couple of ribs.

George stared at Cullie and panted, his face smudged with ashes and seared to a light pink. He stomped his feet impatiently before he finally managed to put out the flames licking at his laces.

"You killed Cullie." Mark shook his head, numbed to the point where he didn't stop himself from opening his mouth.

George turned sharply on one heel and pivoted a scorched fist into his face, splitting his lip and snapping his head backwards with the force of the blow. Before Mark could recover, George bulldozed forward and hit him again, a third time and a fourth.

Mark fell back and crashed into the broken pews, once again completely unsettled by the events around him. He ignored the edge of wood that pressed into his back as he saw George stumbling around like a drunk.

Finally George settled himself against the far wall and drew into a nearly fetal position. Mark watched as the man he thought he'd known well enough to call a brother started crying, his head resting against his drawn up knees.

He had no anger left in him. There was nothing but a hollowed-out feeling and the pain of the scrapes that George's fists had reopened. Mark eventually rose and limped to the closest opening in the side of the church before he dry retched a few times. The smell of cooking meat was overpowering inside the building. Even though the air outside was cold, it was purer, sweeter than the stench inside.

* * *

They did not speak as they walked through the deep snow. They merely kept moving. Mark's feet were wrapped in the inner lining from his jacket to keep his feet warmer. Even that wouldn't have happened if George hadn't done it for him.

Mark was physically there, but nobody was home. That was just as well, because if he'd said the wrong thing, George might have killed him.

George didn't much care about anyone or anything anymore; he couldn't afford that luxury. He wanted to get out of this alive and he wanted to get back to his house and the world he'd left behind.

The blizzard had blown itself out during the long night, but not before dumping close to two feet of snow over the entire area. The map was almost useless, but after close to an hour he'd managed to find the stream again and begun moving in the opposite direction, using the runoff as his marker. A little after noon he found the bridge where everything had gone down the night before. There was no sign of a police car, or of the vehicle that had pushed partially through the guard railing.

It was close to four in the afternoon before they made it back to the place where they'd initially been dropped off. George saw the SUV idling at the edge of the snow covered road and openly sobbed.

The vehicle was running, and he increased his pace, stumbling several times but never quite falling. He made it to the curb next to the Ford and stared at the driver for several seconds, almost afraid to believe his eyes.

Eric Fulford looked so beautiful in that moment that he would have gleefully kissed him. It was only Eric who stepped out of the idling vehicle. Scott was not with him, and neither were any of his family members. He stood ramrod straight and did nothing to help either of them as they came forward. But when they were close, his hard features softened and he hugged George briefly before moving to help Mark into the back seat.

The road conditions were still hellish; though it was obvious the area had been plowed.

"Where are we going?"

"Local hospital." Eric kept his eyes on the road, and they crawled slowly through the frozen wasteland. "Scott's already there. Allison is in labor, or she was the last time I checked in."

"Is your... Are Sarah and the boys all right?"

"Yeah." Eric slowed down to a standstill and looked at George for several seconds. "I don't know about Cheryl or Mark's little ones. I haven't seen them yet."

"How did you know where to find us?"

"You had a visitor last night. John." Eric's face turned to stone again, a sure sign that he was trying not to let his anger get the best of him. Long before he'd signed up for the military Eric Fulford had been the sort to bottle up his negative feelings.

"John..." George knew what Eric was thinking. He didn't have to say *the man whose wife you let get murdered,* for George to know that was what he was holding inside.

"Way I understand it, he's the one that decided you got to live. He went back to where you were last night and watched over all of you. He told me what happened with Cullie."

George tried to catch his breath, but it didn't seem possible. Even thinking of the nightmare from earlier was enough to put a crushing pressure on his rib cage.

"I can't talk about that." George barely recognized his own voice.

"Fair enough." He accelerated, but carefully. Eric was always a careful man. He seldom let his emotions get the better of him. George had always admired that about him.

They rode in silence the rest of the way.

* * *

Roland padded across the snow and watched the SUV as it moved. John was beside him the entire time, moving just as quietly. They made it to their stashed clothes long before the men in the vehicle had parked and sought help for Mark Loman.

Susan was still in the waiting room. He smiled for her and she returned the smile before standing up and coming into his arms. It had been a bad night and though she'd been worried about him being angry for taking Lassiter to this place, he was fine with it. She'd saved him the extra trip.

It wasn't long before Eric Fulford joined them in the room. He sat by himself and waited to hear about the birth of Lassiter's child. They all waited, though they had different reasons for wanting to know what happened.

Scott Lassiter came next, his pale face showing the strain of waiting. Allison Lassiter was fine. He shared that information with Fulford moments after he entered the room. Roland and his people sat at the far end of the waiting area and said nothing.

The baby might live. The baby might die. That was the way of things.

Fulford and Lassiter left the room after a few moments and were gone for close to half an hour. George Heatherly came in and sat down, holding a Styrofoam cup of coffee in his trembling hands. He didn't look at them even once.

"They'll ask, you know." It was John who spoke, his voice soft and careful. This was, of course, the dangerous time. Whatever Roland said would be accepted, but the decision could well break apart his authority within the group.

Roland looked at his wife and then at his son-in-law and nodded. "If they ask, I'll say yes."

He was rather surprised when both nodded their approval.

It was Fulford who actually asked. Lassiter was still too stressed, apparently and didn't trust himself not to lose his temper.

The man came up and asked to speak to Roland in the hallway. Roland nodded and instead of stopping there, walked outside into the cold.

Lassiter and Fulford both stood with him, but it was Fulford who finally posed the question. "Your kind heals quickly?"

"Yes."

He spoke to the captain, but looked at the father-to-be.

"Scott's son is very small, and very weak. His chances aren't so good." Roland simply nodded and waited again. "Is there anything that can be done to save him? By you and your people, I mean?"

He stared levelly at Scott Lassiter as he spoke. "We heal well. We tend to our own. Are you asking if he could be changed?"

"Well, yes." Lassiter looked at the ground, probably afraid of what the answer might be.

Roland's hand was gentle when he caught Lassiter's chin and made him look into his eyes. "I can arrange for him to become like us. If he does, there will be a brief fever and then he will either live through it or he will die. If you are asking me to do this, I'll do it. But you need to know the risks. What we become, what you have seen, is not a normal state for us. Unless he is trained, he'll change at random times and become a very real danger to anyone around him. Those without the proper training… well, they are the things you hear about in legends."

Lassiter nodded.

"Listen carefully to me Scott Lassiter. If I do this, he will have to stay here. You and your wife will have to stay here. You will be among friends, and you will be protected, but if you want your boy to have a normal life, it means staying with us and once you join, there is no way to quit."

Lassiter looked to Fulford, who in turn could do nothing but shrug.

Roland finished. "Speak with your wife. Explain the risks. When you've made your decision, you can come back to me and let me know. I'll either be here, or in the waiting room. I owe you at least that much."

Lassiter nodded again and went inside to find his wife and the courage to explain what he planned.

Fulford looked up at Roland. "So that's it?"

"Of course. You are free to go. You have been ever since I found out who killed my daughter."

"Why didn't you kill all of them?"

"That wasn't my decision to make." He looked the captain in the face, without any hesitation. "If it had been my choice, they'd all be dead now. John is the one who showed them compassion."

"Aren't you afraid they'll tell about you? That I'll tell my superiors in the military?"

"I can't stop you, Captain. I think it would be a mistake on your part, but I certainly can't stop you."

"You could kill me."

"I could. I won't."

The man was trying to stay calm, but Roland could smell his anger, his confusion. "I don't understand you."

"No, but I understand you, Captain. I know your type, as it were. We're a lot alike."

"How do you figure?"

"When you're out in the field, you do what you are told, you follow your orders and you accept what your conscience will allow you to accept. You live by the rules of the military organization and you fight for what you believe is right. And I'd lay odds that if one of your men is killed in combat you go through all of the proper paperwork and you handle the phone calls to the soldier's family yourself. Am I right?"

Fulford nodded.

"I do the same thing with my people. I care for them, I give them their orders and I handle whatever crisis comes my way." He paced, restless again. His kind was always restless. "Here's the thing you need to know, Captain Fulford. Even if you told your military superiors that you had the perfect recipe for soldiers that couldn't be stopped, even if you told them and they believed you, it would never work."

"Why?"

"Don't you think I've done some checking? Would you go into a new combat zone without at least looking at a map? There's nothing to differentiate us from perfectly normal human beings. There aren't any traceable markers in our cells and you can't grow a culture on a petri dish that will give up the secret to why we are."

"So what is it then? Magic?"

"That or something science still can't quantify. I really don't know."

"Let's change subjects. What happened to Cheryl and Mark's kids?"

"They're safe and at another house. We didn't want them anywhere around you and Lassiter's families. You don't have to worry about them."

They sat in silence for a few moments before Roland asked a

question. "What would you have done in my situation, Captain? What would you have done if it had been Sarah, or one of your children?"

Fulford looked at him and answered immediately. "I've been thinking a lot about that. I would have killed all three of them."

The wind caught the side of the building and pushed at both of them with an arctic chill. They stood outside together and waited for Scott Lassiter to come back and give them his answer.

EDITORS' NOTE

Thanks for reading this Cohesion book.

We hope you've enjoyed it as much as we did putting it together.

Please consider leaving us a review, or even sampling the rest of what Cohesion Press offers, as everything is packed full of action, monsters, and creatures that wish you harm.

+ + +

Geoff Brown - Director, Cohesion Press.
Mayday Hills Asylum
Beechworth, Australia

Amanda J Spedding - Editor-in-chief, Cohesion Press
Sydney, Australia